RAW MEAT

by
Bobby Legend

Raw Meat
Published through Legend Publishing Co.

This is a work of fiction. Names, characters, places, and incidents are the product of the author's imagination or are used fictitiously. Any resemblance to actual persons, living or dead, events, or locales is entirely coincidental.

Interior Book Design and Layout by
www.integrativeink.com

ISBN 978-0615-22552-4

Detective Wells and three other neighboring city homicide detectives have their hands full when a puzzling murder mystery leads them on a wild goose chase. The four detectives become involved together when some exotic Ostrich meat being sold at local butcher shops begins killing innocent citizens. And when it's learned that the meat is actually ground human hamburger, the hunt for the suspects intensifies.

Young teens who had delivered the meat to the supposedly unsuspecting business establishments were the main suspects until it was learned that members of the Mafia owned the butcher shops where the meat had been sold from, and that many local mobsters' DNA were found in the hamburger. So the murder investigation turned its attentions towards the mob. And when it's learned that the CIA is involved with the mob over a white van containing hundreds of kilos of heroin and other illegal contraband, the mystery becomes entangled in a web of conspiricy. But what happens next: You'll have to read the book.

CHAPTER 1

My name is Bobby Legend. I'm a newspaper reporter for an independent news organization and this is my story.

I became involved in a bizarre murder investigation in Hollywood around June of 1999. The case began when Tim Teller, an inspector for the Food and Beverage department for the State of California began receiving complaints of salmonella poisoning from neighborhood hospital doctors. But this investigation escalated when many of the poisoned victims began dying.

After many of the victim's autopsies were completed, and the stomach contents analyzed, the cause of death was traced back to diseased ground meat, which was actually ground human flesh. That's when the case became a murder investigation.

An experienced homicide detective by the name of John Wells was asked by his friend, Teller, to investigate this case that had everyone in his office scratching their heads. Many people were getting sick and six people had already died from the hamburger that was sold to the citizens of Hollywood.

Teller's job was to make sure that the meat that the public bought was safe for consumption. But this meat, after being tested and retested was determined to be totally unacceptable, unless you were a cannibal.

Someone had sold ground human meat to an unsuspecting public. And because it was diseased human meat, it was no longer Mr. Teller's problem or the department of Food and Beverage. It was now a problem for the Hollywood homicide department.

Though called in by Teller, Detective Wells was officially given the case to investigate by his Captain. Wells was from the Hollywood division where fantasy is reality and reality is nonexistent. He had been on the force for nearly forty years, thirty of them as a homicide detective. But he had never been called to investigate a case similar to this one.

Even though Detective Wells had just begun the investigation, he did have a few leads to track down. After speaking with some of the victim's relatives, the experienced homicide detective was able to locate the shop where the meat had been sold. The source of meat seemed to come from only one store and was being sold under the guise of an exotic Ostrich meat.

After interviewing a few of the shop's workers, Detective Wells found out that this specialty market had been selling the Ostrich delicacy for more than two months before enough complaints had been phoned into the state's Food and Beverage department to warrant an investigation.

When the Food and Beverage Department heads became overburdened with complaints, they finally acted on the situation. They investigated as best they could until the diseased meat began killing people.

Now the homicide department had to deal with this situation and find the answers and the culprit or culprits that committed this heinous deed. Wells wondered how these evil beings found their human victims before leading them to slaughter? Were these victims already dead when the suspects found them and then ground up or did the perpetrators kill their victims to get their meat? These and many other questions needed to be answered – and fast.

Detective Wells wanted desperately to question the specialty butcher shop's owner but he was nowhere to be found. The police tried but had been unable to contact him. The other workers at the shop said that Mr. Elmero fled the area as soon as he learned that the homicide department would be getting involved in the investigation. Wells had the uniformed officers try to track him down and also put out an all points bulletin on him, but at that time he was only wanted for questioning.

The police weren't positive that Elmero had fled because he wasn't guilty of any crime so Wells decided to give him the benefit of doubt for the time being. At the present time he was only wanted for selling the human meat. But that could change.

Already six innocent people had died from eating the diseased meat and Mr. Elmero was responsible for selling it to the public. How many more innocent people were likely to die was hard to say.

However, Wells had one slight problem. Not only were the police apprised of the homicide investigation so were the news reporters. They were on the scene like flies on flypaper. Wells had to have some uniformed officers clear Elmero's butcher shop of reporters so they wouldn't interfere in his investigation.

The cameramen with their big cameras and all the reporters turned the place into bedlam. The police wanted them to stay clear of the area. They didn't want to close down the shop and put the workers out of a job. Wells could do a decent investigation with the shop open as long as he wasn't interrupted by outside influences.

Wells called a number of the workers into the main office to get their names and addresses just in case he needed to talk with them at another time. He interviewed them each one at a time. There were a total of five workers, two women and three men, plus the owner.

Wells interviewed the men first. They all told basically the same story – that they started selling the exotic meat approximately two months before. Usually one or two people delivered the ground meat. Most of the time, a young hippie couple brought about twenty-five to fifty pounds of ground meat each time they visited the shop. The couple had told the workers that they owned an Ostrich farm and that they sold the hide for boots and sold the meat to small meat shops.

One of the shop's female workers also mentioned another woman that had delivered the meat a few weeks before the investigation began. One of the male workers thought the owner had loaned out one or two of the shop's machines so the sellers had a way to cut and grind up the meat. The machines hadn't been returned.

Nearly three hours after Wells had arrived at the butcher shop he finally completed his interviews. Once he finished interviewing each of the workers, he finally had something to go on. He had the first name of the woman that delivered the meat and possibly a place where she hung out.

Detective Wells was also looking for a small hand operated stainless steel meat grinding machine and a bologna cutter. He believed these machines could still be in the possession of the sellers and could still have the remains of human flesh in them. But the best piece of evidence would be the composite drawings of the couple that had sold the meat to the butcher shop.

Wells also asked the workers to visit the Hollywood police station and work with the forensic artist. He hoped to have a decent drawing of the three suspects within the next twenty-four hours.

When Wells finally departed, a young, beautiful female reporter stopped him and asked him if she could tag along on his murder investigation, but was turned down cold. He told her she would have to gather her story on her own, without any help from him, just like all the other reporters had to do. But Wells would have a problem with this particular female reporter…because she refused to take no for an answer.

On the way back to the office, Wells had stopped at his favorite eatery to dine on two of his favorite steak and cheese hoagies from Gabrielle's Hoagie House near Hollywood and Vine avenues. By the time he had returned to the station, three of the five butcher shop workers were already waiting for him to lend their support to his murder investigation. Wells guided each one of them to a forensic artist to draw the facial profiles of the three suspects, one male and two females that had sold and or delivered the diseased human flesh to Salvator Elmero. He wondered if Elmero knew that the meat was human flesh or was he ignorant of that fact. Until Wells could speak to him, that question would have to wait.

While the artist worked on the forensic drawings, Wells waited for the reports from the forensic investigators about any fingerprints that they might have found and any other evidence that might give him some insight into the three suspects he was trying to find.

From the worker's interviews, Wells was told that the young male and female suspects always wore thin, clear rubber gloves every time they delivered the ground meat not wanting to contaminate it. But Wells believed they wore them to hide their fingerprints.

Hollywood's homicide department has a standard routine for investigating crime scenes and Wells is the senior investigator coordinating with all departments simultaneously. His investigators feed him information daily, usually through reports until the culprit or culprits are caught and arrested.

Detective Wells sent two police officers to Elmero's residence, thinking that he may be hiding there. He also had the diseased meat sent out to the DNA lab to see if they could find out how many victims were ground up in the meat that had been found in the butcher shop's refrigerator. He believed the forty pounds of diseased human flesh might contain more than one body, especially after reviewing a long list of people reported missing within the last two months.

On that list, Detective Wells noticed one name in particular, Tony Manzelli. He was the brother of Don Bruno Manzelli, one of the most feared crime bosses of this century. Bruno Manzelli was the biggest drug dealer in the country, known for bringing five tons of narcotics into this country each and every month. He has a distribution network that covers two-thirds of the United States, and in California was considered a god among his mob peers. He is the Don of all Dons and is feared by every other mob family. In fact, the other mob families go out of their way to please him.

Tony Manzelli could have easily been killed or gunned down by one of his many enemies. But the detectives in the Missing Person's department didn't think so, particularly a Detective Volope, who recently talked with Don Bruno Manzelli concerning his brother Tony.

Don Bruno didn't believe that his brother had been bumped off, but rather that something else had happened to him. He told Detective Volope that he had spoken with all the other crime families across America and they all promised Don Bruno that they had nothing to do with his brother's disappearance. That's why Detective Wells believed that Tony Manzelli might possibly be mixed up in that diseased ground meat. But it would take one to two weeks or even months before the DNA lab would have the answers.

Detective Wells had a few of Tony Manzelli's hair follicles that had been given to Detective Volope so it could be sent along with the diseased meat to the lab technicians for DNA testing.

While Wells was waiting for the composite drawings of the suspects' profiles, he read the reports of Inspector Teller concerning his investigation of the matter at hand. Wells also waited to hear from the officers that he had sent to Elmero's residence. He was sure that Elmero was close by but was just afraid to come forward thinking that he may be charged with murder.

But at that particular moment, Wells didn't have any evidence that led him to believe that Elmero had anything to do with his murder investigation, other than selling the diseased hamburger meat. Elmero thought he was buying exotic Ostrich meat. At least that was what the evidence indicated.

When the officers finally called Wells, they told him that no one was found at Elmero's residence. So he decided to phone a judge, who was a dear friend of his, so he could get a search warrant issued for Elmero's abode and for any pertinent evidence leading to the capture of the three young suspects.

Within thirty minutes Wells was driving to Elmero's residence, armed with a search warrant. When he arrived, he had one of his fellow officers break down the door so they could enter the premises. But to their frustration all they discovered was that Elmero had up and disappeared. There wasn't one shred of evidence that helped Detective Wells in his investigation of his three murder suspects or of finding the butcher shop owner. So he was back to square one, still waiting for the composite drawings of his three suspects.

However, by ten o'clock that evening, Wells departed the Hollywood police station with the suspects' profiles. By morning, every police unit in the area would have photos of the three young suspects. Now it was just a matter of time before Detective Wells would have them in custody. But he knew he must act quickly before more killings occurred.

By the beginning of the second day that Detective Wells had begun his murder investigation, he only had four pieces of evidence to go on. He had the composite drawings of his suspects and he also had one of the female's first names, which was Kathy.

Detective Wells yearned for the forensic and DNA reports but those were still days if not weeks away. He could only hope that one of his officers in the field would come across these young suspects as they maneuvered about the city of Hollywood in their police cars.

The first thing Wells acted upon was his instinct. He traveled to the hang out that Kathy had been known to frequent. It was a deserted, dilapidated, and run-down building near the intersection of Santa Monica and Hollywood boulevards. But he noticed, as he was driving to his destination, a government vehicle following a few car lengths behind. It was a black sedan and the type that government law enforcement officials use.

When Wells parked his vehicle behind the condemned building, he noticed that the black sedan had pulled up alongside the curb, a few buildings down from the one he was interested in. Wells peeked out from a corner of the building and could see the driver of the black sedan. It was the female reporter that had badgered him into letting her tag along on his investigation. When he refused her request, she decided to do the next best thing and follow him for her story. But Wells didn't have the time to interrupt his investigation to confront this reporter so he let her be. For now anyway.

Wells continued his search for the female suspect and entered the condemned, two-story building where Kathy was supposedly holed up. But the place was deserted. Although there was plenty of evidence that somebody had been living there. In fact, it looked as if many people had been staying there at one time or another.

However, there wasn't any pertinent evidence that Wells had found that would put him any closer to his female suspect. After searching through every room of the two-story building, he departed empty handed. He decided to call the forensic investigative team to filter the building for fingerprints and anything else that might prove helpful. He hoped to find something there that would get him closer to finding his suspects. If they had been in trouble with the law in years past, he was sure their fingerprints would be in the FBI's database.

So Wells waited there until the investigative team had entered the premises and began gathering evidence. Then he drove back to the Hollywood station, all the while being followed by that reporter in her black sedan. He wondered why she was following him – then theorized that she was hoping he would lead her to the suspects' hideout. That way she would have the story all to herself.

When Wells reached the station, he learned that the switchboard operators were being swamped with calls from worried citizens. Some called about their missing relatives and others called to say they too had eaten some of the poisoned meat and wanted to know what they should do.

By the second day of Wells' investigation, more and more surrounding hospitals had called into Hollywood police station's dispatch center to let the authorities know about their sick and dying patients that the hospital physicians thought were related to meat poisoning. Many of their patients, it seemed, had also bought and eaten the ground meat that the doctors had confirmed was the source of their illness.

Even the coroners in nearby cities were overwhelmed with dead bodies due to poisoning. Three were dead at one hospital in Santa Monica. Two at another in Redondo Beach and a few more from a hospital in San Pedro. The coroners all claimed the deaths would continue unless the authorities found the culprits that were selling the tainted meat.

But one call Detective Wells had received was from the World Health Organization. They had analyzed some of the meat in question and learned that these people didn't die just from salmonella poisoning. The meat also had the aids virus, hepatitis B and C and a bacteria strain that was of unknown origin.

The World Health Organization claimed that if this particular meat is sold to an unsuspecting public, the deaths could multiply by the thousands. There wasn't any time to spare. Wells had to find the people responsible for these deaths. Fortunately though, many other homicide detectives from nearby cities were also getting involved in this investigation.

Due to the deaths in other cities, Detective Wells had to meet with the other homicide detectives to coordinate a plan of action. Another butcher shop, this one in the city of Santa Monica, had been found selling the tainted meat to unsuspecting customers for the last month. Victims were just now surfacing. If these detectives couldn't find the culprits that were selling this diseased meat and find them soon, they could possibly sell their tainted meat in another state. This could lead to a massive epidemic if things weren't quickly brought to a head.

Wells left his office to visit another crime scene at a butcher shop in Santa Monica and to meet with the first of three detectives, Detective

Willard Smith from the homicide department of the Santa Monica police department. Then he was to meet a Detective Paul Wilmont at the Redondo Beach police station and lastly, drive to the San Pedro station to meet with a Detective Raul Rodriguez.

All three detectives worked in the homicide department for their respective police departments. They also had copies of the composite drawings of the three suspects that Wells had faxed to them. Wells also had orders to coordinate his investigation with others from the World Health Organization and also with any other police departments that might be affected by this catastrophe.

This case had started as an ordinary assignment for Wells but now it had turned into a nightmare. Coordination efforts with the other police departments were turning out to be a massive undertaking. Two shops had been found that was selling the tainted meat. But the detectives continued to search for any other butcher shops that were involved. The four detectives believed there were one or two other butcher shops, possibly in the cities of Redondo Beach and San Pedro that had also been selling the poisoned and tainted meat.

When Detective Wells reached the butcher shop in Santa Monica, the uniformed officers were placing police tape around the crime scene. Detective Willard Smith decided to close down the butcher shop until he could interview the shop's employees.

Just as Wells entered the premises, Detective Smith was walking out of a walk-in freezer carrying a large cardboard box of ground meat. It weighed over fifty pounds. He sent it out immediately to have it analyzed.

Detective Wells introduced himself to Detective Smith.

"Hello. Are you Detective Willard Smith of the Santa Monica homicide department?" asked Detective Wells.

"Yes, I am. And who are you?"

"I'm Detective Wells from the Hollywood police department. I'm here to coordinate our investigations. When did you begin this investigation?"

He told Wells that he was given the case this morning. "After our switchboard was overloaded with calls concerning tainted meat, our coroner gave us the news early this morning. He had three deaths related to food poisoning from tainted meat. When he found out it was human flesh, it became a homicide. And my case."

"Well, I began mine a couple of days ago," replied Wells. "Did your department receive the artist sketches of my three suspects?"

Smith nodded yes, adding, "I showed them to all three employees of this butcher shop and they agreed that two of your suspects were the same people that sold the meat to their unsuspecting employer."

"Where is the owner of this place?" Wells asked Smith.

Smith answered that he didn't know. "And neither do the other workers. He hasn't shown up for work in the last two days. It seems that once he heard about all the deaths from the tainted meat he left town. But we'll catch him sooner or later."

"What's the owner's name?"

"Tommy Elmero," replied Smith

"Elmero? Is he related to a Salvator Elmero of Hollywood?" Wells asked anxiously.

"I don't know, why?"

"Because," Wells replied, "Salvator Elmero is the owner of the butcher shop that I'm investigating. I'll bet you any money that these two guys are related to each other."

"I'll look into it. You may be right."

"Have you sent anyone to his residence yet?" asked Wells.

Smith nodded. "I sent a patrol car over there this morning to check it out, but the house was locked up tighter than a drum. I have my officers watching the house just in case he returns."

Wells asked Smith if he had questioned the workers?

"I have," Smith replied. "But they couldn't give me any leads other than confirming the identity of the two suspects."

Wells asked Smith if any of the workers had mentioned the names of the suspects?

Smith told him that the female suspect went by the name of Kathy. Adding, "But none of them knew the young man's name. They did mention, however, that the guy had long, wavy black hair, two inches below his shoulders and wasn't too friendly."

"That's nearly the same thing my eyewitnesses said," replied Wells.

Smith reassured Wells. "Have no fear, Detective Wells. We'll get these monsters. It might take a little time…but we'll get 'em."

Wells then asked Detective Smith if he wanted to take a ride to Redondo Beach? Adding, "I have to visit a Detective Paul Wilmont concerning this homicide investigation. They also have dead bodies showing up…and all of them were killed from eating poisoned human flesh."

Smith apologized, saying, "I'm sorry, Detective Wells, but I have other things to do right now. How about if we get together tomorrow and go over our notes? I'll call you in the morning and we can get together around lunchtime. What do you say?"

"That's all right with me," replied Wells. "Right now though, I have other things to do. Once I finish visiting Redondo Beach, I have to head over to the San Pedro police department and contact a Detective Raul Rodriguez."

"Don't tell me," retorted Smith. "They also have dead bodies due to eating poisoned human flesh."

Wells nodded, adding, "I have to coordinate my investigation with all three of you, plus the World Health Organization and the state's Food and Beverage Department. I hope we catch these suspects soon. This investigation is beginning to give me a headache."

"Me too," replied Smith.

"Well then, Detective Smith, I'll hear from you in the morning unless you come up with something concrete...or catch the suspects. If that happens, call me immediately."

"Will do, Detective," said Smith, as Wells walked out of the butcher shop.

After Detective Wells entered his car, he looked into his rearview mirror and noticed the female reporter sitting in her car waiting for him to drive away so she could follow him. But as long as she didn't make a nuisance of herself, Wells didn't care if she followed him or not.

Detective Wells started the engine, put his car into gear and headed towards Redondo Beach to meet with Detective Paul Wilmont. Wilmont was investigating two deaths associated with tainted human meat. Wells wondered how many more innocent lives would fall to this act of madness before they could corral the perpetrators and bring them to justice.

The dead victims would have had to burn the meat to a crisp to kill any bacteria or virus. Some of the victims, as told by the Hollywood coroner, had eaten the meat raw, mixed with onions, green pepper and parsley. One of the female victims had died less than twenty hours after eating the poisoned ground meat.

The three suspects were now considered serial killers. Usually the cities affected by such a catastrophe would put together a large task force of possibly fifty different law enforcement investigators, including detectives, psychologists, and forensic specialists. But at this moment, Wells was the only detective working this particular murder investigation for the city of Hollywood and as far as he knew there was only one detective in each of the other cities that were investigating these bizarre murders.

When Wells reached the Redondo Beach police station, he placed his gold detective's badge on the outside of his jacket pocket, then asked the desk sergeant to direct him to Detective Wilmont of the homicide department. The desk sergeant escorted Wells to the detective in question and introduced them to each other.

"Detective Wilmont," said Sergeant Palmer, "this is Detective John Wells from Hollywood's homicide department. He's investigating the tainted meat murders. Detective Wells, this young man is Detective Paul Wilmont."

"How do you do Detective Wells? What can I do for you?" asked Wilmont, as the two shook hands.

Wells remained silent for a few seconds looking over the big man in front of him. He was a good six foot two or three, two hundred and fifty or so pounds and fit as a football player. Wells had to look up to him as he was about three inches shorter, nearly eighty pounds lighter and about thirty years older. Smith and Wells were nearly the same size and the same age – in their mid-sixties. Wilmont – in his mid-thirties. Finally, Wells said, "I'm very glad to meet you, Detective." With that said both detectives relaxed in their chairs.

"Thank you, Sergeant Palmer. You may go now," said Wilmont, as the desk sergeant turned and left the room.

Wells began the conversation. "Detective Wilmont, I'm investigating a number of deaths caused by food poisoning. Your Captain mentioned that you were also investigating similar murders. Is that true?" asked Wells.

"Yes," replied Wilmont, "but I just received the case just a few hours ago. I haven't really started my investigation yet. I'm still waiting for the reports from the coroner's office."

"So what are you doing in the mean time?"

Wilmont replied that he had several officers canvassing the immediate neighborhoods where the victims had lived to see if any of their family members or neighbors knew where they had purchased the tainted meat. "I'm also waiting for reports from the DNA lab and the World Health Organization. Our coroner just sent them pieces of the tainted meat to be tested and analyzed."

"Have you interviewed any of the victims' relatives yet or any of the people that survived eating the tainted meat?" Wells asked Wilmont.

He explained to Wells that there was only one person that could answer that question. "But that person is currently in a coma. She's also the sister of one of the dead victims. The others are either dead or have flown the coop. Three of the victims that survived were indigent and illegal immigrants with no known address or phone number. But we're still trying to locate them, that is if they're still in the area."

"Have you looked for any similar circumstances among the three surviving victims?" asked Wells.

"Like what?"

Wells asked if they had eaten from the same restaurant or had eaten the same food? Or if they knew each other?

Wilmont explained to Wells that the medical reports stated that they had eaten tacos. "But from where, we don't know. So we have no idea where the tainted meat came from. Not yet anyway. But like I told you, I have the uniformed officers canvassing the victims' neighborhoods."

"Have you checked any of your missing persons' reports for the last two months?" Wells asked him. "I'm curious to see if you had a higher than normal rate over the last couple of months than previous months."

"Why do you ask that?" Wilmont asked seemingly confused.

"Because our city for the last two months had a missing persons' rate five times the norm. And somebody had to make up that ground meat. Because the meat that our department tested was ground human flesh. We're trying to find out now just how many different people were in that ground round."

Wilmont thought it over for a few seconds and said, "That's a good idea. I'll have to check the missing persons' list for the last couple of months. I just might get a lead from it."

Wells then asked Wilmont if he wanted to have lunch the following afternoon and talk over this bizarre murder investigation with him and a detective from Redondo Beach? Adding, "So far we've determined that there are at least three suspects, if not more involved in this investigation. And we've also learned that two butcher shops in two neighboring cities have sold the same tainted human flesh. So we're gonna put our heads together and try to come up with some more leads. We have to nail these suspects before any more innocent people are killed. I'm sure we could use your help. Would you like to join us?"

"Sure," he said, "I'd like that. What time is lunch?"

"I'm not sure. Detective Smith will call me in the morning and set up a time. Then I'll contact you and let you know where and when. It will probably be around one or two in the afternoon."

"That sounds good to me."

"All right then," said Wells. "I'll see you tomorrow afternoon. Right now, I have another appointment in San Pedro with a Detective Raul Rodriguez. He's investigating murders similar to ours," With that said, Wells stood up and headed to his car.

As Wells drove to San Pedro police department, he thought about his ongoing murder investigation. He didn't want to underestimate the people that he was looking for. He tried to think as his suspects would think and then stay one step ahead of them. His strategy never failed him. And once he was on a murder suspect's trail, he reeled them in as though he was fishing for Blue Gill.

But suddenly something interrupted his thoughts. Wells believed he saw two of his suspects walking down a busy San Pedro street. So he quickly pulled to the curb and parked his car. However, by the time he had opened his driver's door, the young couple he thought were his suspects had merged with a large crowd of shoppers and he lost sight of them.

But Wells didn't give up. He jumped out of his car and began giving chase. But he was too far behind to catch up to the young male and female suspects. He decided at that point to return to his vehicle, make a U-turn and search for them by car. But just as Wells made his U-turn, the crowd of shoppers suddenly turned a corner and once again he lost sight of his suspects. Though he wasn't sure that the couple was really his suspects, he believed they resembled the drawings enough to warrant questioning them.

However, as Wells turned down the street to follow the crowd of shoppers that the couple had merged with, the people had suddenly vanished. The couple and the throng of shoppers were no longer visible to the naked eye. At least twenty-five people vanished into thin air. Wells was stupefied and had no choice but to give up the chase for the time being. He believed the shoppers had gone their separate ways along with the couple.

Wells made another U-turn, this time heading for the San Pedro police station two miles away. His thoughts returned to his murder investigation. This time he thought about his forensic team. And wondered how they were doing at the condemned, two-story building near the intersection of Santa

Monica and Hollywood boulevards? He left the team as they began searching the premises for any evidence that might give them the identity of the female suspect known as Kathy and any others that might be involved in his horrendous murder investigation.

Detective Wells also hoped that one of the uniformed patrol officers would run into the two suspects that he had just lost sight of. And that the police officers canvassing the streets of Hollywood – particularly a four-square block area in the heart of the city and around the butcher shop's neighborhood – would run into someone that knew the suspects who could possibly lead them to the suspects' hangout and maybe even help apprehend them. Detectives Smith and Wilmont working the case in their respective cities were also doing the same with their uniformed officers.

Detective Wells also wanted desperately to question the two people named Elmero. For some strange reason he thought they were up to their eyeballs in this investigation. He believed that if they were innocent, they would have stuck around to be questioned by the police and not run away and hide out like a bunch of criminals.

Wells' thoughts were suddenly interrupted as he turned into the San Pedro police station parking lot and parked his beat-up, old Ford. After catching his breath he stepped out of his vehicle, pulled his gold shield out of his jacket pocket, clipped it on the outside of the pocket and walked through the front doors of the station. He then stepped up to the front desk and introduced himself to the officer standing behind it.

"Hello, Sergeant Gelber," said Detective Wells as he read the officer's nametag.

"Yes, can I help you?" he asked.

"I sure hope so. I'm Detective Wells and I'm here to see Detective Raul Rodriguez of the homicide department. Is he here?"

"Yes sir, he is. If you would sign in, I'll show you the way."

Wells signed the sheet then Sergeant Gelber escorted him to Detective Rodriguez.

A minute later Sergeant Gelber introduced them to one another. "Detective Rodriguez, this is Detective Wells." With that said Sergeant Gelber turned and left the room while the two detectives got acquainted.

Rodriguez looked to be around forty years of age and was a small, petite character who was no more than five feet tall, and couldn't have weighed more than a hundred pounds sopping wet and wore a nicely trimmed beard and mustache to hide his achne. He could have been a jockey at one time in his life. Wells was a giant standing next to him.

Wells said hello and told Rodriguez that he was from Hollywood station investigating the tainted meat murders. "You are too, aren't you?"

"Yes, I am," replied Rodriquez. "Who told you?"

"Captain Helfman," Wells replied. "He heard about my investigation and telephoned me and explained that you were investigating some murders similar to mine."

"Well, we do have many dead from tainted meat and the coroner stated that it was human flesh that these victims had digested and died from. I just received the composite drawings of your three suspects this morning and I've already got nearly the whole department out canvassing the city, showing the drawings to every citizen of San Pedro."

"Did any of your witnesses verify the suspects' drawings?" Wells asked, hoping.

"We don't have any witnesses," replied Rodriguez. "The ones we had are dead and the ones that survived were either homeless with mental handicaps or illegal aliens of Mexican or Indian ancestry that refused to speak with the police."

Wells knew then that Rodriguez would have to do some heavy investigating.

"So Detective Rodriguez, what you're telling me is that you don't know where the diseased meat was sold from that killed your victims or who sold it to them. Is that what you're saying?"

"That's exactly what I'm saying, Detective Wells," replied Rodriguez matter-of-factly.

"So what have you done besides canvass the area?" Wells asked him.

Rodriguez gave Wells a dirty look and said, "I've been on this case less than three hours. But I've sent uniformed officers to each and every butcher shop, meat market and grocery store that sells exotic meat. Hopefully, they will at the very least find traces of the poisoned meat so we have a lead to go on."

"Well," retorted Wells, "I've got two days on you but I'm still no closer to finding the suspects. I thought I saw the male and one of the female suspects a few miles from here walking down the street but they got lost in a crowd, turned a corner and disappeared."

"Where did you see them?" asked an excited Rodriguez. "Were they in my city? Are you sure it was them?"

He told Rodriguez that he wasn't sure if they were the suspects. Adding, "If I could have gotten closer for a better look then I would know for sure. But I could never catch up to them."

Rodriguez reassured Wells telling him, "I have my investigative team along with many uniformed patrol officers out canvassing the city, so if the suspects are anywhere in this area, we'll nab their behinds."

"Detective Rodriguez, you might also want to check your missing persons' list for any person reported missing within the last two months."

"What for?" Rodriguez asked Wells seemingly confused over his statement.

Wells answered rather bluntly. "Because the meat that those victims died from was diseased human flesh. Someone had to die to get ground up into hamburger and then be sold to the public."

"So you think that some of the people that's been reported missing lately might have been digested in somebody's stomach?"

"That's right," replied Wells. "The diseased meat that was found at two different butcher shops in two nearby cities has already been sent to their labs to be analyzed and tested for DNA to see how many different people were ground up together. You may want to go over that missing persons' list and pick four or five that you think might be involved in our investigation and interview their family members. Ask them to give you any hair fibers from the victim's hairbrush. Then when the DNA tests are completed the evidence can be checked and matched against the DNA from the ground up meat."

"That's a very good idea. I'll look into that. It just might bring us closer to the suspects," said Rodriguez.

"I will be doing the same in my city as soon as my investigative team can make the time. I have maybe six people on my list that I want to get hair fibers from," Wells told him.

Rodriguez nodded, saying, "I'll definitely look into that. But right now I'm waiting for reports from my investigative team. I should be out there with them canvassing the city."

With that said Wells was ready to hit the road. "Well, its getting late and I should be heading back to Hollywood. I have many things to do before the day is out. I also have to regroup with my investigative team. I'm waiting for reports from my forensic team who are searching a condemned building in Hollywood on Santa Monica boulevard for any evidence that might lead me to the suspects in question. We believe this place was a hangout of one of the female suspects known as Kathy."

"Let me know what happens. Any information that can help me in my investigation will be deeply appreciated. So please, Detective Wells, keep me abreast of any new leads that you might get concerning your investigation, would you do that?"

"Of course I will. And you do the same for me. In fact, I'm having lunch tomorrow afternoon with Detective Willard Smith of the Santa Monica homicide division and Detective Paul Wilmont of Redondo Beach homicide. We're gonna talk over our investigations and put our heads together to see if we can't find a way to get these suspects off the street and get these murders solved as soon as possible. If you want to join us, you are welcome to do so. In fact, we'd appreciate it if you'd come."

"Sure. Where and when?" asked Rodriguez.

"I'm not quite sure. Detective Smith will phone me in the morning and let me know what time he can get away from his work and then I will telephone you and Detective Wilmont to let you know."

"Sounds good to me. I'll be waiting to hear from you."

Wells stood up, shook Rodriguez's hand and left the San Pedro police station heading for Hollywood. He hoped to find a few reports sitting on his desk concerning his murder investigation that he could take home and read. It was getting late and his shift was nearly over. He only wanted to return to Hollywood police station to sign out, check his desk and then go home and have a few stiff drinks. And that's just what he did.

When Wells entered the station and returned to his desk he was disappointed to see that there were no reports left for him from his forensic or investigative teams. They were still working and getting much deserved overtime pay but Wells put in his overtime at his home. He would be either reading up on his reports or exercising his arm drinking the night away. And this night he would be exercising his right arm.

CHAPTER 2

Detective Wells partied all night long and ended up falling to sleep on his couch. When he awakened in the morning, he cleared the phlegm from his throat, lit a cigarette, cleared his vision and slowly stood up before stumbling to the bathroom. Once there he straightened out his disheveled suit, splashed a little water on his face, and then went into the kitchen where he drank a big pot of black coffee trying to get rid of his massive hangover.

It had been awhile, at least two weeks since Wells had gotten as drunk as he had, but he needed it to get rid of his anxiety and stress that was brought on from his new murder investigation. Until he had completed each new investigation, he had a habit of getting soused nearly every night and returning to work with a hangover each morning. This morning was no different.

After Wells finished a second pot of Colombian nectar, he was ready to start another day. And anxious to find out if there were any investigative reports waiting for him on his desk. He was sure that the forensic team would have at least one report waiting for him after their search the day before on that condemned building.

Wells walked out the door, jumped into his beat up vehicle and headed for Hollywood police station. Not only was he anxious to read any reports on his murder investigation but he was also waiting anxiously for a phone call from Detective Smith so he could tell Detectives Rodriguez and Wilmont the time of their luncheon engagement. Wells wanted all three-homicide detectives to meet him for lunch at his favorite restaurant, Gabrielle's Hoagie House. Because they made his favorite hoagie sandwiches – steak and cheese smothered in mushrooms.

As Wells was driving down Hollywood Boulevard, heading for work, he thought he saw his two suspects again. They walked towards him as he slowly passed them in his car. They noticed that he was looking at them and bolted from the scene. So Wells slammed on the brakes, put his car into reverse and raced backwards trying not to lose the young couple. But when the light behind him suddenly changed to green, the oncoming traffic stopped him from following his suspects. So he did what he had to do.

He double-parked and left his car in the right hand lane, blocking oncoming traffic so he could give chase. But he was too late. Again they disappeared from view and he lost them. That was the second time in two days that the suspects escaped his grasp and remained at large.

Hurriedly, Wells returned to his car and drove around the block, hoping to run into them again, but it wasn't to be. But before Wells left the scene, he radioed into Hollywood dispatch to have uniformed patrol units search the area for the two suspects more thoroughly.

Just as he was about to leave the area, he looked into his rearview mirror and noticed that same black sedan stopped about six car lengths behind him. Sitting behind the wheel of the car was that same female reporter. But he didn't have time to confront her and ask her why she was following him.

However, the dispatcher at Hollywood station told Wells that there had been an unexpected development in the case and that his Captain wanted to speak with him about it, forth with. Captain Lawson ordered Detective Wells to return to the station house immediately for further consultation with him.

Wells reached Hollywood station in record time with the black sedan following him every step of the way. He parked his car, jumped out of it and ran into the station looking for Captain Lawson – a small and rotund, bald headed, Danny Devito type character.

But when Wells entered through the front doors, he noticed his peers crowded around a television set watching a local news program. He couldn't believe what he was watching. Somehow the media got a hold of the three suspects' composite drawings and exposed the murder investigation to the public.

Detective Wells, along with his superiors, believed this news report about the three suspects would throw a big wrench into Wells' murder investigation. The media somehow received the composite drawings much sooner than the police wanted them to. Now the Hollywood police investigators were worried that the suspects would be aware of the situation and flee the city and possibly the state to start anew somewhere else.

Captain Lawson called Wells into his office and belittled him for letting the drawings get away from his investigative team and into a reporter's hands. However, Wells explained to his Captain that he had no idea how the reporter received the drawings but he promised he would investigate and find out.

Wells also promised Captain Lawson that nothing like this would happen again. At least not on his watch. Captain Lawson was satisfied with Wells' answers and let him return to his duties. So Wells walked out of Captain Lawson's office and directly to his desk and was happy to find a few reports trickling in about his murder investigation.

The first investigative report he read was from his forensic team that had searched the condemned building. It stated that there were a number of different fingerprints found at the location along with a number of empty prescription bottles that at one time contained either heavy pain medication or sleeping pills.

There was also an empty bottle of hydrochloride morphine and a number of used needles and syringes lying throughout the premises. The only problem was that all the information on the prescription bottles had been scratched off except for the drug's name.

The investigators, however, did find and remove a few partial prints from the medicine bottles and found nearly a dozen other complete prints. In fact, when the forensic team returned to the station they ran the prints into the FBI's database and found hits on seven of the twelve prints.

Now Wells had names to go along with the prints that were found in the hideout. As he read more of the report, it also stated that seven out of the twelve prints collected had police records. But when the prints were run through the FBI's database for photo identification none of the hits matched or resembled the suspects in the composite drawings. So Wells filed the names away for safekeeping. Because he knew that many of these people could still be staying in the area and would sooner or later end up at the Hollywood police station.

Just as Wells finished reading the forensic report, his desk phone rang. It was Detective Willard Smith of the Santa Monica homicide division calling to coordinate the time and place for their lunch date. It was set up for one o'clock that afternoon at Gabrielle's Hoagie House.

Wells explained to Detective Smith that two other homicide detectives from San Pedro and Redondo Beach police departments would also be joining them so they could talk over their murder investigations. After receiving directions to Gabrielle's Hoagie House, Detective Smith agreed to meet Detective Wells at the restaurant for lunch.

After Wells hung up his phone, he picked up another report – the list of missing persons for the last two months. After glancing over it, he noticed that most of the names were Italian so he picked out a half a dozen that he thought might possibly be intertwined in his murder investigation.

Wells then sent out his investigative team that included many uniformed patrol officers, to visit the families of the missing people and gather hair samples in order to run DNA tests and compare them against the DNA testing of the ground meat.

However, the investigators could only ask the victims' families for the hair samples. The families didn't have to cooperate with the police department at all. In fact, some did refuse to help in the murder investigation not wanting to believe that their loved ones were dead.

When Wells noticed that lunch was only two hours away, he telephoned Detectives Wilmont and Rodriguez to tell them the time of lunch and gave them directions to Gabrielle's Hoagie House. The two homicide detectives agreed to meet Wells for lunch at the prescribed time.

As Wells hung up the phone, he took special notice of another investigative report sitting on his desk in front of him. While reading it he learned that Tommy and Salvator Elmero, the owners of the specialty butcher shops that sold the poisoned meat, were known mob members and soldiers of the Don Bruno Manzelli crime family.

Wells sat back in his chair and thought about his murder investigation. He wondered how the mob was involved in it. Were the Elmero brothers just innocent buyers of the human meat or were they somehow the killers that got rid of their evidence by grinding up their victims and then selling it to the public out of mob owned butcher shops? Even Manzelli's brother was missing.

Wells also wondered if Tony Manzelli was mixed up in this murder investigation? These and many other questions were clouding his mind, when he looked at his watch and noticed it was time to leave for his luncheon engagement. So he headed out the front doors to the parking lot.

As Detective Wells reached his car, he noticed a pretty and lanky young woman with short blond hair, dressed in a sweater and blue jeans coming towards him. She had just stepped out of her black sedan. It was the reporter that had been following him and his vehicle throughout his investigation. She introduced herself before Wells could get away.

"Hello, Detective Wells. My name is Susan Pelk. I work for an independent newspaper. If you could give me a minute of your time I'd like to ask you a few questions concerning your murder investigation and the three young suspects."

"I'm sorry Miss Pelk but I'm really in a hurry at this time. I have an important meeting to go to."

"Does it concern your investigation?" she asked him.

"I can't say. I'm really sorry but I must leave now. You'll have to catch up with me at a better time. Maybe then I'll be able to answer some of your questions. But if my Captain sees me speaking with you it could mean my job," said Wells as he opened his car door and jumped behind the wheel.

Before Pelk could say another word, he started the engine, put his car into gear and roared out of the parking lot as Susan Pelk held onto the driver's door handle. Luckily she was able to release her grip as the car raced away. She then ran back to her car, started the engine and raced out of the parking lot trying to catch up to Wells' vehicle. Susan Pelk was anxious to see where he was headed. And wanted any information that could help her with her story. But Wells was hesitant to help in her endeavors.

After a five-minute drive, Wells pulled into Gabrielle's Hoagie House parking lot. Once out of the car he looked around for any of the other homicide detectives. He had planned to stand outside and wait for their arrival until he saw that black sedan carrying Susan Pelk. He then decided to wait inside the shop for his guests.

Susan Pelk walked into the shop and sat a few tables away from Detective Wells. He could only give her a cold, disgusting stare. But it didn't faze the woman in the least. She seemed to be a cold and calculating she-devil. Wells wanted nothing to do with her, but America was a free country and Susan Pelk could go wherever and whenever she pleased. Of course to politicians it was a free country. But that was another story.

Finally, at about 1:05 p.m., the first of the three detectives arrived. It was Paul Wilmont of the Redondo Beach police force. Wells stood up and shook his hand as he reached the table.

"Detective Wilmont, it's good to see you," said Wells smiling. "Can I order you a drink?"

"Sure," replied Wilmont. "Do they serve alcoholic beverages here?"

"Yes they do. What would you like? It's on me today."

"I'd like a Long Island iced tea."

Wells ordered one Long Island iced tea for Detective Wilmont and a double scotch for himself. By the time their drinks had arrived another of Wells' guests had appeared. It was Detective Willard Smith. Wells directed him to his table and introduced him to Wilmont.

"Detective Willard Smith, this is Detective Paul Wilmont of the Redondo Beach homicide division. Willard works out of Santa Monica. I'm surprised you two have never met before."

"Well, I just started my job only three months ago. I'm still new to the neighborhood," said Wilmont.

"Not me. I've been working for Hollywood division for over forty years and nearly thirty of them in the homicide department. What about you, Detective Smith?" asked Wells.

But just as Smith was about to answer the question, the last of the homicide detectives had arrived. Wells stood and directed him to their table. Detective Rodriguez walked over and extended an outstretched hand to shake the others hands as he introduced himself.

"Hello. I'm Detective Raul Rodriguez from San Pedro police department. I work in the homicide department," he said, as he grabbed a chair and sat down with the others.

"If you weren't a homicide detective you wouldn't be here right now," said Wells, as he lit a cigarette.

"Detective Wells and I just ordered drinks. Would you guys like anything to drink. They serve alcoholic beverages," said Wilmont.

"I can't drink alcohol, I'm on duty at the moment," interjected Rodriguez.

"So am I," said Wilmont as he lit a large cigar. "But when I get stressed out from a case I'll have one or two stiff drinks at lunchtime. It loosens me up."

"I'll order one. I'll have a rum and coke," said Smith.

"Guys, lunch and drinks are on me today. So order what you like," said Wells.

"Well, in that case I'll have a Margarita, if you don't mind," said Rodriguez.

After they had consumed a few drinks and had eaten it was time to get down to business. But before they could speak about the investigation, Wells had to lay the ground rules. He pointed out the female reporter, Susan Pelk, to his fellow homicide detectives and made sure nobody spoke loud enough so she could hear their conversation. Wells didn't want her stealing any of their secrets that they might expose while talking.

"Did any of you guys watch the local news this morning?" asked Wells.

"Yep," said Detectives Wilmont, Rodriguez and Smith in unison.

"How did the media get a hold of your suspects' composite drawings?" Wilmont asked Wells.

"I don't know," Wells replied. "But I hope they don't get any other information on our investigations."

"Let's do the best we can to keep our evidence under our hats. We don't need any more headaches than we already have," said Smith.

"That's why we have to be careful as to what we say. You don't know who may be listening," said Wells, pointing to Susan Pelk's table.

"You got that right," said Rodriguez.

"Did any of you guys check your missing persons' lists for the last two months?" asked Wells.

"I did," said Wilmont.

"I did, also," said Rodriguez.

"What are you guys talking about? Why are you checking the missing persons' reports?" asked Smith.

"Well," said Wells as he lit a cigarette, "in the Hollywood area I checked our missing persons' reports and noticed that the statistics were up more than five times the norm for the last two months. That meant quite a few people have turned up missing. And under weird circumstances. So I figured if there were dead bodies ground up in that tainted meat…it's quite possible that some of the human flesh could have come from some of these missing people."

"That sounds logical. I'm surprised I didn't think of it myself," said Smith.

"Well, I'm not really sure if anything will come of it or not, but I thought it was worth the time to check it out," said Wells.

"So did anything pan out from it yet?" asked Smith.

"I don't know. I sent out my investigative team to the six families that I picked from the missing persons' list to retrieve hair samples from the victims' hairbrush. That should give us enough for DNA testing to check against the results from the ground meat."

Rodriguez also mentioned that he had sent out his investigators to speak with a few families of the missing people to ask for hair fibers. Adding, "We hope we won't have any trouble from them but my investigators haven't reported in yet."

"What about you, Detective Wilmont?" asked Wells.

"No, I haven't had the chance. We are too busy searching for the three suspects."

"My investigators found one good piece of evidence regarding the tainted meat murders," interjected Smith.

"What have you got?" asked Wells.

"Well, when we showed the employees of Santa Monica butcher shop the drawings of the three suspects, one of them told my investigators that she didn't recognize any of the females. The woman she saw deliver the meat was somebody different than the ones in the drawings."

"Detective Smith, did you have a composite drawing made of your female suspect?" asked Wells.

"Please, call me Willard. And to answer your question, yes I did. In fact, I brought each of you copies for your investigations," he said as he opened up his briefcase to retrieve the drawings. He handed one to each of the detectives.

"You know, I think I've seen this girl before, but I just can't put my finger on it. Do you have a name to go with the photo?" asked Wells.

"No, I don't. The eyewitness couldn't remember what the girl's name was. The drawing is all we have to go on at this time."

"My investigators found out some information that might be helpful," said Rodriguez.

"What did you find out?" asked Wells.

"We found at least one specialty butcher shop in the city of San Pedro that had been selling the tainted meat. And we have our team out now combing the area to search for any other establishments that might be involved."

Wells asked him what the owner of the butcher shop had to say? And what excuse he used for selling the meat? "Did he tell you the names of the people involved that sold him the tainted meat?"

"Not exactly," he said as he kept his face down, drinking from his glass.

"What do you mean, not exactly?" asked Wells.

He told Wells that the owner of the shop hadn't been seen for two days. Adding that, "The employees said he came into the store two days ago, then gave the keys of the place to the manager and told him he would be on vacation for at least two weeks."

"Detective Rodriguez, did you speak with the owner's family or relatives yet about his whereabouts?" asked Wells.

"It's Raul. And yes, I sent my investigators out there to question every family member and relative. I should have the report sitting on my desk by morning or maybe even late this afternoon."

"What's the butcher shop owner's name?" Wells asked Rodriguez.

"Johnny Vega," replied Rodriguez. "He's the brother-in-law to a pair of mob brothers by the name of Elmero."

"You're not talking about Tommy and Salvator Elmero are you?" asked Wells, scratching his head in disbelief.

"Yes, I believe that's their names. Why? Have you had trouble with the Elmero brothers before?"

"Tommy Elmero owns the butcher shop that sold the tainted meat in my city," interjected Smith.

"That's right," said Wells. "They are the owners of the butcher shops that were selling the poisoned meat."

"What does the mob have to do with our murder investigations?" asked Smith scratching his bald head.

Just then Rodriguez interjected his thoughts. "Do you guys think these mob guys are killing their competitors and then grinding them into hamburger to sell to the public to get rid of the evidence?"

"That's a very good possibility," Wells replied. "But what about our three, excuse me, four suspects?"

"Maybe they were just hired to deliver the meat," Wilmont surmised.

"That's also a possibility," interjected Wells. "This case seems to be widening instead of narrowing down. At first I thought the owners had run away because they were afraid of going to jail for buying the tainted meat and that the young couple were the evil killers. But now I realize it could be the other way around. It could be the shop owners are guilty of the murders and the four young suspects are innocent. Boy, how the tables turn."

"Well," said Smith, "don't get too concerned about who murdered who until we have our four suspects and the butcher shop owners in custody to question. That's the only way we're gonna figure this out unless somebody comes forward and confesses to the crimes. But we still won't know for sure until we do a thorough and complete investigation."

Wells told Smith that he was absolutely right. Then he asked Rodriguez if he had any other surprises to tell them concerning the investigations?

Rodriguez replied that he didn't have anything more. Adding, "Possibly by tomorrow something might shake loose."

Wells then told the guys that he still had a few reports to read that might be of interest.

Smith asked Wells if he had anything more to tell that might help them in their investigations?

"Yes, I believe I do," Wells replied. "One of the reports I read was a forensic report on a suspected hangout of my female suspect named Kathy. She was supposedly holed up there recently."

"Evidently you didn't find her there, did you?" asked Smith sarcastically.

"No, she wasn't there when I or the forensic team searched the place. In fact none of our suspects showed up at the condemned building."

"Detective Wells, did your investigators find anything worth talking about?" asked Rodriguez.

"It's John. And yes, they did find some decent evidence that still needs to be analyzed, which included twelve different prints. The prints were run through the FBI's database and seven came up as hits. Unfortunately, none of their photos or body statistics matched my three suspects."

"Now you can check my female suspect against your seven photos. Maybe she'll resemble one of them. How many hits were female?" asked Smith.

"Five were female, two were male," Wells replied.

"Hell, who knows, maybe we'll get lucky for a change," said Smith.

"Tell me about it. I thought I had seen two of my suspects two different times already and in two different cities but I lost them both times. And one of those times was just this morning," said Wells.

"Detective Wells, I mean John, are you sure it was your suspects? I had my investigative team canvass our city for ten hours after you told me that you had seen them yesterday in San Pedro, but we didn't find them," said Rodriguez.

"Yes, but I also told you I wasn't close enough to them to really see their faces clearly. I thought it was my suspects. Just like I thought I had seen them this morning."

"Don't worry, Wells, we'll get them sooner or later," said Smith. "But I want to talk more about the mob and their possible involvement in our investigations. That's really got my curiosity. Maybe Rodriguez <u>had</u> something when he wondered if <u>they</u> hired these kids to deliver the meat to their stores to make <u>them</u> the main target. That way it takes the heat off the mob and places it solely on the kids."

"And where are the owners of these butcher shops?" interjected Wells. "All three suddenly decided to vacation at the same time. Something just doesn't add up."

"Let's hope our teams close the noose around them and bring them in for questioning real soon," said Wilmont.

"I second the motion," said Smith, as all the detectives toasted their glasses in the air.

"Well guys, it's getting late and I have to return to Hollywood station to finish reading my reports and see what my investigators have dug up. They'll page me if they find anything of importance or need me for anything," said Wells.

"You're right. It is getting late. Damn, time sure flies by when you're having a good time," chuckled Smith.

"Here, here," said Wilmont.

"Okay, guys, the check's on me today. Let's keep in close touch and let's have lunch here again in the next couple of days. Or sooner if something breaks," said Wells, grabbing the check and paying the waitress.

All four homicide detectives stood up and shook hands before walking towards the front door of the hoagie shop. And before they entered their cars Wells promised them he would keep in touch daily – and asked that they keep him abreast of their investigations – they agreed. With that said, they jumped behind the wheel of their cars, started the engines and roared off in three different directions.

Detective Wells headed straight back to Hollywood station. He hoped to find a few more reports sitting on his desk when he returned. During the five-minute drive, he looked at Smith's drawing of his female suspect. Wells couldn't get her out of his mind. He really believed he had seen her before but couldn't put his finger on it.

Once Wells entered the city limits of Hollywood he folded up the drawing and began looking on both sides of the street hoping to see one or more of his four suspects. However, by the time he reached Hollywood station he gave up looking for them and concentrated on other matters – like pulling into the station's parking lot and parking his car.

Wells suddenly, for some reason, wondered where Susan Pelk had gone? He had actually forgotten about her while he was driving and studying Smith's suspect's drawing. But then, just as he pulled into the station's parking lot he suddenly remembered her and noticed she hadn't followed him. But he didn't worry about her. He had other things on his mind.

As soon as he signed in at the front desk, he started towards the snack room but was stopped by Captain Lawson.

"Detective Wells, can you step into my office for a few minutes, I need to speak with you," said Captain Lawson.

"What have I done now, Captain?" he joked, as they entered Captain Lawson's office.

"Please close the door. I don't want any of this getting out of this office," he said, as Wells obeyed his command.

"What's on you mind, Captain?"

"Some of your fellow detectives have told me that you were seen speaking with a female reporter. Is that right?"

"Yes," replied Wells looking down at the floor, "I've spoken with a female reporter. But not about my murder investigation."

"They said she has been following you every place you go," scowled Lawson. "Is that true?"

Wells confirmed his captain's suspicion, saying, "Yes, I've seen Susan Pelk's car following a few car lengths behind mine. But she stays in her car. That is, except for today. She followed me into Gabrielle's Hoagie House while I was meeting with three other detectives involved in similar murder investigations."

"I hope she didn't hear anything of importance from your meeting that she could use in her story," snapped Lawson.

Wells retorted, "Unless she has ears of a wolf, she couldn't overhear us. We made sure we spoke softly and quietly. Plus, she was sitting two tables over from ours."

"Let's hope that's the case. We don't want to find ourselves in the news before we're ready."

"Don't worry about me, Captain. I know how to handle Susan Pelk."

Before dismissing Wells from his office Lawson asked if the meeting with the other detectives brought out any new evidence to help in his investigation?

Wells replied, "Actually I did find out a few new things. Detective Willard Smith, the homicide detective from Santa Monica, came up with a new suspect – another young female approximately sixteen to eighteen years of age. Here is her drawing." Wells pulled the folded paper out of his jacket pocket and handed it to him.

Captain Lawson unfolded the paper and looked closely at the drawing of the young female. He seemed to be staring a hole right through the suspect's face. After a long minute, he handed the drawing back to Wells, saying, "Let's see if we can't get these people off the streets real soon. Have you learned anything about the whereabouts of the butcher shop owners that sold the diseased meat?"

"Not yet," replied Wells. "But Detective Raul Rodriguez of the San Pedro homicide division found a shop in the heart of his city that had been selling the poisoned hamburger. But get this, it's owned by the brother-in-law of the Elmero brothers and all three are in the mob."

"The mob. What the hell do they have to do with your tainted meat murder investigation?"

Wells remained silent for a few seconds trying to find the right words before saying, "Sir, we won't know that until we find and question the shop owners. But Captain, what if the mob hired these young kids to deliver the meat to their shops just to take the heat off of them and hide their evidence? Maybe some of these people that were ground up were actually mob members or somehow related to the mob."

Lawson thought it over for a few seconds and said, "That sounds logical. What about the missing persons' list? Have you checked to see if any of the people on the list were mob members?"

"I know of one for sure. Don Bruno Manzelli's brother Tony is missing."

"How do you know that?"

"Because Don Bruno came into the station and filed a missing persons' report on his brother. He's been missing for nearly a week. So if the mob killed him, they're not saying."

Lawson, scratching his head said, "Boy, this news really throws a monkey wrench into your investigation, doesn't it, Detective Wells?"

"Not really," replied Wells. "I just need to find and question some people. Once they are in custody, I'll get the answers I want."

Lawson told Wells to keep up the good work. And then dismissed him.

Wells turned and walked out of Captain Lawson's office and headed for his desk. But when he entered his department, everyone was gone. There wasn't one other homicide detective in the room. He was alone and wondered where everyone had disappeared to? But he quickly forgot about his peers when he saw a pile of new reports sitting on his desktop.

Wells plopped down into his chair and picked up a report to read. As he began to glance through it he remembered the drawing of Detective Smith's female suspect. He began reading the eyewitness's description of the suspect in question. The eyewitness stated the young woman was between sixteen and eighteen years of age, with very short cropped, blond hair, just like the other females but wearing a flowered headband and weighing about one hundred and fifteen pounds.

She had crooked front teeth, wore bell-bottom jeans and a white halter-top, just like the hippies did back in the sixties. Suddenly a light went off in his head. He remembered the seven hits from the FBI's database that he had filed away earlier in the day. He dug them out of the file cabinet and began looking through the photos of the five women.

After looking at three out of the five photos without any luck, he figured he would strike out with the other two also. But when he matched the composite drawing to the last photo, the resemblance was so similar that he was sure the two females were one and the same, even though the photo showed the young woman with shoulder length hair.

The report stated that she was five feet six inches and one hundred and twenty pounds with thick, shoulder length, fuzzy, brown hair, crooked upper front teeth and dressed like a hippie of the sixties who liked to wear bell-bottom jeans and halter tops. That was the same description that Detective Smith's eyewitness had described, except for the hair. The suspect's name was Katie Brown.

The report also included information about her life with her drug-addicted mother. Wells was sickened by the abuse this young girl had to sustain. Katie Brown was sold by her mother to male drug addicts for their sexual pleasure. And had lost her virginity at the age of five. By age six she had been sold as a sexual toy for perverts more than one hundred times, ending up in the hospital more than a dozen times. After her first few visits to the hospital she was returned to her drug-addicted mother. And after her third visit, when she suffered massive internal injuries she was given to the state and put in foster care.

And then when Katie Brown went to live in her foster care home, she was raped within two days of her arrival by both foster parents. They also used her as a sex object until the couple was caught in the act by a social worker making a surprise visit to see how the child was adjusting to her new home. The foster couple received five years in a minimum security prison for raping a six year old girl more than once. What justice?

Katie Brown's second foster care home wasn't much better. She stayed in that home for a total of two years before the law caught up to the foster couple. They had been raping the young girl nightly for the two years she had stayed there. The state took Katie back and placed her in a mental institution instead of another foster home, hoping to calm her fears. But when Katie became antagonistic and out of control during her two-year stay, they strapped her into a straightjacket, locked her into a padded cell and fed her antidepressants and tranquilizers.

When the doctors released her back to the state social department, Katie Brown was again placed into foster care. She had just turned nine years of age. Things seemed to be going all right for the first eight months of her incarceration in foster care until her foster parents began using her to steal for a living. She was caught more than once and her foster parents denied having anything to do with the thefts. So the social worker allowed Katie to remain in their care and that was nearly a fatal mistake. They nearly beat her to death for telling the social worker that her foster parents made her steal. She was saved when a neighbor, while walking his dog on the sidewalk in front of the foster couple's home, heard loud screaming and crying coming from a child. He raced home and called the police. If the neighbor had waited just five more minutes to make the phone call, Katie would have gone to the morgue instead of the hospital.

Katie Brown was in and out of foster care until she ran away at age thirteen. She had been raped, abused, beat up, bruised, battered and taught a life of crime. By the time Detective Wells had finished reading her police report he was visibly sickened and upset. He just couldn't get over the terrible life this young girl had to live through. She had been treated worse than an animal.

But Wells still had a job to do. Now Hollywood division could put out an all points bulletin on Katie Brown. He also had to telephone the other detectives working the investigation. They deserved to learn this information immediately. But just as Wells reached out to pick up his telephone, Captain Lawson came into the room. He looked around and saw that Wells was the only one in the room so he handed him a piece of paper with an address written on it.

"What's this, Captain?" Wells asked.

The Captain replied, "The coroner just called from a murder scene four blocks from here. Seeing you're the only homicide detective in the room, I want you to head over there."

But Wells was already overworked. And pissed that Captain Lawson would put this new responsibility on his shoulders, telling him, "With all due respect, Captain, I've got my hands full <u>now</u>. In fact, I just found out some very important information to help in the tainted meat murders."

But Captain Lawson refused his excuses, saying, "Just handle it for now and I'll see if I can pass it on to one of the other detectives in a day or so. But right now Dr. Jack Terry is waiting for your expertise. And the forensic staff is also there. They need a homicide detective to lead them."

"I'll leave now sir," said a dejected Wells as he started walking towards the station's front door.

"Don't forget Detective Wells," yelled Captain Lawson as Wells walked outside to the parking lot, "I want to hear about this new information you have on the tainted meat murders as soon as you return."

Wells jumped into his car, started the engine, and then raced out of the parking lot pissed as hell. And another headache was right behind him. It was Susan Pelk following in her black sedan.

CHAPTER 3

The murder scene was only four blocks from the Hollywood police station. It was at one of the older and seedier motels in the area. Wells was there in less than three minutes. The coroner and forensic team were outside standing around waiting for a senior homicide detective to show up.

When Wells parked his car in the motel's parking lot he noticed Susan Pelk had parked a few cars away from his own. For some reason he couldn't shake her.

Wells walked into the small motel to check out the murder scene and the coroner and the other investigators followed. Once inside they huddled in the corridor to figure out their next plan of action.

But Dr. Jack Terry, an old and wise coroner was confused and asked Wells why he was here? Adding, "I thought you were investigating those tainted meat murders? How come you were given this case to investigate?"

"Don't ask me, Dr. Terry," replied Wells angrily. "Ask Captain Lawson. He's the one that handed me the case. All the other homicide detectives were away from their desks at the time…so Captain Lawson ordered me here."

"Well, I guess there's not a whole lot you can do about that except obey your boss and do your work," said Dr. Terry, a Telly Savalis look-alike – bald head and all.

"I guess so," said Wells as they walked to the room where the body lay.

Before allowing Wells to enter the room Dr. Terry had him put on surgeon's slippers and thin rubber gloves so he wouldn't contaminate the crime scene. Once that was done, Dr. Terry slowly opened the door. Wells felt a cold chill in the air as the air conditioner was going full blast – the thermostat was set below fifty degrees – and then was taken aback for a few seconds after seeing a mutilated body laying face up on the thin carpeted floor. Wells was startled by the brutality of the killer's action. Dr. Terry believed the body to be three to four days old, but due to the near freezing temperature in the room he couldn't be sure until a complete autopsy was performed.

Once Wells had caught his breath and settled into his work mode, he was ready to begin his investigation – and quickly looked at all areas of the room while standing in the doorway.

In the far corner of the room sitting on a small bed stand under a dusty lamp were two empty glasses. To the right of the nightstand was an unmade bed and an old wooden chair with a pair of pants neatly folded and hung over the back of it. Lying next to the chair on the floor was a pair of dirty white socks and directly in front of Wells lay the semi-nude male victim dressed only in white jockey shorts.

Even though the victim's hands and feet were cut off and parts of his skin in many different areas on the body had been peeled away, there wasn't one drop of blood on the carpeting. Yet Dr. Terry believed that the victim died in this motel room but couldn't be sure until the autopsy was completed. And if the coroner was right...that meant the victim wasn't killed somewhere else and then had his body dumped here, but that the killer or killers had murdered him right here in this motel room.

Once Wells had a good look at the murder scene, he and Dr. Terry entered further into the room. When they kneeled down to review the victim's mutilated body, Dr. Terry mentioned something about the victim's mouth.

"Detective Wells, look into the victim's mouth and tell me what you see."

Wells looked into the victim's wide-open mouth and was very surprised at the sight.

"He's got no teeth," replied a surprised Wells. "By the looks of it, somebody pulled them out. The inside of his mouth is really torn up."

"That's putting it mildly," retorted Terry.

"And what happened to the victim's eyeballs?" Wells asked the coroner.

Terry told him that the killer must have ripped them out.

"But Dr. Terry," asked a confused Wells, "why isn't there any blood if he was murdered here?"

"Look here on his neck," said Dr. Terry pointing to the victim's jugular vein.

"Is that a needle mark or is it an old boil?" Wells asked him.

"A big needle punctured the victim's skin. I believe we have a vampire on the loose," replied Terry.

"Why do you say that, Doc?"

"Because the killer or killers drained him of his blood before mutilating him."

"Maybe he used it to give himself a blood transfusion," replied Wells trying to bring a little humor to the subject.

"Well Detective, that's for you to find out. I'm just giving you my opinion. I'll know more when I do the autopsy."

"So evidently," Wells surmised, "the victim was already dead when they cut off his hands and feet and pulled the teeth out of his mouth. What do you think, Doc?"

"You're probably right."

"Do you think the victim was drugged before the killer started mutilating him?" Wells asked him.

"I would think so. The killer might have injected him in the same spot that they sucked out his blood," theorized Dr. Terry.

"Or they might have drugged his drink," replied Wells. "Those two empty glasses sitting on the night stand might have traces of a sedative or narcotic."

"That could very well be. Have the forensic team analyze them," Terry told Wells.

"Oh I plan on it," Wells replied. "Is there any identification on the victim?"

"I don't know," replied Terry. "I didn't touch anything in this room other than the victim. You might want to check the pants that are hanging over the back of the chair."

"That's a good idea," replied Wells as he walked the few steps to the chair and grabbed the pair of brown suit pants. "By the way, who called the station about this murder?"

Terry told him he thought it was the manager of the hotel. "I think he found the body when he checked the room to see if it was clean enough to be used for a convention that is coming to town in a few days. He said that this room is only used when the motel is full."

"Why is that, Doc?"

He explained to Wells that the room was next to the vending machines and many of the customers used them during the night. And if they lost money in the machines they would kick and bang on them, which sometimes ended in a fight with the person that rented the room. "At least that's what the manager told me. You should probably talk to him yourself."

"I'll do that," replied Wells. "But at another time. I'll get one of the uniformed officers to take the manager's statements. Right now I've got more important work to do. I have to find the people who killed and mutilated this guy."

Terry interjected that he didn't think the victim rented the room.

"Why do you say that?" Wells asked.

"Because the manager told me the room should have been empty," replied Terry. "This victim should have never been here."

"I think that manager may know more than he's saying. Somebody had to know that this room was rarely used, except on special occasions. I believe this to be an inside job. Somebody that works here at this motel knows something about this murder. I'd bet my life on it," theorized Wells

"Detective Wells, I see you have a lot of investigating to do on this case."

"Tell me, Doc, is there anything of importance on the victim's back side that I need to see?"

"No, I checked. However, there is a large piece of skin that has been peeled away on the right shoulder blade that maybe contained a tattoo or birthmark. Something that the killers thought would identify the victim. Just like the other sections that have been peeled away."

"What type of sick human being are we dealing with?" Wells said to no one in particular.

"Evidently someone that's ten degrees off plum," replied Terry.

"Boy Doc, you got that right."

Terry then told Wells that he'd give him the complete lowdown on the body as soon as he did the autopsy.

"Well, I guess I'm about finished here. I'll let the boys on the forensic team take over," said Wells.

"Can I remove the body now?" asked Terry, looking into Wells' tired eyes.

"Yeah," replied Wells, "but before you do...let the photographer shoot the murder scene from top to bottom without destroying evidence, and then have the forensic crew bag the victim's underwear and check the body for any microscopic evidence. Once that's finished make sure they bag the rest of the clothes, the two empty glasses and any other pertinent evidence."

"Will do, Detective Wells. I'll let the photographer get started then."

"Very good, Doc. If anybody needs me, I'll be interviewing the manager to see if I can't get some answers out of him. Like I said, this has got to be an inside job."

"I thought you were going to let someone else question the manager," said Terry.

"I changed my mind."

Wells left the crime scene and walked the fifty yards to the other side of the run down motel. Just as he reached out to grab the doorknob to the manager's office, someone from inside beat him to it. While he stood aside waiting for the person to exit he was surprised to see that the person leaving the office was none other than Susan Pelk.

"Hello, Miss Pelk," said Wells reluctantly. "What are you doing here?"

"I thought I would rent a room. What else?" she snapped as she walked past him.

Detective Wells didn't say anything more and entered the manager's office. The middle-aged man sitting in a beat up old chair behind the counter was sound asleep and snoring. Even when Wells slammed the door behind him, the man still didn't awaken. He was definitely in dreamland.

Wells had to reach over the counter and wake the guy up by grabbing him by the shoulders and shaking him like a rag doll.

"Wake up, buddy," shouted Wells as the sleeping man finally came around and awoke from his slumber.

"Yes, sir. Do you need a room?" asked the man behind the counter.

"No. I'm Detective Wells," he said, showing the man his badge and identification. "I'm investigating that dead body in room 1001. Do you know where the manager is?"

"I'm the manager," he said.

"Are you the one that called in the dead body?"

"No. I work the night shift. The person you want to speak with is the day man, Ray Santo."

"What is your name?"

"I'm Dan Gold."

"Where can I find this Ray Santo?" Wells asked.

"Right at this moment," Gold said looking at his watch, "he's probably at home getting drunk."

Wells then asked him what time Santo started work?

"We're both on twelve hour shifts," Gold replied. "He starts at five a.m. and ends at five p.m.."

"Mr. Gold, what do you know about the mutilated body that ended up in room 1001?" asked Wells.

"I don't know anything about it."

Wells then asked him how long he had been working at this hotel?

"Nearly six months," he replied.

"Have you ever been in trouble with the law?" Wells asked him.

"Yeah, a few times."

Wells wanted to know if it was hard time?

Gold told him that the judge gave him ten years but he was out in two.

Wells wanted to know what got him ten years.

"Murder," Gold replied softly. "But I copped a plea to second degree manslaughter and the judge gave me ten years like he was handing out candy."

"How in the hell did you get out so quick?" Wells asked him.

"Overcrowding," Gold snickered. "I heard a pot smoker took my place. The judge gave him twenty-five years for one ounce of pot. And then the D.E.A. confiscated his parents home and threw them out into the street."

"I don't believe it," snapped Wells.

"It's true," replied the ex-con. "Not only that but one of the D.E.A. agents bought the house that they confiscated, real cheap."

"Mr. Gold, I don't care about pot smokers. I want to know about that dead guy in room 1001. The coroner says that the victim's been dead for at least three or four days. Did you kill him?" asked Wells, staring directly into the night manager's beady little eyes looking for a reaction.

He didn't say anything for a few long seconds and stared at the floor before blurting out, "No I didn't. I don't know anything about that dead body except what Ray Santo told me about it."

Wells wanted to know what Santo had told him.

"Not much," Gold replied. "I only spoke with him for maybe five minutes."

"So what did he tell you?"

"Just that somebody was dead in room 1001 and to keep all employees away from it until the police said otherwise. That was it. That's all he told me. I swear."

Wells then asked him who rented the room to the dead victim?

"No one," snapped Gold seemingly rather nervous from Wells' questioning. "Room 1001 isn't used but maybe once or twice a year if at all. It's used only on very rare occasions when all of our other rooms are filled."

"Why didn't anyone working at this hotel ever notice that the air conditioner was going full blast? The thermostat was set to run continuously and not shut off. Why didn't someone go into the room to shut down the air conditioner?" asked Detective Wells.

"Room 1001 is way at the very end of the motel. I don't go that way unless I absolutely have to," said Mr. Gold.

"It looks to me like you don't leave that chair unless you absolutely have to."

"You're right about that, Detective."

"Okay Mr. Gold, tell Mr. Ray Santo that Detective Wells or one of his investigators will be back in the morning to speak with him about the dead body laying in his motel room."

"I'll tell him."

"Mr. Gold, if you can think of anything else that might help me in this case," Wells said, handing him his business card, "give me a call, day or night. But I'm sure you and I will be speaking to each other again very soon."

Detective Wells opened the office door and stepped outside only to see Susan Pelk sitting behind the wheel of her car and staring in his direction. He began walking very quickly towards her black sedan to confront her about her ethics and why she was stalking him. But just as he approached her car, a rookie patrol cop intercepted him.

"Sir, are you Detective Wells?" asked the rookie cop.

"Yes, I'm Detective Wells. What do you need son?"

"Sir, I was sent here by Captain Lawson to find you. He wants you to go over to this address to investigate another murder scene," said the rookie cop, handing Wells a scrap of paper.

Detective Wells quickly read the address on the scrap of paper.

"Hell, this is on the other side of town," snapped Wells. "Isn't there any other homicide detectives that can handle this crime scene?"

"I don't know," replied the rookie. "I'm just following Capatin Lawson's orders."

"Don't worry, kid," Wells reassured him. "It's not your fault. I'd just like to know what's going on in this town. Don't these murderers ever take a day off to relax?"

"Maybe they murder and kill people to relax," suggested the rookie. "Maybe that's their way of having a good time."

"You could be right. You're pretty smart for a rookie cop. I can tell you're gonna go far in the Hollywood police department."

"Thank you, sir. I have to get back to my patrol car and protect the innocent citizens of Hollywood," said the rookie cop as he walked back to his patrol car before driving away.

Wells jumped into his beat up old Ford and left the hotel parking lot a few minutes later, with Susan Pelk following in her black sedan. He had to drive to the opposite side of the city to reach this most recent murder scene. All the while wondering why he had been selected to investigate.

The address took Detective Wells to another seedy part of the city. It led him to an abandoned and condemned building, just like the hangout he had searched for his female suspect, Kathy. By the time he had parked his vehicle, the coroner, Dr. Terry was already there waiting for him. But this time they entered the premises together. Although without the use of the surgeon's slippers – due to all the fecal matter and garbage strewn all over the dirty floor – Wells still wore the thin, clear rubber gloves.

The investigators had to step very gingerly so that they didn't destroy any evidence – as they walked across the smelly, rat infested floor – which included empty pill bottles, used needles and syringes thrown about in every direction. It looked to be the home of a number of runaways. It reminded Wells of the same scene he had seen at the other condemned building that was searched just the day before.

As the photographer snapped photo after photo and the forensic team placed different pieces of evidence into plastic bags, Detective Wells and Dr. Terry walked from one stinky room to another until they came across a mutilated corpse laying on the floor similar to the one found at the motel.

But this time the corpse was a little different. The one at the motel still had its head intact and had jockey shorts on. This one was completely nude and had no head. It had been cut off just above the Adams apple. But the similarities included the hacking off of the hands and feet – and large pieces of skin had been peeled away, just like the motel corpse. And again, not one drop of blood in the immediate area. Then Dr. Terry noticed the victim's jugular vein had that same indentation and huge, bruised needle mark on it – as did the motel corpse.

They surmised that this man's blood had been completely drained of every drop before his body was mutilated. Detective Wells and Dr. Terry knew that they were dealing with a mad man and vampire that evidently liked blood.

The motel corpse had been dead for more than three days. This corpse had been dead maybe one or two days. But Dr. Terry had a hard time deciding when and how the victim died. Without any blood in the body to give him the signs that he would need to make a decision on the time of death, it was almost impossible to give Wells a positive answer. Dr. Terry would know more after the autopsy had been performed.

It was getting very late and Wells was very tired. He also needed a drink or two soon – or the shakes would overtake his body. However, he had a job to do and that always came first with him.

Wells also had a few reports to read over and catch up on. His work was never done especially when Capatin Lawson kept adding murder investigations to his already full docket. When Wells felt that he had done enough at this crime scene, he decided to let the forensic investigators take over and keep him abreast of any new breaks in the case. He wanted to get home and get off his feet.

"Dr. Terry, I'm going to leave this crime scene to you and the forensic team. If you need me for anything, I'll be at my house getting soused," said Wells.

"Good. We're just about ready to wrap it up anyway. You should have my autopsy reports on your desk in a day or so concerning this body and the one found at the motel."

"That's great. But right now I'm working on three different murder investigations with detectives in three different cities and now Captain Lawson orders me to investigate this crime scene and the one from the motel. I can't work like this anymore. I'm getting too old for this," said a dejected Wells.

"Detective Wells, I know exactly how you feel. I have to do the autopsies. Why don't you go on home now and get some rest. I can take over from here."

Wells gladly left the crime scene. As he walked towards his vehicle, he noticed that Susan Pelk was sitting behind the wheel of hers, waiting to follow him to wherever he was headed. He wanted to confront her about her stalking but was just too tired to argue with her. He decided that a confrontation could wait until he was in a better mood.

As Susan Pelk started her engine and put her car into gear, Wells just smiled at her and jumped behind the wheel of his car, started the engine and raced away from the crime scene to his quiet residence. Keeping an eye on his rearview mirror, he watched as Susan Pelk continued following his vehicle just a few car lengths behind. He just couldn't figure out what she wanted from him. But when he parked in his driveway and saw that she parked only one house away from his, he decided to confront her. Detective Wells stomped over to her car and opened the passenger door to get her attention.

"What do you want, Detective Wells?"

"I want you to stop stalking me everywhere I go."

"I'm not stalking you," Pelk snapped. "I'm working on my story for an independent news organization.

"Then quit following me," Wells shot back. "If you keep it up, I warn you, I'll arrest you for obstruction and stalking a law enforcement official."

"I told you, Detective Wells. All I'm trying to do is gather the facts so I can write a decent story on these tainted meat murders."

"Well don't do it on my time. Follow somebody else. Go follow Detective Smith in Santa Monica or Detective Wilmont in Redondo Beach. Why don't you bother them instead of harassing me?"

"Detective, I'm not harassing anyone. That's in your mind. I'm just trying to get a story. Won't you help me?"

Wells retorted, "If you promise not to follow me anymore I'll think about it. Now please leave me alone and get out of here or I'll call a patrol car to bodily remove you." With that said, he slammed her passenger door, ran up the steps and into his house.

After Wells closed his front door he walked directly to his kitchen cabinet and retrieved his bottle of twenty-five year old scotch and a shot glass. Then waltzed into the living room and plopped his butt into the thick plush cushions of his two hundred dollar couch. There he opened the full bottle and began pouring shot after shot into his glass, drinking them just as fast as he poured them.

After ten or so shots, Wells stood up and wandered to the front window to see if Susan Pelk was still sitting behind the wheel of her car or if his words had finally sunk into her pretty little head? To his surprise her black sedan was gone. He couldn't see it anywhere. Detective Wells was quite happy with himself for setting down the law with her. He hoped that she would be out of his hair for good.

That was the last thing Wells remembered as he passed out and didn't awaken until early the next morning, still in his suit and shoes. He couldn't even remember returning to the couch after he peered out the front window. However, that wasn't important to him at the time. He had to get ready for another long day of work.

Wells slowly stood up and straightened out his wrinkled suit clothes and went into the kitchen to put on a pot of fresh coffee. Once that chore had been completed, he turned on the television set and sat at the kitchen table waiting for his coffee.

While Detective Wells waited, he watched the local news and was very surprised and upset to hear the newscaster talking about his tainted meat murder investigations. They again showed the drawings of his three suspects but never mentioned their names. Wells really didn't think anything about it, until the newscaster put up the drawing of Detective Smith's female suspect. But was relieved when no name was mentioned.

Wells wondered how the news media got hold of the four suspects' drawings. He just hoped that his suspects hadn't left the area and were still around so he could arrest them and throw away the key.

And because of his new investigations he had forgotten to telephone Detectives Smith, Wilmont and Rodriguez concerning the information he had found concerning Detective Smith's female suspect, Katie Brown.

Wells would have to make time in the very near future and let the other three homicide detectives know just exactly what he had found out about Detective Smith's suspect. He would telephone them as soon as he had a free minute.

The first thing Wells wanted to do to on this particular morning was to visit the seedy motel and speak with the day man, Ray Santo. Wells believed somebody at that motel had committed the murder and mutilated the body. He was sure of it. How else could the killer or killers know that that particular motel room wasn't used but once or twice a year? This was the question he needed answered.

After Wells drank his coffee and his hangover had subsided, he was ready to start another workday. He quickly washed and shaved and then headed out the front door. A few seconds later he was in his beat-up vehicle – and was quite pleased with himself when he didn't see Susan Pelk at the heels of his feet. Her black sedan was nowhere in the area. Wells hoped she was out of his hair for good – and had gotten the hint that he wasn't gonna take anymore guff from her or she would have to suffer the consequences.

Wells started the engine of his car and backed out of the driveway, heading for the seedy motel that he had been to the day before. He was anxious to see and question the day man that had called the police to report the mutilated body. He wasn't able to do a background check yet on Ray Santo or for that matter Dan Gold. Although he knew most of the seedy background of the latter, he knew nothing about Ray Santo. But very shortly would be interviewing him.

Wells had a feeling in the back of his hungover head that Ray Santo was somehow involved in the grisly murder of room 1001.

Detective Wells finally arrived at the motel's parking lot and parked near the manager's office instead of fifty yards away. A minute later he had entered the manager's office. A rough looking character was awake and sitting in the dilapidated chair behind the counter.

"Are you Ray Santo?" asked Wells.

"Yeah, I'm Ray Santo. Who are you?"

"I'm Detective Wells," he said, showing the man his badge. "I'm the homicide detective that's investigating the dead body in room 1001 that you called about. Who was he?"

"How should I know?"

"Didn't you rent him the room?" Wells asked him.

"No sir, I didn't. We don't rent that particular room out but once or twice a year."

"Then who let the victim into room 1001?"

"I don't know," Santo replied.

"Who knew besides you and the manager that that particular room wasn't being used?" But Santo remained silent. Wells snapped, "Think boy. This guy's murder was an inside job. Somebody who works at this motel let him in that room and maybe even killed him."

"Believe me, if I knew something I would tell you," said a shaken and nervous Santo.

"Boy, how old are you? Do you want to end up spending a good part of your life in jail? 'Cause that's the way you're headed."

He told Wells that he was only twenty-two years old and hadn't done anything wrong.

"Listen, kid," Wells said, looking him straight in the eye. "The only people that run this motel are the day manager and the night manager. And the night manager swears he doesn't know a thing. So that leaves the day manager. And that's you."

"No, I'm not the day manager. I'm just the assistant manager. The day manager isn't here right now."

"Where is he at?"

"I don't know. He hasn't been in for nearly a week. Well, four days anyhow."

"Where did he go, Mr. Santo?" asked Detective Wells.

"I don't know. He just handed me the keys to the manager's office and left without saying anything. But don't worry, Detective. He'll be back."

"Why do you say that? Are you a mind reader?" asked Wells.

"Of course not," Santo replied. "But the day manager is also the owner of this establishment, so he's got to come back."

"What's this day manager's name?"

"His name is Johnny Vega. We call him Johnny."

"Johnny Vega," said Wells thinking out loud, then lighting a cigarette. "That name sounds familiar. I swear I've heard that name before. Has this Johnny Vega ever left you in charge before, Ray?"

"No, this is the first time. I didn't even know he was leaving. He just surprised me and gave me the keys to the place. That was it. I guess Johnny's trying to see if I can handle the responsibility."

"Have you ever been in trouble with the law, Ray?" asked Wells looking him directly in the eyes.

"Yes I have," he answered.

"What for?"

"Attempted murder."

"Hell, what kind of place is this," Wells asked him as he exhaled a big cloud of cigarette smoke. "What type of people does your boss hire? The night manager just got out of the joint for murder and pleaded it down to manslaughter. The assistant manager was in jail for attempted murder. Who did you try to kill?" But Santo remained silent. Again Wells asked him, "Who did you try to kill, Ray?"

Finally Santo replied, "Somebody I didn't like. He tried to rape me while I was staying in juvenile hall."

Wells told him he was sorry to hear that. And asked him when he got out?

"Just recently. Maybe two months ago."

"Well, I just hope you're not involved in that mutilated murder in room 1001. If you are, I'm gonna nail your ass to the wall," said a confident Wells.

"I told you, Detective. I'm not involved and don't know anything about it."

"Well, kid. For your own sake, keep your nose clean."

"I plan on it."

"Well Ray, if your boss returns have him get in touch with me at the Hollywood station. Here is my card." Wells then handed the kid his business card and left the room.

He had completed his interview with Ray Santo, but left feeling sorry for the guy for having to go through such a harrowing experience while at juvenile hall. No boy should have to suffer like that, Wells thought to himself.

Before Wells left the motel he had to take one last look at the crime scene in room 1001. When he tore away the yellow police tape from the doorway, he grabbed the doorknob and slowly opened the door. Detective

Wells almost thought he'd see another dead body lying on that light beige carpeting, but the room was empty and quiet. You couldn't even tell that something had happened there if it wasn't for that yellow police tape all over the doorway...because the room was spick and span. And you couldn't hear the hum of the air conditioner anymore. Somebody evidently had shut off the thermostat.

Wells had seen enough and slowly closed the door. He wondered where the victim really died. Was it in room 1001 – or did the murder take place somewhere else and was then moved to the motel room? He wouldn't know for sure until Dr. Terry had completed the autopsy. But the body had very little decomposition. So it had to be in an air-conditioned room from the time of death. Although, it could have been taken out of a cold room and moved into another cold room like room 1001.

Why take all the blood out of the body? Was there really a vampire on the loose or was it done so it wouldn't leave any blood evidence when the hands and feet were cut off, the teeth pulled out and the eyes cut out of their sockets? And what about the large areas of the victim's skin being peeled away? Why would the killer or killers do that? Was it to hide identification marks or was it some sick ritual that a devil cult had to perform? Detective Wells wondered about these questions and more but didn't have an answer for any of them – yet.

But after thinking it over for a few minutes Wells figured that the mob must be involved in these grisly murders and most likely the tainted meat murders. But these questions and many others needed to be answered – and fast.

While walking to his car, Detective Wells dwelled on the different motives someone would have for committing all these crazy mutilations that were suddenly popping up all over Hollywood.

Suddenly that name Johnny Vega resonated inside his head. Wells remembered where he had heard it before. Detective Rodriguez, at their meeting mentioned that Johnny Vega was the owner of the butcher shop in San Pedro. And Wells learned that he was also the manager of the seedy motel where the first mutilated body was found in room 1001. Putting two and two together and connecting the dots, Wells had found a connection between the mutilations and the tainted meat murders.

Wells also knew that Johnny Vega was related to the Elmero brothers by marriage. Now he wondered if they were in the same mob family as Don Bruno Manzelli – or in feuding families?

Until Detective Wells could question the shop owners or those four young kids that delivered the tainted meat, he would have to rely on the DNA testing and investigative reports to find his answers.

Wells also hoped that Detectives Rodriguez, Smith and Wilmont would find something new to help him with his tainted meat murder investigation. Then he remembered that he still needed to telephone them and tell them about the mutilated, dead bodies that he had recently investigated and also about finding the identity of Detective Smith's female suspect. And he also wanted to telephone and check with the family of Johnny Vega to find out if they knew of his whereabouts.

Detective Wells wondered why Vega and the Elmero brothers would suddenly disappear if they weren't involved in these murders. Was it just a coincidence or was it a conspiracy? That's the torment Detective Wells had to deal with.

His thoughts were suddenly interrupted as he hopped into his car and headed to the station – anxiously wanting to speak with his Captain to get a few things off his chest.

And to make his important telephone calls.

CHAPTER 4

Wells drove directly from the Hollywood motel to the Hollywood police station all the while thinking about his murder investigations. He wanted to tell Captain Lawson to take him off one or the other. He didn't want to work two different investigations at the same time. The tainted meat murders were more than enough work for one investigator.

Now Detective Wells had two mutilated bodies to contend with and was at his wits' end. While his fellow detectives were sitting around doing nothing, he was doing the work of four homicide detectives.

Just then something familiar suddenly caught his eye. Wells looked into his rearview mirror and saw his shadow and pest, Susan Pelk. Evidently she hadn't gotten it into her pretty little head yet that if she crossed him again he would see her in jail. He let her have her way for now. But he was certain that their paths would cross and he would come out the victor. At this time Wells had more important things on his mind. Susan Pelk at the moment was only a slight nuisance.

If at anytime she committed a blatant act of misconduct or obstruction, Wells would have no other recourse than to incarcerate her. But right now he wanted to speak with Captain Lawson instead of confronting little Miss News Reporter. She hadn't stepped on Wells' feet yet; she just scuffed them a little.

Wells entered the Hollywood police station and saw Captain Lawson standing to the side talking with another homicide detective. He quickly walked over to the front desk, signed in and then walked over to speak with his Captain.

"Excuse me Captain Lawson for interrupting your conversation but I really need to speak with you for a few minutes," he said standing next to him.

"Oh, Detective Wells…before you speak with me you have an urgent message sitting on your desk."

"When did it come in?" Wells asked.

"About ten or fifteen minutes ago."

Wells asked him why the dispatcher didn't get a hold of him over the radio?

"They tried, but you must have been away from that beautiful car you drive. If you'd carry your hand held radio like you're supposed to do, you would have received your message," said Captain Lawson sarcastically.

"Captain," answered Wells, "I don't like carrying that radio. It weighs damn near five pounds. Not only that but it's practically obsolete. Hell, it was made over ten years ago."

"Detective Wells, that's irrelevant," Lawson told him. "The radio still does the job that it's made for. I want you to start carrying it with you or you'll continue to miss dispatcher calls when you're away from your automobile. That is…if you call what you're driving an automobile."

"Captain, do you know offhand who left the message?"

"Yes, it was a Detective Smith from Santa Monica homicide division. I believe he needed your expertise. He said it was very urgent and to get back to him immediately."

"But Captain," pleaded Wells, "I need to speak with you about the two murders you ordered me to investigate. It's just too much for me to do. I can't investigate these two mutilations and also the tainted meat murders. I just can't do it."

Lawson ordered Wells to call Smith. Adding, "I believe he needs your attention more than you need mine. Talk to him and then come back and speak with me."

"Damn it, Captain," Wells whined. "I just can't win with you."

Lawson promised him that they'd work out any problems he had concerning his murder investigations. And to smooth Wells' ruffled feathers and build up his confidence, he said, "I must tell you though, John, I have the best man working those cases."

"I have something I need to tell Detective Smith anyway…but I've been too busy investigating murder scenes to get to a telephone."

"See. It works out perfect then. Now you have the time. So go and make your phone call. I'll see you later," said Captain Lawson. With that said, he turned and walked back into his office.

Detective Wells walked away feeling frustrated and went directly to his desk. As he grabbed the phone and made his urgent phone call, he looked around the homicide department and saw many of the other detectives sitting at their desks, drinking coffee, smoking cigarettes and making jokes to each other. Wells was disgusted with this whole episode. He was working his butt off, while the homicide detectives played the leisure life. Just as his anger began building thinking about this disparity, Detective Smith answered Wells' phone call.

"This is Detective Smith. It's your dime."

"Hello Willard. This is John Wells and I'm returning your urgent message. I needed to speak with you anyway. Because I've found some information that could help you in your investigation."

"John, I'm currently at a crime scene that I need you to see. I really need your opinion on this murder."

"Why, what's up?"

"Can you get away from your duties and drive over to check out this murder scene?"

"I guess I can if you really need my expertise."

"I'd appreciate it," Smith replied. "I'm not sure if this murder has anything to do with the tainted meat murders or not, but I really want your opinion."

"Why? What have you got?" Wells asked him.

Smith didn't want to say over the phone. He wanted Wells to <u>see</u> the crime scene.

"All right," Wells said half-heartedly. "Where are you? I need to talk with you anyway. I have a few things to tell you concerning the murders. By the way, did you happen to watch the local news this morning?"

Smith said that he didn't. Adding, "I've been too busy with my murder investigations to enjoy any free time. In fact just this morning I was ordered to this crime scene to investigate this murder, when there are other homicide detectives in my department just sitting on their asses doing nothing but yet I have to do their work."

Wells snickered, "You have the same problem I seem to be having. But we have more pressing issues to worry about."

"Like what?" Smith retorted.

"Like the news media. I hate to have to tell you this but somebody in the news media got a hold of the drawing of your female suspect and showed it on television. We can't continue to let this happen. These suspects are gonna leave the area and start again in another state."

"I don't believe it. This can't be happening to me." Smith said, disgusted by the thought of it.

But Wells quickly cheered him up with some good news. "Don't worry Willard, I have found the identity of your female suspect. Her name is Katie Brown. I'll bring you a copy of the girl's background. I hate to say this but I actually feel sorry for her. I'll tell you more about it when I see you. Give me thirty minutes and I'll be at your side."

Smith gave Wells the address of the crime scene and hung up the phone. Then Wells hurriedly walked to the parking lot to his beat up car, jumped behind the wheel and drove to Santa Monica in record time. He had no trouble finding the address that Detective Smith had given him – which was a dilapidated building in a rather seedy and dirty part of the city. It was déjà vu all over again.

Wells quickly parked his car in an already filled parking lot comprised of the coroner and forensic vans, three patrol cars and Smith's vehicle. And just as he got out of his car he noticed his shadow, Susan Pelk, who had parked a few buildings away. He just ignored her presence and continued on his way as Smith was waiting for him outside the building.

"Detective Wells, I'm glad you could make it," he said with a concerned look on his face.

"What do you want me to look at?" asked Wells as Smith handed him a pair of thin rubber gloves and directed him into the dilapidated building.

"It's in the next room," he said pointing in that direction.

As they walked through the hallway of the building, Wells couldn't help but notice a foul-smelling, putrid odor emanating from the small room directly ahead of them. The two detectives walked through garbage, fecal matter, empty pill containers, dirty used syringes and empty food boxes of cereal and crackers. It reminded Wells of the hangout that he had searched looking for his female suspect.

When the detectives neared the crime scene, Wells put on his rubber gloves. He saw another man dressed in a white smock standing over the covered dead body.

Smith introduced the man to Wells. "Detective Wells, this is Dr. Fredrick. He's the coroner for the city of Santa Monica."

"I'm very glad to meet you Dr. Fredrick," said Wells as they shook hands.

Dr. Fredrick then bent down and removed the plastic tarp that was covering the body. Wells rubbed his hands together in anticipation but was startled and taken aback when he saw a mutilated, nude male corpse lying on the dirty and cold cement floor – and not one-drop of blood nearby.

The victim's body was in the early stages of decomposition which had started, Wells surmised, maybe two or three days before and gave off such a putrid odor that everyone in the room had to hold their noses so they wouldn't gag. Wells had seen this crime scene twice before. The first thing he noticed was that the mutilated male body had no hands, feet, or head and large parts of his skin had been peeled away, just like the last crime scene he had investigated earlier.

The first thing that Wells looked at was the jugular vein of the victim. It had a large needle mark on it. The head had been cut just above the victim's Adam's apple and the needle mark stood out like a sore thumb. He knew when he saw no blood around that the male victim had to be mixed up with the two mutilated bodies that were found in his city.

There was one difference though between Detective Smith's mutilated body and the two mutilated bodies that Wells had investigated. The hands and feet were not just hacked off but it looked as though somebody tried to grind up what was left of the victim's arms and legs in a meat grinder. The bones were sharpened to a point, as though the killer stuck each wrist and leg into a meat grinder and started grinding away until each arm was ground down nearly to the elbow and each leg ground nearly to the kneecap.

Not one drop of blood, a piece of ground flesh, or piece of skin was anywhere to be found in the room or building for that matter. The Santa Monica coroner wasn't certain if the victim had been killed in the dilapidated building or if he had been killed some place else and then moved to this building. He would have to wait until the autopsy was completed. Wells' two mutilated bodies gave him the same problems.

"John, what do you think?" asked Smith.

"Well I'll tell you, Willard," Wells replied. "I just investigated two mutilated bodies in the city of Hollywood that had the same things done to them that had been done to this victim's body right down to the needle mark in the jugular vein and the large patches of peeled skin. Detective Smith, it looks to me like we have another murder investigation that spans two different cities and requires both of our expertise."

"I came to that same conclusion more than an hour ago," Smith retorted. "I also didn't mention the fact that we had two more people die from eating tainted ground flesh and more innocent people will follow, unless we can stop these evil fiends from committing these atrocious, despicable acts."

"I don't know if our city has had any more deaths relating to the tainted meat because I've been too busy investigating other murders similar to this one," said Wells pointing down to the body.

"I know what you mean, John," Smith replied. "I haven't had a minutes free time since I began the tainted meat murders – and now I've been ordered to investigate this murder."

Wells told him that he'd been so busy investigating recent murder scenes that he hadn't been able to even read his messages, let alone his reports…or for that matter, to take or make phone calls.

"I was ordered by my Captain to investigate two recent murder scenes just like this one, plus I'm also investigating the tainted meat murders while the other homicide detectives sit around the office, crack jokes and do nothing but smoke cigarettes and run their mouths," bristled Wells.

"I also have the same problem with my Captain and with my brother homicide detectives," retorted Smith.

Wells then asked him if he had learned anything new about the tainted meat murders?

He nodded, saying, "I know that Detective Rodriguez learned that another young female suspect delivered the meat with our male suspect. The eyewitness said the female couldn't have been but fifteen or sixteen years old."

Wells snapped, "Willard, we don't care about her age, we just need to find her."

Smith told Wells that there were now four young women that were involved in delivering the human hamburger – and to at least three different butcher shops.

"Did Rodriguez get a name to go with the face?" Wells asked him.

"If he has," Smith replied, "he hasn't faxed it too me yet. He told me that they were just sending the eyewitness to a forensic artist as we spoke."

"Oh by the way, here is your suspect's photo and background report," said Wells, handing Smith the photo. "It'll tell you everything you want to know about her and then some. The color photo is so much better than your composite drawing."

"You mean you found out her identity?" he asked

"I sure did."

"How did you find it so fast?" Smith asked him.

He told him that he looked through the seven photos that were found in the records when he got hits on the fingerprints that were found in a condemned building in Hollywood that was supposedly used as his first female suspect's hangout in the tainted meat murders. Adding, "I mentioned this at our luncheon."

"That's right. I remember now," Smith said, rubbing his chin with his hand.

Wells continued, saying, "Your female suspect looked familiar, so on a hunch I got out the seven photos and matched them to your drawing and this is what I came up with."

"Good work, John. Why don't we step outside for a smoke and a breath of fresh air? I could use it," said Smith. Then both men turned and began walking out of the foul smelling room.

"Detective Smith, can I place the victim in a body bag now?" asked Dr. Fredrick as Smith entered the hallway.

Smith stopped, turned and said: "Be my guest." A half minute later he pushed open the front door and stepped outside into fresh air.

"Boy that place stinks," Wells told Smith. "How long has the body been dead?"

"Dr. Fredrick thinks three to four days," replied Smith as they both lit up cigarettes. "But without any blood evidence he won't be able to know for sure until the autopsy is completed."

As they smoked their cigarettes, Wells told Smith: "In the last two days I've investigated two crime scenes with the same type of mutilated body. One had his head and one body didn't – and there wasn't any blood at those murder scenes either. Not one drop. Nor were their feet, hands or pieces of peeled skin. Not only that but one of the victims had all of his teeth missing. When I checked the inside of the victim's mouth, it showed a lot of damage as though someone had used pliers on him. But no signs of blood. Our coroner thinks we have a vampire on the loose."

"He could be right. But we definitely have a maniac on the loose and we have to get that person off the street and fast," said Smith puffing on his cigarette.

Wells asked Smith to have lunch with him, Rodriguez and Wilmont the following afternoon. "And then we'll be able to go over any new information that we might have on the tainted meat murders and we can also fill them in on these recent mutilations."

"That sounds good to me," Smith replied. "Are you going to call the others and make sure they can make the luncheon engagement or do you want me to do it?"

Wells told him he could if he wanted. "That way I can concentrate on reading my reports that are mounting up on my desk."

Just then Smith's cell phone rang. He pulled it from his jacket pocket and began speaking with the person on the other end.

"Speak of the devil. It's Rodriguez," Smith whispered to Wells.

Wells smoked his cigarette and listened intently to the phone conversation. By Smith's facial reaction, Wells could tell it was an important phone call. Something was up, but what? After five minutes of conversation with Rodriguez, Smith finally hung up his phone. Wells wished he had one, but couldn't afford it. He could barely afford the fuel to drive him home from the station.

"What's up, Willard?" asked Wells. "What did Rodriguez want?"

Smith told him that they needed to take a ride to San Pedro. "Rodriguez has something of importance to show us. He wouldn't say exactly what it was, but I think it has something to do with the tainted meat murders – and a dead body."

"Where is he at?" Wells asked anxiously. "Does he know I'm with you?"

"He does," Smith replied. "And he wants us to meet him at the medical examiner's building in San Pedro to show us his victim before the autopsy is started. I _think_ that's what he wants us for. But I could be wrong. He has that Spanish accent and when he speaks too fast, I can't understand him. But I understood enough of what he had to say."

"Would you like me to drive?" asked Wells.

But when Smith got a good look at Wells' car, he decided against it.

"Is this your car?" asked Smith pointing to what looked like a wreck and death trap.

"Yes it is. She's nothing to look at but she gets me where I want to go."

"How about if we take my car and I drive?" Smith asked.

"That's all right by me," replied Wells.

Just then Smith noticed a woman sitting behind the wheel of her parked car, smoking a cigarette and looking in their direction.

"John, do you know that young woman sitting in that black sedan? It looks as though she's waiting for someone."

"That, Willard…is my shadow. It's Susan Pelk, a newspaper reporter for an independent paper. Or so she says. Remember…she was sitting near us at the Hoagie House. She's been following me since I began investigating the tainted meat murders. Now she can follow you."

Using the remote control on his key chain, Smith pushed a button and the two doors to his new Mercedes Benz opened automatically. The two detectives got in and Smith started the purring engine.

"Nice car," remarked Wells enviously.

"_I_ like it. You could have one too if you wanted."

"Are you kidding?" Wells replied. "Not on my salary. I can't even afford the car that I have." They both laughed.

"Well," said Smith, putting the car in gear and accelerating like a bat out of hell, "we should be in San Pedro within twenty minutes. We'll take Pacific Coast highway. I like driving along the coast…especially the scenery. It'll take our minds off of these horrendous murders."

"That sounds good to me," Wells said.

As the two detectives talked about the exploding murder rate in their county, Smith became upset and said: "What the hell is happening to our country, John?"

Wells replied, "If I had that answer, Willard…then I could afford a new car, 'cause I'd be a millionaire."

Two finished cigarettes later, the detectives arrived at San Pedro's medical examiner's building. After shutting off the car's engine they both hopped out of the vehicle and headed for the coroner's office. They entered through the revolving doors of this modern building and went directly to the autopsy room. They saw Rodriguez sitting in a chair just outside the autopsy room door smoking a cigarette. And he saw them at about the same time that they saw him.

"Raul, how are you?" asked Smith with a wave of his hand. "Wells and I are at your service." Rodriguez stood up and shook their hands. As they stood by the doorway of the autopsy room, Smith told Rodriguez that Wells had come up with some good information that might help lead them to the killer of the tainted meat murders.

"That's right," interjected Wells. "Willard's female suspect has been identified. Her name is Katie Brown."

"We can talk about that later," Rodriguez said to Wells. "Right now though I want you guys to take a look at the dead body waiting to be autopsied. I think it may have a bearing on the case Willard was just investigating – the mutilation murder."

"When did you hear about that?" Wells asked him.

Smith interjected that he had talked with Raul earlier that morning when he called about his female suspect in the tainted meat murders. "He told me that he was on his way to another murder scene and I told him I was investigating a mutilation."

"Well, Raul, what have you got for us to look at?" asked Wells.

As they walked through the doors and into the autopsy room, Rodriguez told them about his most recent crime scene. He thought it had something to do with the tainted meat murders. But when he and his investigators arrived there and saw what it was, he had different thoughts.

A few seconds later all three detectives and the coroner were standing around the table that contained a body bag. And inside the bag – a corpse. But before Rodriguez had the coroner unzip the body bag, he introduced the two detectives to him.

"Detectives Smith and Wells, this is Dr. Melvin, San Pedro's coroner." Dr. Melvin nodded in acknowledgement and then unzipped the body bag and spread it apart so all could get a better look at the body.

"My god. Is this deja vu all over again, Mr. Smith?" asked Wells as they both stared at the headless body.

The head, feet and hands were also cut from its torso. And the arms – about two inches of meat and bone – had been ground away by some type of meat grinder. But the stumps – where the feet had been attached – had not been ground up. And just like the other three mutilated bodies, large parts of the skin had been peeled away and a large needle mark protruded from the jugular vein.

"Detective Rodriguez, was there any blood evidence at the crime scene?" Wells asked.

"None. Not a drop. How did you know?"

Wells explained that he had just finished investigating two mutilated dead bodies at two different crime scenes in Hollywood. "And there wasn't a drop of blood evidence found there either. Then this morning I was called by Detective Smith to view his corpse, which also had no blood evidence at the crime scene and then Detective Smith was called by you to view your mutilated body so I came along."

"We definitely have a vampire on the loose," said Smith to no one in particular.

"You know, the way the arms are ground up I thought maybe this mutilated body and those that were ground up and sold to the butcher shops were connected somehow," surmised Rodriguez.

"It's possible, but not probable," Smith interjected.

"I wouldn't say that," said Wells, putting his two cents in. "After what I've been investigating, anything's possible."

"Where did you find the body?" Smith asked Rodriguez.

He told them that he found it in a cheap and run down motel out near the city limits.

"What did the owner or manager say about the mutilated torso being in their motel?" Wells asked him.

"Was it found in a room or outside on the motel's property?" asked Smith.

"It was in one of the motel rooms," Rodriguez replied. "The owner hasn't been around to be questioned. He hasn't been seen in four days. He also owns another rat-infested motel in Hollywood. But he hasn't been seen there for the last few days either."

"What's the guy's name?" asked Detective Wells.

"If I remember correctly, I believe his name is Johnny Vega. He's the brother of Joseppi Vega, the mob enforcer for the Elmero brothers."

"Wait a minute," said Wells. "That name sounds all too familiar. The guy that owns the motel in Hollywood is also named Johnny Vega. If he's the brother of Joseppi Vega and brother-in-law to the Elmero brothers, then maybe the mob is mixed up somehow in these murders."

"I believe that," Rodriguez replied. "The mob has to be involved in these murders. It's just too much of a coincidence."

"Hell, maybe the mutilated murders and the tainted meat murders are connected," said Smith.

"Yeah," Wells interjected, "but we won't know that for sure until we find our suspects. We also need to find the owners to these establishments where all these murders are taking place and where the tainted meat was sold from."

Remembering the conversation when Wells and Smith had first arrived, Rodriguez asked Wells if he had a photo of Smith's female suspect that he could have?

"Willard has it," he replied, looking to Smith for an answer.

Smith told Rodriguez that he had one in the car that he could copy. "I'll make sure you get it before John and I leave," Smith promised.

"Very good," Rodriguez replied. "That'll help me immensely."

Smith then reciprocated and asked Rodriguez if he had a composite drawing of his new suspect?

He shook his head no, saying, "Not yet. The eyewitness still needs to come in and sit down with the forensic artist. I think she's coming in this afternoon. As soon as I get the composite drawn I'll fax you a copy."

"Good," replied Wells and Smith in unison.

Wells, after lighting a cigarette, then asked Rodriguez if his eyewitness knew the female's name?

"I don't think so," Rodriguez replied. "She just saw her deliver the meat with the male suspect. When we showed her the drawings of our female suspects, she didn't recognize any of them."

"Well at least we know the name of one of our suspects," said Wells.

"Oh," interjected Rodriguez. "I forgot to tell you guys before, but I think we have a suspect in my mutilation case."

"What did you find out, Raul," Wells asked anxiously.

"Well, we found an eyewitness that saw a young woman walking near the area where the body was found. But until we get the composite drawing done and interview the woman more thoroughly, we don't know what we have."

"Let's hope somebody saw something," remarked Wells. "Whoever's doing these mutilations…are some really sick individuals."

Smith agreed, saying, "And we need to get them off the street – and fast."

Wells then told Rodriguez that he, Smith and Wilmont were going to lunch the following afternoon to coordinate the murder investigations so as not to step on each other's shoes. "What do you say, Raul? Can you make it for lunch tomorrow afternoon at Gabrielle's Hoagie House?"

"Sure I can," he replied. "I wonder if Wilmont has learned anything new on the tainted meat murder suspects?"

"I don't know," answered Wells. "I've been too damn busy working two different murder investigations. I don't even have time to sleep anymore."

"With these tainted meat murders and now these mutilations, I don't think any of us will be getting much sleep," said Smith.

"You could be right about that," said Wells.

Smith told them that he hadn't heard from Wilmont since the luncheon engagement the other day and asked Wells if he had sent Wilmont the report and photo of Katie Brown?

"No, I haven't had time," Wells replied. "I only brought one copy of the report and one photo. And that was for you, Willard. If I had known ahead of time that I was coming here, I would have brought an extra copy for Raul."

"Well, Raul can copy mine. In fact I'll go get 'em now," said Smith, before turning and walking away, heading for the parking lot and his Mercedes.

As Smith walked away, Rodriguez asked Wells his opinion on why his victim's skin was peeled away?

"To hide his identity of course," Wells answered. Adding, "One of my victim's had his teeth completely pulled out but yet they left the head on his torso. The second body I investigated <u>had</u> no head, so the teeth are probably still intact, wherever it is."

"That's unbelievable," remarked Rodriguez shaking his head in disbelief.

Wells then asked Rodriguez if his investigators had found any fingerprints on or around the body or any evidence that could lead to the identity of the killer or killers?

"We don't know yet," he replied. "But I believe a few prints were found on a few pill bottles that were lying on the floor about five yards from the torso. I doubt if it will pan out though. But we have to try."

Wells then explained that he identified Smith's female suspect from fingerprints found at a suspected hangout of his first female suspect.

"But Willard didn't find any fingerprints of his female suspect," interjected Rodriguez.

"I know," replied Wells. "But when we ran one set of the fingerprints we found at that hangout through the FBI's data base, the computer spit out the girl's photo and I matched them to the drawings we had of all our suspects. Luckily one out of the seven photos I had…matched the composite drawing of Willard's suspect."

Just then Smith came back into the room carrying Katie Brown's photo and background report, then handed them to Rodriguez to make copies.

"Did I hear somebody call my name?" Smith asked.

"We were just talking about how I found your female suspect's identity," said Detective Wells, lighting another cigarette.

As the three homicide detectives continued their conversation, Rodriguez walked to the photocopy machine and made copies of Katie Brown's report and photo, then handed the originals back to Smith.

"Raul," said Smith, "when you get those composite drawings done of your two female suspects, please fax them to me and John. Maybe we'll get lucky and find a name to go along with the face. Wells found a name to go with <u>my</u> suspect's face, maybe he can do the same for yours."

"Will do," Rodriguez promised. "But I still feel the mob is somehow connected in all of these murders that have begun popping up. Everywhere we turn, the mob is involved. They own the butcher shops where the human ground round was sold and now we learn that the mob owns the motels where two of the three mutilated bodies were found. This isn't just a coincidence…this is a conspiracy. And I think it's a mob conspiracy."

"You could be right," said Smith.

"Well, don't forget about lunch tomorrow," Wells reminded Rodriguez before taking a long drag on his cigarette. "I'll contact Wilmont and make sure he comes. This meeting will be important because most of the reports will be in from our respective teams. So maybe there'll be something in them that can give us the break we need to crack these murders and mutilations. We won't get the DNA reports for another week at least and I too believe the mob is somehow involved in all of this."

Smith was anxious to return to his home base and mentioned it. "Well I guess John and I should be heading back to Santa Monica. It's getting late and we all have lots of work to do. The sooner we get into dissecting the evidence and autopsy reports, the sooner we can find the killers to these mass murders. I know our homicide statistics have gone up fifty percent in the last week."

Rodriguez thanked the two detectives for coming. "Now that I know that you two had mutilations committed in your cities, we should work together on these investigations along with the tainted meat murders."

"We will," replied Wells. "Three heads are much better than one."

"Four heads," interjected Smith. "Wilmont is also included."

"Yeah," said Wells flicking his cigarette butt to the floor, "but he hasn't investigated a mutilation like the rest of us have."

"Maybe he's the lucky one," remarked Rodriguez as he followed Wells and Smith out to the parking lot and to the Mercedes.

As the two detectives got into the car, Wells waved goodby to Rodriguez, saying, "We'll see you tomorrow, Raul." Seconds later, Smith started his car and roared away, heading for Santa Monica.

As Smith and Wells were driving through Palos Verdes to return to Santa Monica, Smith's cell phone began ringing. He quickly answered it and heard Paul Wilmont's voice on the other end. He was calling for the two detective's help. After Smith finished his phone conversation and hung up, he quickly explained the situation to Detective Wells.

"Paul Wilmont needs us for our expertise and opinions. He wants us to meet him at a crime scene in his city of Redondo Beach. He first called Hollywood station to speak with you but found out that you were with me. Do you mind checking out his crime scene?" asked Detective Smith.

"No, I don't mind. We have to pass through Redondo Beach to get to Santa Monica anyway, so why not. Maybe we'll learn something."

The two detectives headed towards Redondo Beach and were only minutes away from Wilmont's crime scene. When they pulled up to the address, they soon realized it was another abandoned and condemned building in the seedy part of the city. Detective Wilmont was standing outside smoking a cigarette and watched as Smith parked his vehicle.

The two homicide detectives stepped out of the Mercedes and met Wilmont in front of the doorway. Once Wilmont explained the situation, he proceeded to show them the crime scene.

The three homicide detectives entered the premises and put on rubber gloves, then proceeded to walk into the filthy, dilapidated building. There were already ten or so investigators from the Redondo Beach coroner's office and forensic lab securing any evidence that might be at the crime scene.

The weather outside was very hot. And inside must have been over one hundred and five degrees, which made the place smell of rotten eggs. The putrid smell was so bad it was hard for the investigators to breathe. The human waste mixed in with the garbage and spoiled hamburger lying on the floor made the detectives gag. So they held their noses as they checked out the crime scene.

Over to one side and in a corner of the small room stood a fifty-five gallon round plastic container filled to the top with stinking, spoiled, ground up meat, which the three detectives believed, after talking amongst themselves, was ground up human flesh. An empty fifty-five gallon plastic round container sitting next to the full one had been filled at one time. Not with human flesh but with human blood.

The sides and bottom of the plastic container had traces of dried blood. Lying to the right and behind the fifty-five gallon plastic containers was a headless, mutilated body just like Detectives Smith and Wells had seen more than once before. It was deju vu all over again.

The mutilated body had no head, hands or feet and it had the same telltale signs that Wells and Smith had seen before. Large patches of skin had been peeled away, but most of this torso had already been ground up into hamburger. Pieces of ground up flesh lay all around. The killers had evidently been in the process of grinding up the body, when for some reason they became frightened and left the crime scene without getting rid of the evidence.

Also lying near the torso was a small meat-grinding machine that had some ground up flesh still in it. Wells tried to turn its handle but it was stuck. He then tried to correct the problem and noticed a large bone had lodged into the turning screw that mashed up the bone and meat.

Wells stopped messing around with the meat grinder and returned to view the torso. He knelt down and checked the jugular vein and found what he was looking for – a large needle mark where the blood had been drained. There wasn't one drop of blood near or on the mutilated body. Which meant that there wasn't any way to identify the torso until DNA tests were completed. Detective Wells hoped that this male victim was one that had been reported missing by his family.

After letting Smith and Wells view the torso, Wilmont lit a big cigar and asked them what they thought. But before they could answer, Wilmont said: "What do you think, Detectives? You two guys act as though you've seen this before, have you?"

"Yep," replied Wells. "We've seen it before, haven't we, Willard?"

Smith nodded and said: "We sure have. And more than once. In fact Wells and I just came from San Pedro where Detective Rodriguez showed us a mutilated torso. And both Wells and I have also run across these same crime scenes in our respective cities."

"We had just left the San Pedro coroner's office when you telephoned Willard," said Wells.

54

"Did Rodriguez have a similar murder scene?" Wilmont asked them.

"Not just Detective Rodriguez," Wells answered. "Mutilated bodies have been popping up all over. Now we've found dead torsos in four different neighboring cities. I've had two in Hollywood. Smith has had one, which we viewed earlier today. And while we were investigating that crime scene Rodriguez telephoned and asked us to view his mutilated victim."

"You're kidding," said Wilmont in disbelief.

"No we're not," replied Smith. "All four of us that are investigating the tainted meat murders now have mutilated murders to investigate. Now that we see the meat grinder full of your victim's flesh, I have to believe the tainted meat murders and these mutilated bodies are connected somehow."

"What do you think, John?" asked Wilmont.

Wells told him that he agreed with Willard, saying, "The mutilated bodies and the tainted meat murders are definitely connected."

"Somebody is killing and mutilating these people and we better find out who's doing it and fast," said Smith with a concerned look on his face.

Wells then asked Wilmont if he had any suspects yet that he thought were connected to this murder or any eyewittnesses that might have seen the killer or killers leave the building?

He told them that he had investigators canvassing the neighborhood and hoped to find someone who saw something.

"Good luck," Wells said half-heartedly. "These days people just don't like to get involved."

Just then Smith's cell phone rang. He answered the call and immediately handed the phone to Wells.

Wells took it from his hand and asked him who was on the phone?

He replied that it was Captain Lawson.

Wells talked with his Captain for nearly five minutes. Evidently there had been another murder in Hollywood that needed to be investigated and Captain Lawson chose his best homicide investigator to handle it. Wells finished his conversation with Captain Lawson then handed the cell phone back to Detective Smith.

"John, what's going on?" Smith asked him as he placed his cell phone into his jacket pocket.

Wells told him that his Captain wanted him to investigate another murder scene in Hollywood. "It seems a rookie patrol officer found a body while searching the building. Would you guys like to tag along?" he asked the two detectives.

"I would like to," replied Smith, "but I have to be getting back to Santa Monica and check in with my investigators. I have murder investigations to investigate too."

"Me too," added Wilmont, puffing on his smelly cigar. "I'm too busy right now with this one. But keep me informed of any information that might help us catch these psychotic murderers that have been mutilating bodies."

"Yes, please do," Smith told Wells.

"Oh, by the way, Paul," added Wells, "we're having lunch tomorrow afternoon at Gabrielle's Hoagie House at one o'clock. Rodriguez will also be joining us. We'll be able to compare and go over our notes and evidence. Maybe something will come out of it so we can catch these sick killers. I still say it's the mob killing these people. But we can talk about that tomorrow at lunch. Right now I have to get to Hollywood and Vine. I guess our work is never done." With that said Wells then turned to leave the building.

"Detective Wells," said Smith, "wait for me unless you want to walk or take the bus. You rode with me, remember?"

"That's right," Wells replied. "I have so much on my mind right now I completely forgot. I guess my age is catching up with me."

Detectives Smith and Wells said goodbye to Wilmont and then left the building. A minute later they were in the Mercedes and heading for Santa Monica. Ten minutes later, Wells was in his beat-up old Ford heading for Hollywood to a building near the intersection of Hollywood and Vine to investigate yet another homicide.

CHAPTER 5

Detective Wells hurried to the intersection of Hollywood and Vine to check out another murder scene. Captain Lawson didn't make it clear if this murder was related to his tainted meat murders but Detective Wells would soon find out. He parked his car near the address in question. As he got out of his vehicle he noticed the coroner's van was already there along with four other law enforcement vehicles.

Wells quickly sought out the rookie cop that had found the victim. There were four uniformed patrol officers standing outside near the door of the building talking and smoking cigarettes, so Detective Wells called out to them.

"Who was the lucky officer that came across the crime scene?"

"I am. I guess I was the lucky one," said a young patrol cop stepping away from the group.

Wells recognized the young lad immediately. He was the same rookie officer that had delivered a note to him for Captain Lawson about the murder scene at the seedy motel where Wells' first mutilated victim was found.

Reading the officer's nametag on his shirt, Wells asked Officer Diehl what he had found?

"Something that I don't want to run into again," replied the rookie. "I had Captain Lawson call you because I knew you were working the mutilation murders. And this may also lead to the tainted meat murders."

"Why do you say that?" Wells asked him, as Officer Diehl opened the front door.

"Because I saw two of the suspects from the tainted meat murders and began following them. But when they saw me they ran and I gave chase. It was Katie Brown and one of the Elmero brothers that's wanted for questioning for selling the tainted meat to the public."

"I take it you didn't catch them?" Wells asked the rookie.

"Yep, I lost them. But we have the canine unit out looking for them now. As well as other officers canvassing the area for any eyewitnesses."

"Good work, Officer Diehl," replied Wells. "Do you know which Elmero brother you saw?"

"I'm not certain but from looking at the photos I would say it was the younger brother, Tommy."

Wells then followed Officer Diehl into the abandoned building. Dr. Terry met him at the door and handed him a pair of rubber gloves to put on so he wouldn't contaminate the crime scene.

"John, get ready to be sick," said Dr. Terry as they walked into a third room before a hideous sight confronted them.

This wasn't a murder scene it was a slaughter. Three more nude male torsos lay on the dirty floor that had been mutilated by a psychotic killer or killers not more than two days before.

As Wells checked the victims' nude bodies, he couldn't help but notice that all three victims had their heads, hands, feet, arms and legs removed. Only the male genitalia and torsos remained. Wells knew this crime was also related to his other mutilated victims. And when he saw a round, plastic fifty-five gallon drum filled to the brim with ground round, he knew that this was also tied to the mutilated murder scene in Redondo Beach.

Wells had the forensic team test samples of the meat to verify if it was human or animal. The tests would be complete within the day. DNA tests would also be needed if it was found to be human flesh but those tests would take nearly a week or longer depending on the labs work load.

These three male victims also had needle marks on the lower part of their jugular veins. Dr. Terry believed that the victims' many body parts were hacked off after their bodies had been emptied of their blood because there was none found anywhere. That is until the investigators found another round, plastic fifty-five gallon barrel. And this time it wasn't full of tainted meat, it was full of blood. It wasn't known if the blood was human or not, but Detective Wells and the coroner believed it was. The barrel was more than half full of it, and in a thick liquid form.

Everything was taken to the forensic lab to be analyzed – except for the nude bodies. They were taken to the morgue for an autopsy and identification. And no clothes, wallets or identification were found.

However, Wells received a sudden surprise when the forensic crew dumped the container full of ground meat into a body bag and a decapitated head fell out of the bottom of the container. When Wells walked over to check it out, at first it was hard to tell – with the head having no eyes or teeth – but he believed it to be Salvator Elmero, the older of the two Elmero brothers and the owner of the butcher shop in Hollywood.

With this revelation, Wells now had no doubt that the tainted meat murder investigation and the mutilation murders were related. After he found Elmero's head in the fifty-five gallon plastic container, what else could he think?

Wells believed more than ever that the mob was involved in these grisly murders. The mutilated bodies and ground up flesh could only be their work. He believed that one of the crime families in the area had killed their enemies, disposed of their bodies by grinding them up and sold it as ground round using their butcher shops as the means to distribute it to the public as exotic Ostrich meat, thereby getting rid of the evidence.

Detective Wells' gut instinct told him that the young people that were wanted as suspects were just innocent victims that were duped by these evil mobsters. Wells vowed to break this case wide open as soon as he was able to question the owners of the butcher shops. But he figured they might have already been killed and made into hamburger.

These victims were either being killed by enemies of the Bruno

Manzelli crime family or by the Manzelli soldiers themselves to quiet any of Wells' witnesses that could give him the answers he needed to bring his tainted meat and mutilation murders to a close.

Wells needed to return to his precinct to check his reports and all the photos of his suspects including the missing owners of the establishments where the tainted human hamburger had been sold and where the mutilated bodies had been found. He was hoping to discover the identities of the victims, which could lead him to finding their killers.

Wells told Dr. Terry that he was leaving the crime scene and returning to the station. Adding, "Would you get the autopsy reports to me as quickly as possible?"

"Will do, Detective," Terry told him. "Is it all right if I take the bodies away now?"

"Yeah," replied Wells as Officer Diehl stood near his side, "I'm finished with 'em. Has the photographer taken photos of the murder scene?"

Dr. Terry told him he had.

"Then you can take the bodies away," Wells replied. Then Wells congratulated Officer Diehl on his find and patted him on the shoulder. Adding, "You will make a good homicide detective one day."

With that said Wells then left the crime scene, returned to his vehicle and drove back to the Hollywood police station, while Susan Pelk followed in her black sedan. Wells just ignored her and continued on. As long as Susan Pelk didn't overstep her bounds and interfere in his murder investigations he would let her be.

Wells parked his vehicle in the station's parking lot while Pelk kept her distance, parking a few rows away and staying inside her vehicle smoking a cigarette as Wells entered the station. He quickly signed in at the front desk and then walked directly to his desk. As he entered the room there was a dead silence – and not one homicide detective in sight. He was alone and doing more than his share of the investigating.

Wells plopped into his chair and looked at the thick stack of investigative, autopsy and forensic reports sitting atop his desk. He picked up a report and began reading it until he looked at his watch and saw that his workday was finished. He grabbed the stack of reports, placed them in his old and tattered leather briefcase and headed out the door to the parking lot – then jumped into his beat-up Ford and headed for home with his shadow, Susan Pelk in tow.

Fifteen minutes later Wells pulled into his driveway and watched as Pelk parked out on the street three doors away. He again ignored her and walked into his abode carrying his briefcase full of reports. He then headed directly to his kitchen cabinet, grabbed his bottle of scotch and a shot glass, waltzed into the living room, plopped down onto his nice comfortable couch and began pouring shots, then downing them just as fast he poured them. He poured four before he took a break to light a cigarette.

Detective Wells then opened his briefcase and pulled out the evidence report that he hadn't finished reading when he was called to his first mutilation. It explained the evidence found at the first hangout that he had searched looking for his female suspect in the tainted meat murders. Besides many empty pill bottles there was also a bottle of liquid morphine that had been stolen a week before from a hospital emergency room, one block away from the hangout.

The hospital couldn't come up with a suspect for the theft. But the day of the theft a girl by the name of Katie Brown had visited the emergency room for a cut thumb, which the doctor had sutured. Wells wondered if it was just a coincidence or was Katie Brown the thief? He needed to find her and question her before he would know.

At Detective Smith's murder scene, the forensic investigators also found an empty five hundred-milligram bottle of liquid morphine and many empty pill bottles. Wells would have to wait for a copy of Smith's investigative report before he would know if the two empty bottles of liquid morphine had matching inventory numbers and had come from the same hospital.

Wells hoped he would be given copies of the investigative reports from Wilmont, Smith and Rodriguez during their luncheon engagement the following afternoon. He would give them copies of all of his reports pertaining to the homicide investigations that he was currently working and he hoped they would do the same for him.

The second report Detective Wells read was the missing persons' report for the city of Hollywood. There must have been over one hundred names on the list, six of which were known mobsters. And four others that could be mob associates or mob connected. He added the four names to the six that he already had hair samples of, given to him by the missing persons' families.

One person Wells had added and then scratched off the list was the name of Elmero, Salvator Elmero. But he wouldn't know for sure if Elmero was one of the dead until the DNA tests were completed. Once the autopsies and DNA tests had been completed on the three torsos that had just been found, and Elmero was found to be among them, an Elmero family member would be called down to the morgue to view and verify the remains.

Wells also read the autopsy report on the first mutilated torso that had been found at the seedy Hollywood motel room. He didn't quite understand the test required but Dr. Terry used the spinal fluid to find out if the body had been killed in the motel room or had been moved from another location and then dumped there. And the test proved just that – that the victim had his blood sucked out from the jugular vein before being killed and mutilated in the motel room.

While the other three detectives thought there was a vampire on the loose, Wells didn't believe it. Now he did. Except he believed the vampire was from the Manzelli crime family or one of the rival families that were in competition with them. In fact one eyewitness report stated that three men were seen near the motel room where that first mutilated body was found.

As Wells looked at the composite drawings of the three men, he thought one of them was his male suspect from the tainted meat murders and that the other men were members of the Manzelli crime family.

One drawing looked like Johnny Vega, owner of the seedy motel in Hollywood where the first mutilated body had been found, and the other man looked to be Tommy Elmero, owner of the butcher shop in Santa Monica where the tainted meat had been sold. But Detective Wells wouldn't know for sure until he looked at the photos that were in his desk drawer at the station.

But if it were the two men that Wells believed them to be, then they were still alive. He began thinking that maybe these men and others were killing these people for the Manzelli crime family.

Detective Wells set the stack of reports onto his coffee table and walked into the kitchen for another bottle of scotch. Just to pass the time he looked out his kitchen window to see if Susan Pelk was still in the neighborhood. She was. Pelk was sitting behind the wheel of her car in the pitch black of night smoking a cigarette. Wells could see the glow of the ash of the cigarette as she puffed away on it. He couldn't believe she could be getting a story just by sitting in her black sedan all night watching his house. Wells wondered what she really wanted from him?

But again Wells ignored Pelk's stupidity and returned to his living room where he plopped his butt onto the plush cushions of his couch, poured and drank four more shots, then continued reading his investigative reports until he passed out – not waking up until the next morning.

Wells heard the loud ring of his alarm clock but ignored it. It took him another ten minutes before he stirred from his couch to confront his horrendous hangover. First thing he did was light a cigarette, which helped clear his throat of phlegm that had accumulated during the night. Slowly raising himself up from the dead he stumbled into the bathroom with a bloated head that felt as though it would pop, turned on the faucet and splashed some cold water onto his face to ease his pain and wake him up.

Wells didn't shave because he thought his shaking hands might cut his own throat. But at least that would have stopped the pounding in his head. With his bathroom chores completed he shut off the water and stumbled into the bedroom to change into a fresh suit. He only owned three and two of them needed cleaning. So he took his only clean suit out of the closet and slowly changed into it, combed his greasy black hair – what little he had left – and stumbled into the kitchen to warm a fresh pot of coffee.

While his coffee perked, he smoked a cigarette and turned on the five-inch, black and white television that he kept on his kitchen table. He tuned in to the local news station to find that the reporter was blabbing about the tainted meat that caused many innocent deaths throughout Santa Monica, San Pedro, Redondo Beach and Hollywood.

The reporter went on to say that many other bodies had been found in those same cities but hadn't died from tainted meat. But rather, they <u>were</u> the meat. The local reporter stated that several mutilated bodies may also be connected to the tainted meat deaths and that their blood had been completely sucked out before they were ground up into hamburger and sold to the local butcher shops.

The reporter also stated that there was a vampire on the prowl and for the local citizens in those four cities to be leery and to stay away from any exotic Ostrich meat. The station also showed three of the four composite drawings of the young suspects in the tainted meat murders and named one of them – Katie Brown.

That was too much for Wells to handle, especially the way his head pounded. So he shut off the television and poured himself a cup of hot, black coffee. As he stood near the kitchen window, he looked out to see if Susan Pelk was still outside in her car watching his house. Sure enough, she was sitting behind the steering wheel. She hadn't moved since she followed him home the night before.

Wells returned to his kitchen chair and finished drinking his coffee. When he accomplished that task, he stood up, walked into the living room, grabbed his thick stack of reports and placed them into his briefcase. With briefcase in hand, he stumbled out the front door and jumped behind the wheel of his beat-up Ford.

Wells then slowly backed out of his driveway and passed the black sedan. But as he peered through his car window towards Pelk's vehicle, he noticed something very strange. There was a dark red substance covering the windshield and Pelk's body was slightly slumped to the right. Wells stopped his car in the middle of the street, jumped out and ran to the black sedan to check on her. As he ran towards her car, he called out her name.

"Susan Pelk. Are you all right?"

But she didn't move. And when Wells reached her vehicle he could see that she was dead. He reached through the open driver's window and gently shook her body, but to no avail. She had been shot during the early morning hours. He could see that a large bullet had entered into the back, left side of her head, just behind her left ear. The blast covered the car's dashboard and windshield with her splattered blood.

Wells wondered why Susan Pelk was killed? He hadn't heard any gunshots at all during the night. Even though he was in a drunken stupor, he believed he still would have heard them. But not if the killer had used a silencer. And Detective Wells knew only the mob used silencers to kill their enemies. But why would the mob want to kill a reporter? What did Susan Pelk know about the mob that Detective Wells didn't?

Wells couldn't believe this was happening. He turned and ran to his vehicle, then reached through the open window and grabbed the radio's microphone. But he couldn't get through. There was too much static during his radio transmission so he ran to his place and phoned in the murder to Hollywood police dispatch. Within fifteen minutes the coroner and forensic investigative crews had arrived. Detective Wells met them at the dead reporter's black sedan. His hangover didn't make it any easier for the crusty old homicide detective.

"Detective Wells, did you call this in?" asked Dr. Terry.

Wells said he had.

Looking at the body through the open window, Dr. Terry asked himself, "What do we have here?" Then as he opened up the driver's door of the black sedan he asked Wells if he knew the woman's identity.

"She's a female reporter," Wells replied. "Her name's Susan Pelk. Her I.D. should be in her purse. Isn't her purse near her body?"

"No, I don't see it," answered Dr. Terry. "Maybe she didn't carry one. Maybe her driver's license is in her glove compartment."

Thinking Terry could be right Wells opened the passenger door, then looked into the glove compartment for Susan Pelk's identification.

While Dr. Terry looked over the dead woman's body and the photographer took pictures of the crime scene, Wells checked the glove compartment and backseat for any evidence that might lead to her killer.

The glove compartment was empty, as were the back and front seats. The only thing the investigators had to go on was the license plate number. So a young patrol officer was given the task of running it through the D.M.V. database. Five minutes later the tag came back...not as Susan Pelk's car, but as belonging to the FBI's home office in Los Angeles.

Detective Wells couldn't believe it when he learned that the car belonged to the FBI.

The forensic team took the woman's fingerprints to run them through the FBI's database for identification. But it would be more than an hour before the investigators could return to the station to run the prints through the computer.

When the scene had been thoroughly investigated, Wells allowed the coroner to take the body away for an autopsy. He wanted Ballistics to compare the slug that killed Pelk to other slugs that were kept on file from past murders. Wells believed the mob had killed the woman. And they use their weapons only once and then get rid of the evidence, so he knew there wouldn't be a match to the deadly slug. But the ballistics' test had to be done and procedure had to be followed.

"Dr. Terry," said Wells, "if you need me for anything, I'll be at my desk until lunchtime. That is unless I'm called away to another murder scene."

"I'll get you the information on the slug and autopsy as soon as I can," Terry replied.

With that, Detective Wells returned to his car and left the murder scene...heading straight for the Hollywood police station. He wanted to see if he could match the three male composite drawings to the three men that had been seen leaving the area where the three mutilated torsos had been found.

While Detective Wells was driving to the station, he looked into his rearview mirror and thought Susan Pelk was following him in her black sedan, but he realized that couldn't be. She was just found murdered in her car. Wells continued to watch in his rearview mirror as the black sedan followed three car lengths behind. But the sedan's windshield was too dark to see who was driving the car. He wondered who was following him now and why? Was it another reporter, the Manzelli crime family or was it the FBI?

But as Wells turned into the parking lot of Hollywood police station and parked his car, the black sedan turned in the opposite direction. It wasn't following him after all, Wells thought. He figured he was just too paranoid after Susan Pelk's murder.

After catching his breath Wells got out of his car and headed into the station. Seconds after he signed in at the front desk Captain Lawson stopped to speak with him.

"Detective Wells, would you follow me to my office? I need to talk to you about the Susan Pelk murder."

"What do you need to know, Captain?"

He asked Wells if he had any suspects or eyewitnesses to the crime?

Wells replied, "I won't know until the investigators return and hand in their reports. I sent the uniformed officers to canvass the neighborhood for anyone that might have seen something early this morning."

"Didn't you hear or see anything last night?" Lawson asked him.

Wells shrugged his shoulders. "I was pretty drunk last night, Captain," he replied. "But I did look out my kitchen window around ten o'clock last night and saw Susan Pelk sitting behind the wheel of her car smoking a cigarette. I looked out the window again this morning and she was still there. I didn't think too much about her until I drove past her car and looked in her direction. That's when I saw blood splattered across the inside of the windshield and her body slumped over to one side. I immediately stopped my car and jumped out to check the body. When I saw she was dead I ran back to my car to radio for help but there was too much interference with the transmission so I ran back to my place and called dispatch."

"Who do you think is behind her murder?" Lawson asked.

Wells told him that he didn't know but would find out. Adding, "I believe she was killed by the mob to silence her. But for what...I don't know. We also ran the car's license and it came back as a FBI vehicle. I'm waiting now for her fingerprint identification. Her purse was gone and the car's glove box had been ransacked. We had no way of positively identifying the woman. I want to find out why she had been following me for the past several days."

"Didn't you ask her?" Lawson snapped.

"She was a news reporter," Wells told him. "I figured she was trying to get a story. Now I'm wondering if Susan Pelk was the person that was giving the local news media the drawings of my suspects."

Lawson then said something that surprised Wells. "I think I'm going to give Susan Pelk's investigation to Detective Lenda. He's been working the old unsolved murder cases and I think it's time he get involved with an ongoing murder investigation."

"Why him?" Wells asked. "I believe the Susan Pelk murder is linked to the tainted meat murders and possibly the mutilations. I don't have anything to support my beliefs yet, but I hope to when my investigators report back to me."

But Lawson told him to concentrate his efforts on the tainted meat murders and the mutilations. "If you think they are somehow intertwined, prove it. But in the meantime, I want Detective Lenda on the Susan Pelk murder case. If the investigation leads to her involvement in the tainted meat murders or mutilations, then I'll let him work with you. But until then, I want you to forget about Susan Pelk and work your other cases. Is that understood?"

But Wells was adamant. He wanted to investigate the Pelk murder – and again told Lawson that the Pelk murder was somehow linked to his other murder investigations. "I don't know how, but I feel it. Captain, I really think you ought to let me add the Susan Pelk case to the ones I'm already investigating. I want to investigate her murder."

Lawson got a little peeved, saying, "Wells, I'm gonna say this once and only once. If any more dead bodies surface due to the eating of ground human flesh, we'll have the news media hounding us for an answer and then we'll have to start a task force and our budget can't afford one. It's damn near depleted now and we still have more than three months left in this fiscal year. But right now we have four homicide detectives working those murders in four different cities. You guys should come up with something and soon."

"I'm sure we will, Captain," Wells promised. "In fact, I'm having lunch this afternoon with the other three detectives. We're going to talk over the tainted meat and mutilation murders. There has also been at least one mutilated body found in each of the four cities. And the same ground round that was found at the butcher shops was also found at many of the mutilated crime scenes."

"Well keep me abreast on your investigations," Lawson told Wells. "And remember…Lenda will be investigating the Pelk murder. Is that understood?"

"Yes sir, it is," Wells replied as he looked at his watch and noticed it was nearly lunchtime. "I'm sorry, Captain," he went on to say, "but if I don't leave now I'll be late for my luncheon engagement with the other detectives."

"Then get out of here," Lawson snapped, motioning Wells out of his office.

Wells walked away and headed for his desk. He wanted to retrieve the photos of the missing mob members and compare them to the drawings of the suspects seen leaving the places where the mutilated bodies had been found.

And when Wells reached his desk he was surprised to find another stack of reports waiting for him. He grabbed them, reached into the center drawer of his desk, grabbed the photos and file of the missing suspects in his investigations and hurried out of the station before getting into his old car. Once inside his car he placed the stack of reports into his briefcase along with his others and then raced out of the parking lot heading for Gabrielle's Hoagie House.

Again someone in a black sedan was following – about four car lengths – behind Wells' vehicle. He couldn't see the driver or for that matter anyone else in the vehicle. The black sedan was an exact replica of the vehicle Susan Pelk had been driving. Wells figured this black sedan was also owned by the FBI. So he kept an eye on it as he drove to the restaurant. But as he pulled into Gabrielle's parking lot, the black sedan drove past the restaurant and continued on down the highway.

Wells then turned his attention to his fellow detectives and lunch. He parked his car and waited for the others. A few minutes later the three others showed up within one minute of each other. All four homicide detectives then exited their vehicles and met at the entrance of the restaurant where they shook hands while holding onto their thick stacks of papers or briefcases.

The homicide detectives walked to the back room to Wells' favorite table in the smoking section. Before they sat down they each ordered drinks. In fact, they all ordered Long Island ice teas except for Wells. He ordered his usual double scotch on the rocks.

After smoking their cigarettes, drinking their drinks and ordering their meals, the detectives began talking about their murder investigations while waiting for their meals to arrive.

"Listen up," said Wells. "Before we get started I just want to say that whoever is giving the drawings to the local media, should stop. This morning I saw three of the young suspects' drawings in the tainted meat murders all over the tube. Luckily, only Katie Brown's name was mentioned. But sooner or later our suspects are going to get spooked and leave for another state to start their business elsewhere."

Smith told Wells that he hadn't mentioned anything about his murder investigations to anyone outside of law enforcement.

The others also denied hoof and mouth disease.

"Well, maybe the source that gave our suspects' composite drawings to the media is no longer alive," said Wells as he lit another cigarette.

"Why do you say that?" asked Smith.

Wells replied, "Because this morning a female reporter by the name of Susan Pelk was found murdered in her vehicle only two houses down from mine. She had been following me ever since I began the tainted meat murder investigation. I don't know why she was killed, but I believe her murder is somehow linked to our investigations."

"Who killed her and why?" Rodriguez asked him.

"I wish I knew," replied Wells. "It might be the mob. Somebody shot one slug into the back of her left ear. It has mob murder written all over it.

But why is not known at this moment. After lunch I'm gonna visit the coroner and hopefully get some answers. But in the meantime, let's see what each of us has come up with in our individual investigations. We each have experienced a mutilated murder in our respective cities and I've come to the conclusion that they're linked with the tainted meat murders. Especially after finding the ground meat at the mutilated murder scenes. Do any of you have any evidence that might substantiate my claims?"

All at once each detective began handing out copies of their reports to the others that they deemed important. Eight hands and arms were reaching across the table handing out their important papers.

"Please…let's do this one detective at a time," said Smith. "Who wants to go first?"

"I will," replied Rodriguez. He then set his female suspects' composite drawings in the center of the table for all to see. "As you can see these are the two female suspects that were seen in my city. One drawing is of the woman that delivered the tainted meat to Johnny Vega's butcher shop. The other is of the female that was seen by an eyewitness near the motel where my mutilated torso was found. And that too is owned by Johnny Vega. And he and his brother, Joseppi are both known mobsters of the Manzelli crime family."

"Good work, Raul," said Wilmont as he lit a big cigar. "Do you have any names to go with the drawings?"

"I wish I did," he replied. "Oh, one other thing. My investigators also found a fingerprint that matched one of the unidentified prints that Wells' investigators found at Katie Brown's hangout in Hollywood. We found our print in the seedy motel room where the mutilated body was found."

"Have you been able to identify the fingerprint's owner?" asked Wells.

"No, the identity is still unknown. But we do know that this person was in the hangout of a suspected murderer and also found at another murder scene in San Pedro. So I would say that this person whoever it may be, is mixed up in our murder investigations."

"You might be right, Raul," Wells told him, "but we need more to substantiate those allegations. Does anyone else have anything to add that might help lead us to these suspected murderers?"

"Well," said Wilmont, puffing away on his stinky cigar, "we have an eyewitness that saw two male suspects leaving the murder scene across the way from Redondo Pier where we found our mutilated victim. But nothing more on the tainted meat murders. The victim that could have told us something died last night after being in a coma. We should have the composite drawing done later this afternoon. I'll fax it to each of you the minute I receive it."

"What about you, Willard?" asked Wells.

"Well, we got a few hits from the fingerprints found at my murder scene. The photos I handed out to you guys are of the three men that are wanted for questioning in the mutilation. As you can see, they're mobsters from the Santini crime family and enemies of the Manzelli crime family. We just don't know if they were involved in the mutilations or if they are the mutilations. We're waiting for matching DNA tests from the torso found and the hair fiber that we received from the suspect's family."

"Who are these mobsters? Do they have a name?" Wilmont asked him.

"They sure do. One goes by the name of Sammy "the skinner" Santini. He's the younger brother to Louie Santini. As you all know Louie is the top mob boss of the Santini crime family and arch rival to the Don Bruno Manzelli crime family. Both families have massive drug distribution networks that reach from coast to coast. Now I believe they are trying to get rid of their competition. The other two male suspects are Tony "the ax" Antoli and Carl "meat cleaver" Calletti. So keep your eye out for them."

"Such poetic names," reflected Wells.

"What about you, John? What have you got for us?" asked Wilmont.

Before answering, Wells took a deep drag on his cigarette, exhaled, then told them what had transpired the day before. "Yesterday while visiting Willard in Santa Monica, I was called to a murder scene in Hollywood. There were three mutilated torsos just like all the others, and no blood anywhere. But we did get a surprise. My investigators found a fifty-five gallon plastic container similar to others that have been found at your own murder scenes filled with ground human flesh. Except when they emptied it into a body bag a decapitated head fell out of it which we think is Salvator Elmero. He was wanted for questioning and the owner of the butcher shop in Hollywood that sold tainted meat. Now the question is did a rival crime family kill him or did his own crime family kill him so he couldn't finger anyone else in the tainted meat murders? That's the question."

"Are you sure that the decapitated head belongs to Salvator Elmero?" asked Smith.

Wells replied, "We won't know until a positive identification is made through DNA tests. The head had no eyes or teeth and it was crushed and mutilated. The wife will be called in later today to view the head. We hope she will be able to give us an answer one way or another but through the DNA tests we will know for sure. But that may take a few days or longer."

"What about this news reporter that you found near your house shot to death? How is she mixed up in all of this?" asked Rodriguez.

"I'm not certain," Wells replied. "No identification was found on her person or in her vehicle, but when we ran the tags and license plate, it came back as a vehicle used by FBI agents in the city of Los Angeles. She introduced herself to me as Susan Pelk, but we're checking her fingerprints just to be on the safe side. I should have her identity by the time I return to my precinct."

"John, are you investigating Susan Pelk's murder?" asked Smith.

"I wanted to," he replied. "I believe she is somehow mixed up in our murder investigations. Maybe she saw or heard something that she shouldn't have and the mob silenced her. But my Captain refused my request to investigate. He gave it to an inexperienced homicide detective by the name of Tom Lenda. He hasn't investigated a hot case since the department hired him. His only murder investigations were of old and unsolved cases. He's been working them for over a year and hasn't come up with a thing. So I don't know how he'll do with Susan Pelk's murder case."

"I'm sure he'll do fine," interjected Smith. "We were all in that position ourselves at one time."

"Speak for yourself," Wells retorted.

Finally the waitress brought their meals to the table so work was stopped for twenty minutes while they ate. Afterwards the four homicide detectives sat back and smoked there cigarettes or cigars and ordered more drinks. All the while talking about their murder investigations.

"You know now that I've taken a closer look at Raul's suspect, I believe I have a photo that resembles her," said Wells as he pulled out a photo from his thick stack of papers and placed it in the middle of the table for them to see. "She is one of the seven people that had been identified from the fingerprints found at Katie Brown's hangout."

"Yes, I have that photo, too," said Rodriguez. "If you remember, John, you faxed me the seven photos and twelve fingerprints that were found at her hangout the other day."

"You faxed them to me also," said Wilmont.

"I also received them," said Smith.

Wells shook his head in disbelief that he had forgotten. "You know I've been so busy lately I can't remember what happened five minutes ago, let alone a few days ago," said Wells as he finished his second double scotch on the rocks and then ordered a third.

"You should go easy on those drinks, John," said Smith.

"Oh, that's all right. I'm a big boy."

"You know best," Smith told him.

"Okay guys. Let's get back to the murder investigations," said Rodriguez, trying to calm the situation.

Wells then asked the three detectives if they had sent their DNA evidence from the mutilated torsos to the proper authorities for testing and for cross referencing and matching to DNA evidence from their missing persons' list?

"We all have," Smith replied. "Haven't we, guys?"

"Yes," said Detectives Rodriguez and Wilmont in unison.

"I also sent other hair fibers that were found at my mutilated murder scenes," said Wells as he crushed out his cigarette. "But like I said before, they could be from the mutilated victims themselves. We won't know until the tests are completed."

Smith told him that his investigators from his forensic team were still going over the evidence. Adding, "Anything that can be sent for DNA testing, will be."

"All right you guys," said Wells, "let's get back to the photo and drawing of Raul's suspect." Wells then passed one of Raul's two suspects' photo and drawing around the table and asked the other detectives if they thought the person in them was one and the same? "I think they're a match," Wells told them. "What do you guys think?" He waited anxiously for their answers as they passed the suspect's photo and composite drawing around the table.

"They sure look the same," replied Smith. "What do you think, Raul?"

"They could be the same person," he replied half-heartedly. "But the photo shows the girl with long hair and the drawing shows her with short hair. I didn't want to say anything about it until I got your opinions. But I did do a background check on her."

"So what's her name?" asked Wilmont. "Is she the suspect who delivered the tainted meat or was she seen near the motel room where the mutilated body was found?"

Rodriguez told them that she was the woman who delivered the tainted meat to Vega's butcher shop. Adding, "She was seen with John's long, black-haired male suspect. And her name is Janie Jensen. She's twenty-two years of age but looks and acts seventeen. She's also a nymphomaniac and has been in trouble with the law. She's been busted for many different crimes including prostitution, theft and larceny. She hangs out on the street and is homeless and is known to hang out with four or five other homeless street urchins who have been known to congregate in Hollywood, as well as Santa Monica, Redondo, Manhattan, Hermosa and San Pedro. They've also been seen at different beaches in Palos Verdes, such as Lunada Beach and other nearby beaches in that area. She's been on the streets since she was a child of eleven and has done anything and everything just to survive. That's about all I have for now. My investigators are still checking her background. They are trying to get her juvenile records but aren't having much luck."

"You know," interjected Wilmont, tapping her photo with his finger, "I think I've seen this girl and a few of her friends near the Redondo Beach Pier. Yes, I'm sure of it. I'll have to have my investigators check that area with a fine tooth comb."

"Well I've put out an APB on her in connection with the mutilation murder at the San Pedro motel," said Rodriguez.

Smith told them that he'd get photos of her to all of his patrol officers and investigators. "Sooner or later all of our suspects have to surface."

"Yeah, but let's hope it's not in ground up meat or another mutilated body," said Wells.

"Talking about ground meat," interjected Smith. "I've had two more victims die from tainted meat poisoning. A combination of the E-coli bacteria and the aids virus did them in."

Wells asked Willard how many confirmed deaths he had in Santa Monica that were caused by eating ground up human flesh?

He said there were now a total of five that he knew of.

"We better find these killers and fast," said Wilmont as he chewed on his big cigar. "If the news media ever finds out about all these mutilations popping up all over Los Angeles county, we'll be making excuses for our incompetence for the rest of our lives."

"Well then, let's find out who's doing the killings," retorted Wells. "I still say these torsos are over a mob war between the Manzelli and Santini crime families. I believe it's all about their drug empires. Neither family wants to share the wealth. They're greedy bastards. They want it all for themselves."

"John, now all we need now is the evidence to back up your theories," said Smith.

"I'll have it before too long. I'm sure of it. Mobsters aren't the smartest of people. They'll make a mistake and when they do, I'll come down on them like a load of bricks."

"Let's hope so," replied Smith. "I'm getting a lot of static from my Captain. He wants these murders closed and fast. I hear it hourly from the guy. That's why I try and get away from my desk as much as possible."

"You're not alone. We all have that trouble," said Wilmont, as the other detectives shook their heads in the affirmative.

"It's getting late," Wells reminded them. "I'm going to have one more drink for the road and then I have to get back to the station. I have to see the coroner about the decapitated head and the three torsos that were found yesterday. I want to find out if it belongs to one of the torsos. I also want to see how the Susan Pelk autopsy is going. Even though it isn't my case, I'm still interested in her murder."

"Let us know if you find anything that might help us in our murder investigations," Wilmont reminded him.

"I will," answered Wells. "I'll fax you the material as soon as I receive it if it concerns our investigations."

"Yes, it is getting late. I have to get back too or I'll hear about it from Captain Helfman," said Rodriguez.

"Don't worry about the bill," said a slightly light-headed and drunken Wells. "I'll take care of it."

"Thank you, John. I'll get the next luncheon engagement," said Smith, as the other detectives acknowledged Wells' kindness.

All four detectives had one more round of drinks before the party broke up and each went their separate ways. After Wells paid the bill and left a good-sized tip for the waitress, all four detectives departed the restaurant and drove back to their respective cities to continue their investigations.

Wells headed directly to the Hollywood coroner's office. He wanted to find out from Dr. Terry if an Elmero family member had positively identified the decapitated head. He was anxious to learn anything that would bring him one step closer to breaking his murder investigations.

CHAPTER 6

Wells was not only anxious to learn the identity of the decapitated head, but he was also anxious to read the ballistics report on Susan Pelk's bullet. Because if it was a twenty-two, that would point to a mob hit. But that would just be conjecture until Detective Lenda could come up with corroborating evidence.

As Wells drove to Hollywood's morgue, he again noticed a black sedan following four car lengths behind him. He wondered who it could be? It sure wasn't Susan Pelk. Wells just wanted to find out why they were following him. However at this particular moment his murder investigations were far more important than the black sedan following him.

Wells pulled into the parking lot of the coroner and forensic building and parked his vehicle – then waited to see if the black sedan would also pull into the parking lot. But again, the vehicle and its occupants continued driving on the main highway. Wells wondered now if he was just being overly paranoid or was that car truly following him. But those thoughts would have to wait. He had other important matters to contend with. Seconds later he was out of his car and heading into the building looking for Dr. Terry.

Wells walked directly into the autopsy room thinking that Terry would be doing Susan Pelk's autopsy. But when he entered the room, he saw Detective Lenda, Captain Lawson and other homicide detectives standing on the other side of the room talking. When they saw Wells they all turned in his direction and stared at him as though he had been their major conversation piece.

"Captain Lawson, is Dr. Terry around?" asked Wells.

"Look in the morgue," replied Lawson. "I believe he's trying to identify one of your mutilated bodies."

Detective Wells turned and walked to the morgue. As he entered through the big double doors he could see through the big viewing window, a torso and the decapitated head that had been found the day before.

The head and torso were laying together on a table in the middle of the room as Dr. Terry was speaking with a crying woman whom Wells believed to be Salvator Elmero's widow. By the way she was crying and carrying on Wells could tell that she had positively identified the decapitated head as that of her husband. Dr. Terry consoled the old woman while the torso and head were wheeled away and placed into the morgue's freezer.

After a few agonizing minutes the woman departed the building and Wells was able to speak with Dr. Terry about what had just transpired.

"Dr. Terry, how are you today?" Wells asked him.

"I guess things could be going better. I'm too overworked and underpaid."

"Aren't we all," Wells retorted.

"What can I do you for, Detective?"

"I take it that that woman was Salvator Elmero's widow?"

"How did you know?" Terry replied.

Wells answered: "By the way the woman was crying and carrying on and the way you consoled her, I figured she had identified the head and torso."

"Well, Detective Wells, you were right. The body and head is that of Salvator Elmero. He's one dead mobster. Do you have any suspects in his death?"

"Yeah," Wells replied. "I believe either his own crime family or the Santini crime family killed him."

"Why do you think that?" asked Dr. Terry as they slowly walked towards the autopsy room.

Wells explained: "I believe there's a mob war going on over America's narcotics trade. Each crime family has a distribution network from coast to coast. Either the Manzelli crime family killed Elmero to silence him over the tainted meat murders or the Santini crime family killed him to get rid of their competition."

"Well whatever the reason, I hope you can stop it real soon. The news media found out about all these mutilations popping up all over L.A. County and now it's being played on every local news station in California," said Dr. Terry.

"You've got to be kidding," Wells replied shaking his head in disgust. "How in the hell did the news media get wind of these killings?"

"They didn't say," replied Terry. "But you're the detective. Isn't it your job to find out?"

"It is. But I'm only one person. By the way Doc, I saw Detective Lenda and Captain Lawson in the autopsy room. I take it they are waiting for Susan Pelk's autopsy report?"

"If they are, they'll be waiting for a long time."

"Why do you say that?" Wells asked him.

"Because someone from the federal government came in this morning and carted the body off to some unknown destination."

"You're kidding," Wells answered in amazement. "What would the federal government want with a news reporter?"

Terry asked Wells if he was sure she was just a news reporter? Adding, "The forensic team put her fingerprints into the FBI's database and nothing showed up. In fact when they checked the data base for the name of Susan Pelk...the name came back as deceased."

"Well, she is deceased, isn't she?" asked Wells.

"Oh yes," Terry replied as they walked through the open doorway and entered the autopsy room. "The woman that we had here in the autopsy room that we thought was Susan Pelk...is dead. A bullet in the back of the head did that. But the woman named Susan Pelk, the news reporter had died over two years ago. So whoever that female was I had in this autopsy room...we'll never find out now. The federal government made sure of that."

Wells excused himself to speak with his captain.

Captain Lawson, Detective Lenda and two other homicide detectives were still standing in a circle in quiet conversation as Wells approached them.

"Well Captain Lawson, I guess Detective Lenda has to go back to investigating those old murder cases," said Wells.

"No, I don't think so, John. Lenda will be taking over your tainted meat and mutilation murder investigations."

"You mean, Lenda and I will be working together?" asked Wells.

"No. I mean you are off the murder investigations and Detective Lenda will take over."

"Why? What have I done? Are you putting me on the Susan Pelk murder case?" asked Wells utterly confused by Lawson's words.

Lawson shook his head no, saying, "I'm taking you off all investigations until we can clear up another matter."

"What are you talking about, Captain Lawson? What other matter?" asked Wells completely oblivious to the matter at hand.

"Detective Wells, can I have your gun and badge please. I'm putting you on paid leave until we can get some answers to the murder of Susan Pelk," said Captain Lawson holding out his hand.

"Captain Lawson, please explain to me why I'm being suspended. Do you think I'm somehow mixed up with Susan Pelk's murder? Or whatever her name was?"

"Please, Detective. Hand over your weapon."

As Detective Wells reached into his jacket to retrieve his thirty-eight-caliber revolver, he was surprised to learn that his holster was empty. He figured in all the confusion over Susan Pelk's murder he had left it sitting on his kitchen table.

Detective Wells couldn't believe that he was being accused of something that he had nothing to do with. He wondered if someone, namely Captain Lawson, was setting him up? Was Captain Lawson working for the federal government? If so, for what reason? Wells wondered if it had anything to do with the mob war that he believed had exploded in L.A. County.

It had been over fifty years since the last mob war in southern California. During Mickey Cohen's reign, more than twenty-five mobsters were killed or executed in a two-week period over the drug trade in California. Now it was for total control of the narcotics trade from coast to coast.

"I'm sorry, Captain," Wells told him. "I don't have my gun with me at this moment. I must have laid it on the kitchen table and forgot to put it back into the holster. But why do you want my gun and why am I being suspended?"

Standing nearby, Dr. Terry overheard the conversation and answered Wells' question.

"I'm sorry, Detective Wells," interrupted Terry. "It's my fault. I called Captain Lawson over here just after the federal government carted Susan Pelk's body away."

"So what has that got to do with me?" asked Wells, looking to Lawson for the answer.

"I can explain that, Detective Wells," interjected Terry. "Before the federal agents carted away Susan Pelk's body I extracted the bullet from her head. Then I sent it to Ballistics for testing. The bullet came back as a match to your gun."

"That's impossible," snapped Wells. "The tests are wrong. I was laying on my couch, passed out in a drunken stupor when Susan Pelk was killed."

"That's not what the ballistic tests show. And now your gun mysteriously disappears. What are we to think? You seem guilty to me," said Captain Lawson, looking Wells directly in the eyes.

"Captain Lawson, how can you say that about me? I thought you knew me? We've been working together for thirty years and you act as though I'm a stranger."

"I'm sorry, Wells. I.A.D. will investigate the situation and if they say you're clean, your suspension will be lifted. Do you think I would suspend my best homicide detective if I didn't have too? Especially with all these murders popping up all over town. And now the local news media are pointing fingers at our police department for not disclosing the mutilations that have occurred. I don't want to suspend you, Detective Wells. But I don't have any other choice. It's in I.A.D.'s hands now."

"Captain, it will take Lenda a week to get on top of these murders. By that time there could be another dozen victims. Please sir, I'm begging you, let me keep working the murder investigations. I know I can crack this case. Just give me a few more days," pleaded Wells.

"John, I'm sorry. When you find your gun, please bring it to the station so Ballistics can check it out," said Captain Lawson as he walked past Wells and headed through the doors to the parking lot, while Detective Lenda and the other two homicide detectives followed.

"Dr. Terry, do you have Susan Pelk's autopsy report?" Wells asked him.

"No I don't," replied Terry. "The federal agents took everything but the slug. They even grabbed the woman's fingerprint records from the forensic team. Evidently the Feds didn't realize that they had already been run through their data base and didn't tell us a thing."

"So who signed for the body?" asked Wells.

Terry told him a federal agent signed for it. "He flashed a gold shield in my face and demanded Susan Pelk's body. And when they picked it up, they must have thought that I hadn't started the autopsy…because the body was covered and inside a body bag. When they learn that I have completed it and removed the slug from her head, they'll be back looking for it. I'm sure of that."

"Will you call me if those agents return?" Wells asked Terry. "I know I've been suspended, but this is personal now. I'm gonna crack this case or die trying. All I need to find is one of the mobsters or the young kids who are mixed up in all of this. But keep it to yourself. I don't want it to get back to Captain Lawson that I'm still working the case."

"Just be careful, Detective. "You're liable to get yourself in big trouble…or killed," said Dr. Terry.

"Not tonight. Because I'll be at home getting drunk. But if you hear anything, let me know," said Wells as he and Dr. Terry shook hands.

Wells turned and walked out of the autopsy room and headed to the parking lot to his car. Once outside, he stopped for a second to catch his breath and to see if that black sedan was anywhere around, watching him. It wasn't. So he jumped into his vehicle and headed for his place. But low and behold, not more than thirty seconds after he turned out of the parking lot, Wells noticed it following him, about five car lengths behind.

Fifteen minutes later, with the black sedan still on his tail, Wells pulled into his driveway – then quickly stepped out of his vehicle and ran to the side of the road wanting to get a good look at the person or persons sitting in that car. But when the vehicle got within a hundred feet of Wells' place, it turned left onto another side street.

Wells ran across the street hoping to get a better look, but the black sedan raced away from the scene. Wells again thought he was being overly paranoid concerning that black sedan and left it at that.

He returned to his home and unlocked his front door – then went directly to his kitchen cabinet and his bottle of twenty-year-old scotch.

Wells grabbed the bottle, a shot glass and then waltzed into the living room where he plopped down onto his comfortable couch and began pouring shot after shot of scotch down his throat. After a dozen or more shots, he began phoning Detectives Rodriguez, Wilmont and Smith letting them know about his suspension.

Wells explained to the three detectives that he had been suspended from his job and was a suspect in Susan Pelk's murder. He also mentioned the fact that Detective Lenda would take over his murder investigations. The other three detectives couldn't believe it. However, Wells made it clear to them that he would still be investigating the tainted meat and mutilation murders even though he had been suspended. But without his Captain's knowledge or authority.

Rodriguez, Wilmont and Smith all agreed to help Wells anyway they could and also keep quiet about his ridiculous suspension and about being a suspect in Pelk's murder.

When Wells finished his phone calls he remembered about his missing gun and began looking for it throughout the house. But he came up empty handed. He couldn't understand how his weapon could just disappear. Again he searched the house, up and down, inside and out, but still no gun.

Every room in his house had been turned upside down. Drawers were emptied and thrown all over the floors. Clothes were littered throughout the house as though a tornado had swept through, leaving a mess behind. After more than two hours of looking and searching, Wells finally gave up. He just couldn't figure out where his gun had disappeared to. He knew though that he had it the night before.

Wells phoned his homicide department and asked a fellow detective to search through his desk drawers in the hope of finding his revolver. However, the only gun that was found was his back up piece: a three-fifty-seven-caliber magnum revolver that he kept and used mostly for target practice. Wells hardly ever carried the heavy piece of iron on his person. That's why it was in his desk. But that still didn't answer his question. Where was his thirty-eight-caliber revolver that was supposedly used to kill Susan Pelk?

Detective Wells thanked his comrade for helping him and hung up the phone. He continued thinking about his personal problems. Even though he was stone drunk, he couldn't sit still. He had to get out of the house and breathe some fresh air. But just as he was walking out his front door the phone rang.

Smith was calling from Santa Monica police station. He must have told Wells some good news because the drunken detective's spirits picked up. After Wells had finished his conversation with Smith, he hung up the phone, rushed out the front door, jumped into his beat-up vehicle, started the engine and headed for the Santa Monica police station. But he was so drunk that he didn't notice that the black sedan had pulled out from a nearby street and began following him. His vision wasn't the best either as he drove down the highway towards Santa Monica.

Thirty minutes later Wells pulled into the Santa Monica police station parking lot. Nearly every law enforcement official there watched as he parked his vehicle in their nice, newly paved parking lot. He received glares from them as he walked into their beautiful police station.

When Wells entered through the front door he was surprised to see two of the detectives he had spoken with a few hours before. Wilmont and Rodriguez were standing near the front desk smoking cigarettes and talking.

The two detectives admonished Wells for being drunk as he stepped up to the front desk and signed in. When Wells asked to see Smith, he was told to wait with Rodriguez and Wilmont and that Smith would see all three detectives in a few minutes.

The three detectives waited for nearly twenty minutes before Smith called out to them and directed them into the interrogation room.

"I'm glad you could make it, Detectives," said Smith.

"Why did you call us down here?" asked Wilmont. "All you told me is that you have some good news that could break the tainted murder case wide open. So what have you got, Willard?"

"Did you find one of our suspects?" Wells asked Smith.

He nodded yes and explained to them that his investigators combed the beach area and ran into his female suspect. "Gentlemen, I want you to watch through the mirrored glass as I interrogate Katie Brown. She was arrested and brought in for questioning not more than ninety minutes ago. I phoned you guys as soon as my investigators brought her into the station." The guys were overjoyed and showed it by patting one anothers' shoulders and backs.

"Has she said anything yet?" Wells asked Smith.

"Not yet," he replied. "She knows when to keep quiet. This young girl acts the age of a person in there forties not that of a teenager. The streets have taken its toll on her. But don't worry, Detectives, I'll wear her down. Oh, one other thing, John. I'll have to phone Detective Lenda about this suspect. But because of your situation I'll wait a few hours before I do."

Wells nodded in acknowledging the inevitable and thanked Smith for his help, saying, "I appreciate that. And please tell no one I was here."

"Don't worry about me, John. Just worry about yourself," replied Smith as he opened the door and walked into the interrogation room where his female suspect was already sitting smoking a cigarette.

Wells and the two other detectives quickly positioned themselves in front of the mirrored window so they could watch Smith interrogate his suspect.

Smith sat in the chair directly across from his young suspect, Katie Brown while she stared straight ahead as though she was in a trance. She had very short brown hair, pierced ears and was dressed like a flower child of the sixties – wearing granny glasses, a skimpy halter-top, dungy, dirty faded Levi jeans that had been cut off into short shorts and her bare feet were dirty inside her open-toed sandals.

Before Smith interrogated the young girl he turned on the tape recorder that had been sitting on the table in front of them – along with a full pack of cigarettes and matches that belonged to his suspect.

"Miss Brown," Smith said, "before we get started can I get you a soda pop or a cup of coffee? Or maybe a candy bar or snack?"

Katie Brown didn't answer and sat quietly, blowing cigarette smoke out of her mouth in the form of smoke rings. She ignored Smith's presence and stared into the air. The detectives watching behind the one-way glass believed she would keep silent. But then she surprised everyone by speaking.

"I want to get out of here!" she snapped. "I didn't do anything! Why am I here?"

But her words of innocence didn't have any effect on Smith. He explained to her the reason for her interrogation. "Miss Brown, I'm Detective Smith and I need to ask you some questions to clarify some issues. Will you answer my questions?"

"If I can. I've got nothing to hide."

"You're quite the celebrity, aren't you?" Smith asked trying to get on her good side.

"Why do you say that?" she asked him.

"Your face is all over the local news. Haven't you seen yourself on television?"

She shook her head no, saying, "I haven't watched television in two years. The places I stay don't have televisions."

That was enough of the small talk. Smith was ready to get down to business and get the answers he needed. He then asked her about the ground meat that her and her male friend had delivered and sold to butcher shops in Santa Monica and the neighboring cities?

Chain smoking her cigarettes she told him that the meat was found near a garbage bin.

"Where was this garbage bin?" Smith asked her.

"I'm not sure," she said, stuttering as she spoke. "I didn't find it. I just went for a ride to help deliver the meat so we could get money for drugs."

"Who is this person you're speaking about?" Smith asked, leaning across the table and looking directly into her eyes.

She replied: "I'm speaking about my friend, Jarrett."

"Is he your boyfriend?"Smith asked.

She shook her head no, took a deep drag on her cigarette, then said: "He's just a friend I met on the street."

Smith asked her if he was the one who found the ground meat that she sold to the different butcher shops?

She shook her head yes, saying, "I just went along for the ride – one time."

But Smith knew that he had caught her in a lie and told her so. "But Miss Brown, we have witnesses that state you delivered ground meat to at least three different butcher shops with the same person that you call Jarrett. Do you know Jarrett's last name?"

She told him that she only knew him as Jarrett.

"Do you know where we can find him?" Smith asked her.

She told him no. Adding, "I haven't seen him in more than a week."

Smith asked her if she knew where Jarrett lived or hung out?

She answered: "He lives on the street. He told me that he had been on the street since he ran away from his family at the age of ten."

"Where did you live?"

"A lot of places."

"Name one?" Smith asked her.

Before answering she put out her butt and lit another cigarette. After exhaling a big cloud of smoke into Smith's face she told him that most of the time she slept in abandoned buildings.

"Where at?" Smith asked anxiously.

"A lot of places. It depends on what city I'm in."

As Katie Brown puffed away on her cigarette, Smith reached into his briefcase and pulled out a few photos and drawings of the suspects in the murders including the mobsters and placed them on the table in front of her.

"Katie, do you know any of these people?" he asked her, pointing to the photos.

She nodded, saying, "Yeah, I've seen some of these people. A few of the men are the owners of the butcher shops that Jarrett and I delivered the meat to. I also recognize a few of the girls in the photos." She pointed to one and then another. "This girl's name I think is Janie and this one is Kathy. I don't know about the others."

"Do you know the girl's last names?" Smith asked anxiously, knowing that he was getting closer to solving his investigations.

She shook her head telling him that last names didn't mean too much to her. "Especially when you live on the street. Hell, I don't even know if the names they go by are their real names."

Smith then asked her where her friends were? And if any of them delivered any of the ground meat with Jarret?

"I don't know," she replied blowing a big cloud of cigarette smoke into Smith's face. "But I do know that Kathy and Janie know Jarrett. They might have helped him deliver some of the meat. But you'll have to ask them."

"I would if I could find them," Smith retorted. "Do you know where they stay or live?" She remained silent, refusing to answer that question. Smith again asked her if she knew where they stayed or lived.

Finally, after what seemed like hours but were only seconds, she replied, "They all live on the street and travel from one city to another. When the cops get tired of us hanging around, begging for food and money, they run us out of town and we have to go to another city."

"When you say we, who are you talking about, Katie?"

After a long pause, she answered: "Anyone who was with me on that particular day."

Smith then asked her how they traveled from city to city?

"Usually we hitchhiked or walked."

Smith zeroed in on his target and asked the important question. "Do you know what city Jarrett is staying in right now?"

She told him she didn't know. "He left this morning with two girls."

"What are the girls' names?"

"Kathy and Belinda. Kathy is the one I told you about before. But you don't have Belinda's photo."

Smith continued his questioning, knowing that he was making good headway. "Did Jarrett and the girls tell you where they were going?"

She shook her head no, then said, "I went into a store to beg for food and when I came out they were gone. All three of them. I stayed in the area waiting for them to return but then I was arrested and brought here to this station. I still don't know why I'm here."

"Before we talk about that, Katie," Smith said, "why don't you tell me what you know about this Jarrett character?"

Before answering she lit another cigarette using the butt as the match, took a long drag, exhaled, then said: "What do you want to know?"

"Well for starters…how long have you known him? Where is he from? What type of person is he? A good person or bad person? Just tell me whatever pops into your mind about him."

And she did. More than he expected. Saying, "I've known Jarrett for over four years. He found me when I first hit the street. I think he was thirteen or fourteen years old and I had just turned thirteen. I ran away from home after being abused and molested by my mother's druggy boyfriend. Jarrett took me in and protected me until I could protect myself. I owe my life to Jarrett. So to me he's a very good person. Why do you want to know about him? Has he done something wrong?"

For the first time Smith became angry when she began asking him questions. He was no longer a nice guy and snapped: "I ask the questions here, not you! I just want you to answer my questions." She seemed utterly surprised and scared by the way his personality had suddenly turned from likable to a monster. He leaned across the table, his nose nearly touching hers, then asked her in a loud, angry voice, "Why did you and Jarrett sell this ground meat to butcher shops that were owned by mobsters? Did you know the butcher shops that you delivered the meat to were mob owned?"

From her demeaner, you could tell she was nervous and scared. She replied very meekly, saying, "No, I didn't know anything about that. I just went with Jarrett when he asked me to tag along. But some of the men that drove us to the butcher shops are in the photos that you showed me. I recognize two or three of them. In fact we took the ground meat out of their vehicles. One time we had to lift this big, heavy plastic container out of the guy's trunk that had driven us to the butcher shop and Jarrett and I carried it into the butcher shop."

Smith continued his onslaught of questions, asking her if she knew that the men in the photos that she pointed to were mobsters in the Manzelli crime family?

She shook her head no, saying, "I just thought they were friends of Jarrett. I had no idea that they were mobsters." She took one last drag on the cigarette before lighting another one.

But Smith didn't believe her. "So you had no idea that the men that drove you and Jarrett to the butcher shops to deliver the ground meat were mobsters. Is that what you're saying, Katie?"

"That's right," she replied, her hands shaking. "I didn't know the men. They were Jarrett's friends not mine."

Smith then switched gears from Jarrett to Janie. "Let's talk about this girl Janie," Smith said. "What can you tell me about her?"

"Not much," she replied.

"How long have you known her?"

"A few years," she said, opening up. "She's much older than I am, so we don't have too much in common. I see her usually on the weekends

81

hanging out at different clubs in Hollywood. She's not my kind of person."

"Why do you say that, Katie?"

She paused for a second, took a drag on her cigarette, then said, "Janie is heavy into sex. I think she's a nympho. She just comes around to see Jarrett when she wants sex from him."

"So Janie doesn't hang out with your group all the time then? Is that what you're telling me?"

Again she paused, figuring out what she wanted to say before she said it. Finally, she said: "She stays with us and she doesn't. Usually we go on our own and meet up at different places depending on which city we're in. We follow Jarrett when he wants us to. We get lost when he doesn't."

"So Jarrett tells your group what to do and when to do it. Is that right?"

But Katie seemed more interested in her pack of cigarettes than in Smith's question. She crumpled her cigarette pack, telling Smith, "Detective Smith, I'm all out of cigarettes. Would you please get me a pack of cigarettes and an orange soda pop, if they have it?"

Smith was hesitant and didn't want to stop the questioning because he was making great progress. But reluctantly he gave into her demands and said: "I guess I can. You've been very cooperative so far. Would you like a sandwich to go with your soda pop?"

"That would be great," she said with a smile. "I would like tuna fish if they have it."

"I'll be right back with your goodies," said Smith, as he shut off the tape recorder and then left the room.

Smith was met by the other three homicide detectives who had been watching the interrogation of the suspect through the mirrored window.

"Willard, would you mind if I sit in on the interrogation? I would like to ask Miss Brown some questions also," said Wells.

"John, you can sit in on the interrogation and ask her some questions, just don't say anything about the tainted meat murders until I give the go-ahead. I want to get as much information out of her before I tell her about the tainted meat. Is that clear, Detective?"

"Don't worry about me. I've been in this business too long to screw up now," Wells retorted.

Smith looked at Rodriguez and Wilmont and asked, "What about you guys? Do you want to ask Katie Brown any questions?"

"If I think of any, I'll let you know," answered Rodriguez.

"I don't have anything to ask her, either," replied Wilmont. "You don't need me in there to screw things up. You're doing a fine job without my interference."

Detective Smith excused himself and gathered the items Katie Brown had asked for. Ten minutes after he left the interrogation room Smith returned with Detective Wells in tow. He placed the food, soda pop and cigarettes in front of his female suspect and then introduced Katie Brown to his brother detective.

"Miss Brown, this gentleman is Detective Wells. He's from the

Hollywood police station. He would like to listen in on our conversation and maybe ask you a few questions. If that's all right with you?" asked Smith, as he and Wells sat down in chairs across from the female suspect.

"Sure. I don't mind. I didn't know I was so popular," she replied as she opened her pack of cigarettes and soda pop.

"Katie, I hope you like your sandwich. The vending machine didn't have tuna fish so I got you pickled bologna. I hope you don't mind," said Smith.

"Not at all. Beggars can't be choosy. Heck, most of the time I'm eating out of dumpsters. What can I say? Christmas came early," she said, then took a swig of her orange soda pop, stripped away the cellophane wrapping from her pickled bologna sandwich and began feeding her face.

Smith saw that she was practically starved so he told her that he'd wait a few minutes and let her eat her food before asking her anymore questions. While they waited he and Wells smoked cigarettes and relaxed before continuing the interrogation.

She ate her sandwich in record time and as she finished it, let out a loud burp, then said in a jokingly manner: "Boy, I could get used to living like this. I here you get three square meals in jail." A few seconds later she lit a cigarette then waited for the questioning to begin.

Smith stomped out his cigarette on the floor before continuing his interrogation, starting where he left off. "Miss Brown, we were talking about your friend, Janie. You say she's twenty-two years old and a nymphomaniac. Do you know anything else about her? Like where she came from and why she left her family to live on the dirty streets of California?" asked Detective Smith.

Katie took a long drag on her cigarette, blew out the smoke, looked Smith in the eyes and said: "I believe Janie came from the East Coast. She ran away from her family like all of us on the streets. And why do we run away? What else? Abuse. Either mental or physical." She explained to Smith that Janie's parents left their house one-day and never returned – leaving Janie behind. "So Janie hitched a ride to Hollywood with a neighbor. And that's how she ended up on the streets like me. Janie was the second person, after Jarrett, to reach out and help me. But she has her troubles, too. She's always in and out of jail for one reason or another. Usually for prostitution or stealing."

"Did you know that Janie and Jarrett also delivered ground meat?" Smith asked her.

She shook her head no, saying, "Usually Jarrett asked me to go with him. But if I wasn't around when he needed me, then he would ask someone else to help him."

"Katie, you mentioned two other girls that left with Jarrett earlier today. One you named as Kathy and the other you named as Belinda. You pointed out the photo of Kathy. Is there one on this desk of Belinda?" asked Detective Smith.

She looked through all the photos and said: "No, I don't see one. She's the trouble maker of our group," she said, then inhaled deeply and blew a big cloud of cigarette smoke out of her mouth.

"Why do you say that?" asked Smith.

"Because," she replied, "Belinda's always starting arguments and fights. And then Jarrett has to jump in and break it up. Sometimes she acts like two different people. Like she's got a split personality. Whenever she hangs around us, we know there's gonna be trouble. So I try and stay away from Belinda as much as possible."

Wells suddenly jumped into the conversation. "Katie," Wells asked her, "if you took a guess, where do you think Jarrett and his two female friends are right now? Does Jarrett have a special place he likes to be or hang out?"

"Not that I know of," she replied. "But if I took a guess, I'd say anywhere near the beach. During the week we travel from one beach to another and during the weekends we usually visit Hollywood and the night scene. So Jarrett, Kathy and Belinda would probably be at the beach. But in what city, I couldn't tell you."

Before Wells could ask another question, Smith resumed interrogating his suspect. "You've told us about Jarrett, Janie and Belinda," interrupted Smith. "Now tell Detective Wells and myself what you know about the girl you called Kathy. Is her photo on this table?"

"Not a photo, but this drawing," she said, as she handed Detective Smith the drawing of Detective Wells' first female suspect in the tainted meat murders.

Detective Wells now knew the female suspect's first name but still didn't have a last name to go with the drawing.

"Please tell me all you know about this girl Kathy," asked Wells. "If you don't know her last name, do you know anything else about her?"

Before answering she threw her cigarette butt on the floor, slowly took a cigarette out of the pack, lit it, took a long drag, exhaled, then answered Wells' question, saying, "I believe Kathy is the same age as I am, seventeen. She ran away from a dysfunctional family at the age of ten and she's been on the streets ever since. Her stepfather molested her and when she told her mother about it, she didn't believe her. Kathy told me that her mother was a prostitute and would bring her tricks home and let her kids watch as she satisfied her customers. Her mother was addicted to cocaine and heroin and even injected Kathy with dope when she was only six years old. Her mother did that to make her go to sleep so she wouldn't be bothered by her. Two days after Kathy's eighth birthday, her mother injected her with heroin and she overdosed. Kathy was rushed to the hospital by a neighbor and the doctors brought her back to life. The state was called in and Kathy was taken away and put into foster care. But that wasn't any better."

"Why do you say that, Katie?" asked Smith.

"Because Kathy's foster parents used her as a slave to wait on them hand and foot. And when Kathy was beaten and raped by her foster father, she couldn't take it anymore and ran away to California. She came all the way from Michigan at the age of ten. Janie found her and took care of her for three years before they hooked up with Jarrett. That's seven years on the streets and nobody cared but Jarrett."

"Katie," Wells said, "I can't believe you know so much about this girl and not know her last name. And I believe you know her last name and aren't telling us. I believe you know these other girls' names but aren't telling us. What's Kathy's last name, Katie?"

"I don't know," she asked. "Last names aren't important when you're on the street. I don't even know if their first names that they told me are their real names. When you live on the street, only feeding your head and stomach are important."

Wells continued his interrogation, telling her: "Kathy is also one of the girls that helped Jarrett deliver the ground meat to a butcher shop in Hollywood. Katie, do you know who drove them to the butcher shop? Was it one of the men in these photos?" asked Wells, pointing to the photos on the table.

She shrugged her shoulders, saying, "Like I said before. The only reason those other girls helped Jarrett deliver the meat was because I wasn't there to help him. So if I wasn't around, I wouldn't know who did what now would I?"

"That sounds logical to me," said Wells, as Smith nodded in agreement. "Katie, let me ask you this. The mobsters that drove you and Jarrett to the butcher shops so you could deliver the ground meat, did any of them ever visit your group at any of the abandoned buildings where you stayed or lived at?"

She squirmed in her chair, squinted her eyes, then replied, "I saw some men that visited Jarrett when we stayed at different abandoned buildings in Hollywood and Santa Monica. And I think they were the same men that drove us to the butcher shops."

"But you don't know their names. Is that right?" asked Smith.

She took a big drag on her cigarette, exhaled the smoke in the direction of the two detectives, then rested her chin on her balled up fists that lay on the table and finally replied, "I didn't care about their names. They were talking with Jarrett, not me. Jarrett didn't like any of us sticking our noses where they didn't belong. So I never asked any questions. I only did what I was told."

Wells seemed a little perturbed with her answer and told her so, saying, "You've survived the streets for four years and you want us to believe that you don't have a mind of your own? I don't believe you. Your innocent act doesn't convince me."

"Please, Detective Wells, don't get so upset," Smith said, trying to calm the situation. "Katie has been very helpful answering our questions. She'll keep answering them if we don't get her angry."

"Detective Wells isn't making me angry," Miss Brown retorted. "He can say whatever he feels. It doesn't bother me. Living on the streets for all these years has eaten my heart and feelings away a little bit at a time until they disappeared completely."

"Well, let's continue. Shall we?" asked Smith.

Katie nodded in agreement as she took a long drag from her cigarette and blew the smoke into Wells' face. Detective Wells just ignored Brown's foolishness and kept his calm.

"Miss Brown. Have you ever been treated at Hollywood hospital?" asked Wells.

"Yeah, once. Why?"

"What were you treated for?" asked Wells.

"A sprained ankle."

"There was a bottle of liquid morphine stolen from the emergency room the same time you were being treated there. Would you know anything about that or who stole it?" asked Wells.

"Is that what I was arrested for? You think I stole a bottle of liquid morphine from Hollywood hospital. You're crazy. I didn't have anything to do with it."

"I don't believe you," snapped Wells. "When my investigators were searching the abandoned building in Hollywood, they found the empty bottle of morphine that was stolen from the hospital. And when it was analyzed at the forensic lab we discovered your fingerprint on the bottle. Can you explain how your fingerprint got on an empty, stolen bottle of liquid morphine that you had nothing to do with?"

She shrugged her shoulders and said, "I have no idea. Maybe I picked it up to see what was in the bottle? But I didn't steal it."

"But I believe you know who did," replied Wells, staring deep into her eyes. "Now tell me who stole that bottle of liquid morphine from Hollywood hospital."

"I told you," she whined. "I don't know. It wasn't me."

But Wells refused to believe her, saying, "It was either you...or part of your gang that you hang around with. We found your fingerprints and your friend's fingerprints in the abandoned building where the stolen bottle of morphine was found."

"Well then, ask them about it. But I had nothing to do with stealing it."

Smith interceded, saying, "Let's get off that subject and talk about something else. Katie, how did you get involved with Jarrett delivering the ground meat?"

"Why? What does this ground meat have to do with anything?"

"Please, Katie. Just answer the question," said Smith.

After a short pause she answered Smith's question. "Well...a few weeks ago when I entered the abandoned building that we were staying at, I saw Jarrett and another man standing near a large stack of cardboard boxes, talking. When they finished their conversation Jarrett asked me to help him deliver some fresh meat to a few butcher shops in the area. So we loaded the cardboard boxes into the man's car and delivered them. That was it."

"Do you know who the man was that drove you that day to deliver the meat?" asked Wells.

Pointing to a man's photo sitting on the table in front of her, she answered, "I think it was him."

"That's Tony "the ax" Antoli," Wells pointed out. "He's a soldier in the Santini crime family. Did you know that, Katie? Do you think Jarrett knew the person he was dealing with?"

She told Wells that she didn't know the man and didn't ask Jarrett any questions. Adding, "Jarrett didn't like people asking him questions. He would get angry if we did. So I just did as I was told."

Listening to the way Katie spoke and answered the two detectives' questions, Wells was quite impressed with her and told her so. "You know Katie, you're only seventeen years old but yet you act and speak like a mature woman."

"That comes from living on the streets," she replied. "You have to grow up fast. It's called survival of the fittest."

Wells then asked her where her and her friends lived? "Give us addresses or streets where these abandoned buildings you stayed are located. Can you do that for us, Katie?" he asked.

She shrugged her shoulders and said, "I don't know the addresses. When we go to Hollywood...we find an abandoned building and we sleep there. When we're in Santa Monica, we find a condemned or abandoned building nearby and use it. But where they are I couldn't tell you. One abandoned building looks just like another."

Smith turned off the tape recorder and motioned to Wells to stop speaking.

"Would you excuse us for one minute, Katie?" said Smith. "Detective Wells and I need to get a cup of coffee. Is there anything you would like? Another soda, perhaps?"

After she crushed out her butt and lit another cigarette, she told them that she was fine and didn't need anything, except "to get out of this place as quickly as possible."

Wells and Smith stood up and walked out of the interrogation room. They were met by Rodriguez and Wilmont.

"What gives?" asked Wells, looking at Smith for an answer.

"Katie is being very evasive," Smith replied. "We have to find out what abandoned buildings she stayed at. We know she delivered the tainted meat, but did she know it was human flesh?"

Wilmont jumped into the conversation and put in his two cents, saying, "She acts as though she's completely innocent. She says she was just delivering the meat for her boyfriend, Jarrett. That's the person we need to find and question."

"If we tell her why she's been arrested, maybe she'll come clean," surmised Wells. "If she knows that the meat she delivered with this Jarrett character was diseased, ground human flesh, I'm sure she'll give us the answers we're looking for. What do you think, Willard?"

"I don't know if I want to play it that way," he replied. "If we tell her about the tainted meat, she just might clam up and ask for an attorney. Before I say anything about that, I wanted to get as much information out of her as possible."

"It's not working," Wells told him. "Katie knows what we're going to ask her before we do. She has the answers but not the right answers. I believe she knows a heck of a lot more than she's telling us."

"I'm sure she does," Smith interjected. "But it's my suspect and my interrogation. Right now she's being cooperative. I want her to continue answering my questions. I'm sure she'll screw up sooner or later and then we'll have her. That's when we'll tell her about the tainted meat and not until then. Is that understood, Detective Wells?" Smith gave Wells a look of disdain.

Wells got the message and replied, "Like you said, Detective Smith, it's your suspect and your interrogation. I'm just here to watch."

"Very good. If you're ready, John, let's get back to the interrogation." With that said, Smith opened the door and entered the interrogation room with Wells following close behind.

Wells and Smith took their seats, then Smith turned on the tape recorder.

"I thought you guys had forgotten about me," kidded Katie Brown.

Detective Smith was anxious to get on with the interrogation, believing Miss Brown would give him the answers he wanted. He then asked her if she was ready to answer his questions. "Katie, are you ready to answer some more questions for us?"

But before she would answer another question she wanted to know why she was arrested. She became angry and told the two detectives that they had no right to hold her against her will.

Wells shot back, saying, "Miss Brown, you know exactly why you've been arrested."

But she had no idea. She thought they were holding her over a stolen bottle of morphine taken from a hospital. "Well you're wrong," she told them. "I didn't steal any morphine."

"No, that's not the reason," Wells told her. "It's because of the meat you sold and delivered to those butcher shops. You knew that meat was tainted, didn't you?"

When she heard that, her eyes buldged and nearly popped out of their sockets. She became irate and snapped, "What the hell are you talking about? That was good meat. We ate it ourselves. We made hamburgers with it."

Smith couldn't believe what he had just heard and asked her if any of them got sick after eating it?

She replied, "Some of us had stomach aches and diarrhea. But we didn't contribute it to the hamburger. We thought it was from the water we drank." Wells jumped back into the conversation and asked her if she knew that the meat she had delivered and sold was human flesh.

"What are you saying?" she asked, not believing his words.

Wells asked her again, "Did you know that the meat you sold to those butcher shops was tainted human flesh?"

"No I didn't," she replied with a frightened look on her face.

While Wells and Smith were interrogating the female suspect, Wilmont was called back to his city of Redondo Beach. He had to investigate another crime scene. Wilmont asked Rodriguez if he wanted to tag along and view the crime scene but the detective refused his request and stayed on to watch the interrogation.

"Miss Brown," interjected Smith, "we believe you know more than you're telling."

"Are you kidding?" she answered with a surprised and dumbfounded look on her face. "Are you telling me that I ate human flesh like cannibals do? I think I'm going to be sick." She suddenly doubled over and began making gagging sounds as if she was about to regurgitate.

Wells wasn't going for it and believed she was acting, saying, "You're gonna be much sicker, Miss Brown if you have to spend the rest of your life behind bars. Unless you tell us where you got the meat and where we can find your friend, Jarrett, you're not gonna see sunlight anytime soon."

Hearing that, she became angry and asked for a lawyer. "I'm not saying another word until I get a lawyer," she told them.

"All right Miss Brown," said Smith, trying to calm the situation, "we will stop the interrogation until we can get you an attorney. Until then, you can sit in a cell and think about the situation you're in. But if you tell us where we can find Jarrett we can make your troubles disappear. Personally…I believe you when you said that you didn't know the meat was tainted ground human flesh."

"I didn't know," she answered. "I swear it."

"But that doesn't help the people that became ill from the meat," Smith told her. "Did you know that several people in four different cities where you sold and delivered the meat died from eating it?"

She said she didn't. "I swear to God," she whined. "I didn't know."

Smith continued his onslaught and tried to frighten her into giving him the answers he wanted, saying, "Whether you knew about the meat or not, you're involved. And it's still called murder. So when you're sitting in your cell, think it over. Then if you want to cooperate and help us find Jarrett, I'll help you get out of this place. If not, you can rot in prison as far as I'm concerned."

Again she became angry hearing Smith's words and told him that she wasn't saying another word until she spoke with an attorney.

Hearing that, Smith shut off the tape recorder and told Wells that they could no longer help her unless she wanted to help herself. Adding, "I guess our interrogation of her is finished."

With that said, the two detectives stood up and left the room as Katie Brown sat in her seat biting her fingernails.

A few minutes later Smith had one of the officers return the female suspect to her cell while he and Wells talked with Rodriguez.

"Raul, where is Wilmont?" asked Smith.

Rodriguez told him that Wilmont received a call from his captain and had to return to Redondo Beach to check out a crime scene.

"I wonder what he's got now," interjected Wells.

"I'm sure we'll find out real soon," Smith answered, "especially if it's linked to our murder investigations."

Wells looked at his watch and replied, "I guess it's time for me to get out of here. I had hoped we could have learned something from our female suspect. But she's either too frightened to say...or she's protecting her boyfriend, Jarrett."

"John, you're probably right," replied Smith. "If torture were legal, I'd have used it on her. Because we have to stop these killings...and fast. I believe we have a mob war going on and it's going to get worse before it gets better," Smith surmised.

"What do you think, Raul?" asked Wells. "Do you think mob rivals are killing each other over the drug business?"

"I do," he replied. "But I think Katie Brown is only an innocent bystander and was just helping her boyfriend, Jarrett."

But Wells had a different thought, telling them, "If Tony Antoli brought the meat to Jarrett for him to deliver to his enemies' butcher shops then we've definitely got a mob war in progress. If so, we have to find out why."

"I agree," said Rodriguez.

Wells acknowledged his words with a nod of his head, then said, "I think we need to put pressure on the mob and their businesses. I wish I could help in the investigation fellas...but until Captain Lawson lifts my suspension I have to be very discreet and keep a low profile."

"Good luck, John. I hope everything works out for you," said Rodriguez.

Wells thanked them for their confidence in him and told them he needed to get back to Hollywood station and check in with his department to see what IAD had come up with. Adding, "Someone stole my gun and killed Susan Pelk with it. Now I have to find out why."

"How could somebody steal your gun?" asked Smith.

He shrugged his shoulders, saying, "That's what I want to find out." With that said he shook hands with the two homicide detectives and left Santa Monica police station.

As Wells was leaving the building he happened to see his inexperienced peer, Detective Lenda walking towards the entrance. Not wanting to be seen, Wells quickly hid behind a large bush. It worked. Lenda walked past and into the police station without noticing him.

When Wells reached his vehicle, he noticed a black sedan parked a few rows over. He began walking faster and faster towards the car hoping to find out who was driving it and why they were following him. But before he could reach it, the car raced out of the parking lot. A few minutes later he was in his car, racing after the black sedan. But unfortunately it had escaped his grasp.

CHAPTER 7

Detective Wells drove to his place without seeing that black sedan in his rearview mirror. However, when he reached his driveway and hopped out of his car he saw a black sedan turn down a side street. Being too tired and thirsty to give chase to see where it was headed, he instead, unlocked his front door and went directly to his kitchen cabinet as he had done thousands of times before – and grabbed a new bottle of scotch and a shot glass, then walked into his living room where he plopped his butt onto his couch and began drinking. And thinking – mostly about Detective Lenda, his replacement for his homicide investigations. Wells hadn't heard from him concerning the reports on the murder investigations, which Wells still had in his possession and were now scattered about on his living room floor.

For the next three days Wells kept his thoughts to himself by drinking his cares away. He felt useless and restless due to his suspension from the force. And the only way to keep his mind off of his troubles was to stay in a drunken stupor – which he did for three days until a ringing telephone interrupted it.

After more than thirty rings, Wells finally pulled himself together and picked up the phone and was surprised to learn that Captain Lawson was on the other end. He wanted Wells to come into his office right away to speak with him concerning his suspension over the Susan Pelk murder. Captain Lawson wouldn't be specific over the phone and wanted to see Wells in person.

Wells told his Captain that he would be at Hollywood police station within the hour. How he would do that he wasn't at all certain. He was still groggy and drunk from his three-day binge.

After Wells hung up the telephone, he slowly lifted his hungover body off the couch and was barely able to stand. Finally, after calibrating his gyroscopes, he was able to regain his balance and stumble to the bathroom to wash his face and shave. When he finished his chores in the bathroom and straightened the wrinkles out of his only clean suit, he stumbled into the kitchen to warm up his nearly three day old coffee.

Wells drank two big cups of hot, black coffee, then picked up all the reports off the living room floor and placed them into his briefcase. He then put on his shoes, grabbed his briefcase and headed out his front door, slowly stumbling down the three steps and the ten feet to his beat-up old Ford.

After starting the engine, Wells slowly backed out of his driveway and headed for Hollywood police station. Looking into his rearview mirror he noticed a black sedan following three car lengths behind. Who were these people that were following him, he thought to himself?

Wells hadn't seen the black sedan for nearly three days, but yet the minute he leaves his home, he's followed. He now believed the people following him were most likely FBI agents investigating their comrade's death. Even if Detective Wells confronted them, he was certain they wouldn't be truthful in their answers. So he just continued to ignore their presence. Unless the sedan's occupants stuck their noses where they didn't belong, Wells wasn't interested in their erratic behavior.

At this moment the only concerns Wells had was wondering if Captain Lawson would ever let him return to his duties. His life was only worth living as long as he wore his gold shield. But at this particular moment Captain Lawson had control of it.

Finally, nearly fifteen minutes after he left his home, Wells pulled into Hollywood police station's parking lot and parked his car. Grabbing his briefcase, he stepped out of his car and headed for Captain Lawson's office.

Once Detective Wells entered the police station, all eyes were upon him as he walked to the front desk and signed in.

"Damn, Detective Wells. You look like the living dead. You must have had a rough night last night," said Desk Sergeant Steiner, looking into Wells' bloodshot eyes.

"No. A rough three nights," Wells replied.

"I thought you were suspended," Steiner went on to say. "Are you picking up your paycheck?"

"No," Wells replied. "I'm here to see Captain Lawson. He ordered me here today." He then walked to his Captain's office and knocked on the door.

"Come in," said Captain Lawson.

Wells walked into Lawson's office and stood silently in front of his desk for a few seconds before speaking up.

"What's the problem, Captain? Why have you called me here today? I hope you've found the real killer to Susan Pelk's murder. Have you?"

"No, we haven't, Detective Wells," answered Lawson. "Have you found your gun so we can check it out and give it a ballistics test?"

Looking down to the floor, Wells shook his head no. "I believe someone came into my home and stole it while I was passed out. Then they used it to kill Susan Pelk and framed me for the murder."

"Who would do something like that and why?" Lawson asked him.

"I'm not sure," Wells replied, "but most likely they did it to get me off the murder investigations."

"That sounds logical," Lawson answered. "That is, if you didn't kill the woman yourself, while you were in your drunken stupor. I mean, damn man, look at you. You look like you have one foot in the grave. It looks as though you've been on a drunken binge since you were suspended."

"So what!" Wells snapped. "I have a right to. I'm no longer working, Captain, remember?"

"Let's not argue about that. I have more important matters to contend with."

Just then there was a knock at the door. Wells turned to see who it was and was surprised and a little upset to see Detective Lenda walk into the room and sit in a chair next to his.

"Good morning, Captain. You wanted to see me?" asked Detective Lenda.

"Yes. I want you to join Detective Wells and me in our conversation."

Lenda looked at Wells and his bloodshot eyes and greeted him. "Detective Wells, hello. I thought you were suspended," Lenda said, as the two detectives shook hands.

"As far as I know, I am. Unless Captain Lawson tells me different," said Wells, as Lenda took the seat next to his.

Just then, there was another knock on the door. This time an uniformed patrol officer entered the room that Wells was unfamiliar with.

Lawson told the patrol officer to come in and take a seat and then introduced him to the two detectives. "Officer Jack Tobin, this is Detectives Wells and Lenda from homicide. I want you to tell your story just as you told me earlier today," said Captain Lawson as the two homicide detectives shook hands with this young patrol officer.

With the introduction out of the way, Wells was ready to get down to business and had a few questions to ask his captain. "What's this all about, Captain? Why am I here today?" asked Wells.

"Detective Wells, listen to what Officer Tobin has to say and then I'll explain the situation. Go ahead, Officer Tobin, tell us your story," said Captain Lawson.

Tobin began explaining what had happened to him the night before. "Around six o'clock yesterday evening, my partner, Officer Diehl and I stopped at our favorite cafe to have dinner. I had to use the restroom to relieve myself and while I was in there Officer Diehl saw a crime in progress. He thought the female suspect that was committing the crime was the one in the tainted murders. So he left a message for me with the waiter. It said that he was going after a suspect."

Wells asked him why his partner thought the girl was a suspect in the tainted meat murders?

"I guess he saw a photo or composite drawing of her," replied Tobin.

Wells then asked Tobin if the waiter had witnessed the crime?

"No, _he_ didn't. But once the investigators canvassed the area and questioned the eyewitnesses, a picture emerged."

"So what supposedly happened?" Wells asked him.

Tobin explained that the eyewitnesses told the investigators that two men had gotten out of a fairly new white van and started a conversation with two hookers standing on Hollywood Boulevard. And while they were talking, a young female bumped into the men and picked their pockets. "I believe that's the crime Officer Diehl had witnessed when he went after the suspect," said Tobin. "When the men realized their pockets had been picked they ran after the girl while Officer Diehl followed ten yards behind.

94

That was the last time Officer Diehl and the two men were seen."

"What about the two men? Did they catch the girl that picked their pockets?" asked Wells.

"I don't think so," replied Tobin. "But the investigators were told that a young female resembling the girl returned to the area around midnight with a young man that fit the description of your male suspect in the tainted meat murders. And they jumped into the same white van that the two men had gotten out of."

"So are you telling us that the male and female stole the van?" asked Wells.

"Yes, sir, I believe they did. The girl must have gotten the car keys when she picked the men's pockets…and came back with her male partner when the coast was clear."

After listening to Tobin's story, Wells was confused and didn't understand why he was called in to the station. "Captain Lawson, what has all this got to do with me? Why am I hear?" Wells asked him.

"Because," Lawson replied, "the girl that committed this crime was linked to your murder investigations and I needed my best detective's expertise on this matter. Then Lawson looked at Lenda and said, "Nothing against you, Lenda, but Wells has thirty years of experience over you."

"I understand, Captain," said Lenda.

"But that still doesn't answer my question, Captain," interjected Wells. "Why am I here? I'm on suspension, remember?"

But Lawson surprised him, saying, "You were on suspension. We've got an officer missing. So I want you to work with Lenda and see what you can come up with. This case needs your expertise and know how. We have investigators canvassing the area but they aren't having much luck finding Officer Diehl and the two men. I'm hoping you and Lenda can do a better job."

"Are you telling me, Captain, that I'm back on the tainted meat and mutilation murder investigations?" asked Wells.

"That's exactly what I'm telling you, Detective Wells," replied Lawson.

Wells asked him about I.A.D. "They might have something to say about my suspension being lifted without their authorization."

"Let me worry about that, John," Lawson answered. "You worry about finding Officer Diehl and the suspects in your murder investigations."

Wells turned to Tobin and said, "Officer Tobin, I will need all of your investigative reports concerning this matter."

"I have them," interjected Lenda.

"Well, let's get them and visit the area where all of this occurred," said Wells as he stood up to get back to work.

Just then Captain Lawson's telephone rang. A minute after Lawson answered the phone, he jotted something down on a piece of scrap paper then handed it to Wells – and hung up the phone.

Wells looked at its contents and asked Lawson about it.

Lawson explained that it was the address where the investigators found Officer Diehl and the two men from the white van – and that he wanted Wells and Lenda to go there and take over the investigation. "And Wells," continued Lawson, "until we can get this Susan Pelk murder mystery figured out, Lenda will be in charge of the investigation." But even though he told Wells that Lenda was in charge, he also told Lenda to do whatever Wells told him to do. "Is that clear?" barked Captain Lawson.

"Yes, sir, I understand completely," answered Lenda.

"So I can resume the murder investigations?" Wells asked Lawson.

"That's an affirmative," Lawson replied. "Now get out of my office, all of you." "And Wells," he added, "I want you to check in with me daily."

"Oh, one other thing, Captain Lawson. Were Officer Diehl and the two men found alive or dead?" asked Wells.

"Detective Wells, I wouldn't send you over there if they were alive, now would I?" Lawson said sarcastically.

"That's all I need to know," Wells answered. He looked at Lenda and said, "Let's get going, Detective Lenda."

The two detectives and Officer Tobin left Captain Lawson's office to visit the murder scene nearly three blocks away from the cafe where the chase began.

Before Wells departed the station, he had to make a quick dash to his desk to retrieve his backup piece, his .357 revolver. He never had to fire his gun while working on the job. But investigating a possible mob war was something else. He figured it was better to be safe than sorry. He grabbed his revolver out of his desk drawer, placed it into his empty holster and hurried to catch up to his comrades as they were walking through the front door to the parking lot.

"Detective Lenda, we'll take my car," Wells told him.

"That's fine with me," Lenda answered.

But Tobin told Wells that he'd follow him in his patrol car. "If you don't mind," he added.

"Officer Tobin, I know Officer Diehl is your partner, but you'll have to stay outside the crime scene," said Wells, as he and Detective Lenda got into his beat-up old Ford.

"Detective Wells, I think it's about time you invest in another automobile," kidded Lenda.

Wells ignored his comment, then started the engine and raced to the crime scene. Within five minutes they had reached the address. It was another condemned building just a few blocks from the murder scene of his three mutilated bodies. The coroner's van and forensic investigators were already there. Wells didn't know exactly what he would be investigating – and wondered if the victims' bodies would be in one piece or many.

Detective Wells had seen every type of murder there was. At least he thought he had. But his assumption quickly evaporated as he entered the crime scene. The two homicide detectives stopped in their tracks as they were met at the door by Dr. Terry. He handed both detectives rubber gloves so they wouldn't contaminate the dirty crime scene.

Detectives Lenda and Wells thought they had seen it all, until they came upon this crime scene. They could only stare at the victims, as they had never seen anything like this before. In the southwest corner of the building was a large kitchen table. Sitting around it were three male victims strapped and tied to chairs. Sitting on the table in front of each victim was their skullcaps. These three male victims had the top of their skulls taken off and more than half of their brains exposed.

When Wells and Lenda walked over to get a closer look at the victims' bodies, they noticed that their brain matter had been scooped out in large chunks. In fact, one victim had a teaspoon stuck into his brain, as though somebody had been eating it. Lenda wasn't used to this type of crime scene. He turned away and began regurgitating his breakfast. A few minutes later, he felt much better.

Wells looked over the crime scene and noticed similarities to the mutilated murders he had been investigating. Even though the three victims still had both hands and feet attached to their bodies, they did however, have a large needle mark on their jugular veins, just like his mutilated victims. This was one sick crime scene, Wells thought to himself. All three victims still had their eyes open, as though they had watched each other's brains being eaten while slowly having their blood sucked out of their bodies. Wells looked into Officer Diehl's frightened eyes and thought: He will never climb that ladder of success now.

"Dr. Terry, was there any identification on the two men?" asked Detective Wells as he looked over the three male victims.

Terry told him that Officer Diehl still had his nametag on but the two men had no identification on their person whatsoever – and that the forensic investigators took their fingerprints and should have their identities within the hour. He went on to say that in one of the men's pants pockets a piece of paper was found with a number written on it. "It looks to be a telephone number," he told Wells, handing him the piece of paper. "I hope you find out whose it is."

Wells looked at it and said, "You're right. It does seem to be a telephone number." But he didn't recognize the area code. "When I get back to the station I'll find out. Thanks, Doc."

"Dr. Terry," interjected Lenda, "are the investigators sure that these two men were the ones chasing after the female suspect?"

"They believe they are. But to be sure, they are showing photos to the eyewitnesses as we speak to see if they can identify them. You should have your answer within a few hours…as soon as the witnesses can be found."

"Good work, Doc," Wells told him. Then he asked him about the needle marks on the jugular veins – and whether the victims were dead or alive before their brains were scooped out?

Terry told him that he wouldn't know for sure until the autopsies were done. "But," he added, "I'd bet my life that the victims watched each other as their brains were being eaten...and while their blood was slowly being sucked out of their bodies. It's a terrible way to go. That's for sure."

"You can say that again, Doc," said Lenda.

Terry then told Wells that the forensic investigators believed that this murder scene was linked to the mutilations.

"Why is that, Doc?" asked Wells.

"Because they found pieces of ground meat," he answered. "Not much, but a few ounces. They've taken it back to the lab to have it checked to see if it's human. They also have a number of fingerprints that were found on and around the table. Hopefully, we'll have the identities and background reports within the next couple of hours."

"Doc, when were the victims killed?" asked Wells.

"Around midnight. Maybe an hour before or an hour after. I won't know for certain until I do their autopsies."

While Wells wandered around the crime scene, he saw many empty prescription bottles that had contained mostly sedatives and painkillers. But all the names and addresses of the patients had been scraped off, leaving only the name of the drug.

After nearly three hours at the crime scene, the photographer and many of the forensic investigators had left the building, taking the evidence with them to have it checked and analyzed at their lab. Detectives Wells and Lenda were the last to leave as the bodies were removed and taken to the morgue. Then the crime scene was taped off and secured.

After Wells and Lenda left the building, they headed for Wells' vehicle to return to Hollywood station. But as they walked back to the beat-up old Ford, they noticed a car pass by very slowly. Wells became suspicious and as he ran towards it to get a closer look at the passengers and driver, the vehicle quickly made a U-turn to get away from the area. Wells noticed then that there were three men in the vehicle.

Both Wells and Lenda tried to stop the vehicle from leaving so they could ask the three men riding in it a few questions. But when they got close to the car, two of the male passengers opened fire on the detectives.

Lenda and Wells drew their weapons and returned fire. The gunmen's vehicle suddenly came to a halt in the middle of the street and all three male occupants jumped out and continued to fire their weapons at the detectives. The gunmen hid behind their vehicle for better protection from lead poisoning.

This was the very first time that Detectives Wells and Lenda had ever fired their weapons in self-defense. The fight lasted more than five minutes and before the shooting stopped the two detectives got the best of them. All three had been shot and were lying on the street in pools of blood. By the time the detectives reached the three gunmen and checked their vital signs, two of them lay dead. However, one of the gunmen who'd been hit twice in the left shoulder was still alive and talking incoherently.

Wells, confused and frustrated, nervously wiped the sweat from his forehead with his shaking hands and asked the gunman, "Who are you guys? And why in the hell didn't you stop? I only wanted to ask you a few questions." He rambled on, saying, "I never expected a gunfight. I never killed anyone in my life. Why did you guys shoot at us!"

Wells wanted and needed a drink real bad. This was the first time he fired his weapon to defend himself and ended up killing two people. He realized what he had done and became sick to his stomach. Suddenly, Lenda noticed that he had been shot, too and was bleeding from his upper right shoulder. The second he saw his own blood he passed out and Wells had to catch him from falling and hitting his head on the cement. Setting Lenda down in the street he ran back to his vehicle to radio for backup and the coroner.

Dr. Terry and the forensic investigators had just left the crime scene not more than thirty minutes before. Now they would have to return to the same place and pick up two more dead bodies. Luckily, there was one gunman still alive to question. But that would have to wait. Wells would question him at the hospital after his wounds had been mended.

While the detectives waited for the ambulance and the investigators, Wells helped calm Lenda and tried to stop the bleeding to his wounded right shoulder. When he had calmed down the young homicide detective, Wells checked each gunman's pockets for identification but there was none. He thought they were mobsters, but from what family? He would have to wait for their fingerprint analysis and background checks.

Within fifteen minutes backup had arrived. Two patrol cars and their occupants taped off the crime scene around the gunmen's vehicle and bodies. A few minutes later the ambulance, coroner and forensic investigators arrived.

The paramedics quickly checked out Lenda and the wounded gunman. They loaded them into the ambulance and raced away to Hollywood hospital. Detective Wells let the forensic investigators take over the crime scene as he jumped into his car and followed the ambulance to the hospital to check on his partner and suspect.

Just as Wells entered the emergency room he was told by the chief of staff that surgery was needed for both victims and that he should return in a few hours. By that time, he was told, if everything went as expected, they would be alive, alert and able to speak...to answer any questions Wells might have. Detective Wells reluctantly agreed with the doctors. But before leaving the hospital he told a hospital security officer what had transpired and that his suspect was under arrest.

Wells pointed out the suspect and told the security officer to stand guard over his room and to keep him handcuffed to the bed at all times. Detective Wells assured the officer that he would return to question the suspect in a few hours.

Leaving the hospital Wells headed for home to get a few stiff drinks under his belt. Now that he had time to think, in retrospect he was lucky to be alive. More bullets whizzed past his head on that day than in Korea. He tried to relax but his nerves wouldn't let him. He was in a frazzled state of mind. The three gunmen had nearly killed him and his partner. As the gunfight ensued, he felt two bullets whistle past his ears, just inches from his head. When Wells thought about this and how close he came to dying, he felt weak in the knees and began shaking all over.

Wells stomped down on his car's accelerator to get home sooner rather than later. He needed a drink and needed one fast. By the time he had pulled into his driveway, jumped out of his vehicle and ran up the three steps to his front door only ten minutes had passed. As his hands shook, Wells inserted his key into the lock and pushed the door open. Running directly to his kitchen cabinet he grabbed a shot glass and his bottle of scotch – then while standing at the kitchen sink he poured shot after shot down his throat until he lost count.

When his body stopped shaking, he was able to take his liquor and glass into the living room to relax and think. For the next hour or two he continued his drinking ways – drinking shot after shot while waiting to return to the hospital to visit his wounded suspect and partner.

During this time the investigators telephoned Wells to tell him the identities of the three gunmen. They told him what he had thought all along – that the three gunmen were soldiers in the Manzelli crime family. And one of the bodies found in the abandoned building strapped to a chair was identified as Benny "the baby" Benaldo, a member and soldier of the Sanitini crime family.

Now Wells had to find out what role the three mobsters played in his murder investigations and that of Officer Diehl and the other two victims found in the abandoned building. He was sure he would get the answers from the wounded gunman – if he lived.

The investigators had a few other surprises to tell Wells. One would sadden him. The other would shock him back into reality and sober him up. The first surprise he was told was about the third victim in the table murders – that they were unable to identity him. However, the numbers on the piece of paper that was found in his pants pocket, when punched into the telephone, was the telephone number of the CIA building in Langley, Virginia. They also told Wells that two men from the CIA had picked up the body in question before it was tagged and delivered to the morgue.

Now Wells was really confused. Why would an employee of the CIA and a known mobster hang around together, he asked himself.

But the investigators left the best news for last – and was the biggest surprise yet. It had to do with his missing thirty-eight-caliber revolver, which was found in the hands of one of the dead gunmen. They were sure this news would get Wells off the hook for the Susan Pelk murder. And to say the least, Wells was elated. Now he had a good reason to sober up.

And just three hours later – five hours after Wells had left the hospital

– Lenda's surgeon telephoned to let him know that his partner was alert and doing fine after surgery and that his male suspect was also awake and well enough to answer questions.

Wells hung up the phone and put away his bottle of scotch. After drinking nearly twenty shots of it within that five hour period he wasn't sure if he could drive safely. But he wanted his questions answered so he took the chance. After staggering out his front door and stumbling to his car, he was now headed to the hospital to check on his partner and to question his suspect.

While driving to the hospital, Wells thought about the questions he would ask his wounded male suspect, who went by the name of Mario "the muscle" Morrelli, a known Manzelli soldier.

Wells had to laugh at the nicknames these mobsters gave themselves. Tony "the ax" Antoli, Sammy "the skinner" Santini, Carl "the meat cleaver" Calletti. And the names of the two dead gunmen were Eddy "the fish" Fennetti and Jerry "the jet" Gerabaldi. Both soldiers in the Manzelli crime family.

Detective Wells was quite happy with the way things were working out – especially after hearing the news about his missing thirty-eight-caliber revolver. It was found in the possession of Eddy "the fish" Fennetti. But that didn't mean Fennetti was Susan Pelk's killer. Whether he was or not, Wells believed the answer to that question and others would come from Mario "the muscle" Morrelli.

Nearing Hollywood hospital, Detective Wells, looking into his rearview mirror, noticed the black sedan following about four car lengths behind. And Wells now believed the people in that vehicle were either FBI or CIA. He was sure the federal government was following him, but didn't know why.

However, Wells had other things on his mind and ignored – for the time being – the black sedan as he entered the hospital parking lot and parked his car – the black sedan pulling in a few seconds later.

A few minutes later he was standing at the information desk in the main lobby inquiring about his partner's and suspect's room. But when Wells introduced himself the receptionist handed him a message telling him to phone Captain Lawson's office immediately. He did as he was told and walked to a pay phone just a few feet away and called his captain.

Captain Lawson explained to Wells that Officer Tobin, while chasing one of the female suspects in the tainted meat murders into an abandoned building he came across more dead victims sitting around a table and wanted Wells to investigate the crime scene immediately. Wells was speechless as he jotted down the building's address. It was only two blocks away from the last crime scene he had investigated just eight hours before. Once Lawson had explained the situation to Wells, Wells hung up the phone, anxious to begin the investigation.

Instead of questioning his suspect and looking in on his partner, Wells left the hospital and drove to the crime scene – with the black sedan in tow.

During his short drive, Wells wondered about the three homicide detectives in the neighboring cities that were investigating the tainted meat and mutilation murders. He hadn't seen or talked to them in more than three days and figured that it was time for another luncheon. Wells had many things to tell them. Especially about the situation stemming from the Susan Pelk murder.

Wells was still fairly drunk but had complete control of all his faculties. He reached the crime scene in record time. The coroner and investigators were already there. This was deja vu all over again.

But the first thing Wells noticed that was different from the last crime scene was that a young woman was in handcuffs and sitting in the back seat of a patrol car. He wondered if she was the female suspect that Officer Tobin had chased into the building. But at that moment Wells was more concerned about checking out the crime scene – to see if there were more dead bodies like the ones he had seen earlier that morning. Wells would find out in a few seconds.

As he walked through the door, Wells was met by Officer Tobin and Dr. Terry.

"Officer Tobin, I noticed a handcuffed female sitting in a patrol car. Is she the main suspect to this crime?" asked Detective Wells.

"No," he replied. "She's from a previous call."

"Detective Wells," said Dr. Terry, as he handed Wells a pair of rubber gloves, "what in the hell is going on in this city? How many more killings are we going to have before all of this finally ends?" Wells just shrugged his shoulders as Terry directed him to the crime scene, which was in a small room just twenty-five feet from the front door.

Detective Wells had a strong suspicion of what he was about to see. He was right. Sitting at a kitchen table, tied to their chairs were three more victims, exactly like the ones he had seen earlier that day. Upon closer examination he noticed one of them looked exactly like his male suspect in the tainted meat murders – Katie Brown's boyfriend, Jarrett. And another looked like the one that Katie Brown had picked out in the photos during her interrogation who was identified as Tony "the ax" Antoli. He was a soldier in the Santini crime family and the person that drove Katie Brown and her boyfriend, Jarrett to the butcher shop to deliver the tainted meat. He would know for sure once the fingerprints were done because none of the victims carried identification.

These three victims also had their skullcaps removed exposing their brains – what was left of them – with spoons stuck in each one – and a large needle mark in their jugular veins, just like the others.

But that wasn't the only thing that the investigators found. They also had come across a videotape lying on the floor near the feet of the longhaired victim. Although no fingerprints were found on it, Detective Wells was anxious to view it – to find out its contents.

So he excused himself from the investigation and let Dr. Terry take control. He left the building with the videotape tucked away in his jacket pocket then jumped into his car and sped away from the crime scene – with the black sedan following close behind. This time, instead of Wells ignoring their presence he fooled them and lost them in traffic. He then circled the block, came up behind them and wrote down the license plate number before radioing it in to find out its owner.

Within a few minutes the registration came back as belonging to FBI headquarters in Los Angeles. Wells figured as much, which got his goat. He caught up with the car and pulled alongside it hoping to see who was driving. However, the windows were tinted and he couldn't see into the vehicle. So again he ignored them and raced to his home to play the videotape, not caring about the black sedan.

The minute Wells walked into his living room, he turned on his video machine and placed the tape into it. The beginning of the tape was full of static. At first, he thought it was just a blank tape. However, one minute into it, Wells knew it wasn't for family viewing.

The tape showed three men strapped into their chairs – the same men he had just seen at the abandoned building. Thick belts of heavy rope bound the mens' chests, hands and feet. The tape never showed the killers. But at least two people were at the abandoned building. One videotaped the horrendous activity and the other cut the tops off their victims' heads.

Although the tape had no sound, it showed the victims screaming in their chairs while the killers injected them with a syringe full of drugs. It must have been a mild sedative because it made the victims relax. Then the killer taped each victim's mouth shut before inserting a large needle into their jugular vein which was hooked up to a long, thin tube that went all the way to the floor into a large pale. Afterwards, another injection was given to them intravenously, which again seemed to relax them. A few seconds later the killer removed the tape from their mouths, just long enough to see them screaming for the killer to stop.

A few minutes after giving the injections, the killer began to saw the skullcaps away from the victims' bodies using a small battery operated bone saw. Wells watched in horror as their eyes bulged out of their eye sockets while screaming out in pain. The victims' hands would clench and their bodies would tighten as the killer's saw dug deeper into their skulls. The killer's face was never seen, only the hands, which were encased in thin rubber gloves, so you couldn't see them either.

The videotape showed each of the victims' contorted faces as they went through their torturous journey. It took nearly ten minutes for the killer to slowly and cautiously cut away the skullcaps to expose the brains without causing any damage to them. Then the killer placed the skullcap of each victim on the table in front of them. The victims couldn't see themselves, but they could see the others – and watched as the skullcaps of their friends were removed and exposed. It was quite a hideous sight.

Every five or ten minutes of filming, the cameraman would show the buckets filling up with the victims' blood. As the blood slowly drained out of their bodies, the killer held up a teaspoon in front of the camera lens and then began to scoop out large spoonfuls of brain matter as the other victims looked on.

The killer would dip the spoon into a victim's brain matter and scoop out two or three large spoonfuls – each time holding it front of the camera lens for better viewing – before moving on to his next victim. Then the camera would swing over and show each victim's expression that appeared on their faces as each spoonful of brain matter was ripped away from their bodies, while their blood dripped into the buckets.

And every so often the camera would show the buckets – full of blood – as they were being taken away and replaced by an empty bucket and then emptied into a larger container. Each bucket was emptied three times into a larger container within a fifty-minute period.

Then the camera was again aimed at the victims' faces. As the brain matter disappeared from each victim's skull and as their blood escaped from their bodies into a bucket, their breathing slowed, their bodies relaxed and their faces became expressionless as their eyes stared straight ahead, until their last dying breath.

Wells, after watching the grotesque and sick videotape, needed a drink badly. But he didn't stop at one. He continued drinking shots of scotch as he rewound the videotape and played it again and again. He wanted to make sure he didn't miss something important, like a shadow that showed the length of the killer's hair or height: Anything that might bring the victims' killers to justice.

As Wells watched in horror, he wondered what kind of sick minds were behind these acts of torture. Acts of vengeance by the mob were really no surprise to law enforcement officials – a bullet behind the ear was usually sufficient. But having ones brains and blood depleted in such a grotesque manner was too outlandish even by mob standards. Who, Wells asked himself, would have such a sadistic mind to torture his victims this way? Maybe, he thought, the killers were trying to extract information from them? If that was the case, what was so important to them that they had to scoop out large spoonfuls of brain tissue? Wells surmised that maybe they did it just to feed their egos – or stomachs.

Every so often the video showed the killer ripping the tape from the mouth of one of his victims, presumably to answer the killer's question or so Wells assumed. About what, Wells didn't know. But he was sure of one thing, the three male victims shown in that video weren't being tortured for fun.

Wells was sure the victims had information that the killers wanted. Whether the victims spilled their guts or not, their blood had been spilt. Wells wondered how the victims could talk at all while their brains were being scooped out of their heads.

Wells again wondered what type of sick mind would go to this extreme of endless torture? He seemingly understood the grinding up of bodies was a good way to get rid of the evidence. But why torture someone to such an extreme? This was not the mob's usual way of doing business. Especially leaving their victims in such a way that their identities, in time, would be known.

Before Detective Wells became too drunk, he decided to share this new evidence and information with his three comrades, Detectives Rodriguez, Wilmont and Smith. It had been nearly four days since he had talked with them. He needed to speak with them and tell them that he was off suspension and back on his murder investigations.

There were many new revelations that Wells needed to speak with the other detectives about. So he began telephoning them, one by one. First, he phoned Detective Rodriguez, then, Wilmont and lastly, Smith. Each agreed to meet him for lunch at Gabrielle's Hoagie House at one o'clock the following afternoon.

Detective Wells also asked Smith if he could interview his female suspect, Katie Brown concerning an urgent matter. He didn't want to tell Smith the reason over an open line but he explained that there were many surprises he wanted to talk about.

Detective Smith agreed to let Wells interview Miss Brown the following morning, then they would ride together to their luncheon engagement. Wells made no mention to the three detectives about the videotape – or Jarrett's death, the male suspect in the tainted meat murders until he was positively identified. And the forensic investigators would know for certain, hopefully by the following morning, the identities of all three recent murder victims.

Detective Wells also had to make time to speak with his wounded suspect, Mario "the muscle" Morrelli and find out what he and his friends were up to on the day of the shootings and why they fired their weapons at him and Lenda.

Wells decided then and there, even though he was quite drunk, that there wasn't any time to waste. So he put away his shot glass and bottle of scotch, ejected the videotape from the machine and put it into his jacket pocket before getting behind the wheel of his car – and after a few tries, he finally put the key into the ignition, then started it. But backing out of his driveway, he nearly hit a passing vehicle before heading for the hospital. Even though Detective Wells had two near misses with other cars, driving into the opposite lane each time, he arrived safely at the hospital.

As he stumbled from his car and neared the main entrance of Hollywood hospital, he saw the black sedan pull into the parking lot. But he completely ignored their presence and continued through the revolving doors heading first to his partner's hospital room. He was anxious to give his young friend a pep talk. And wanted his partner to know that he needed to get well fast so he could help in the murder investigations.

CHAPTER 8

A s Detective Wells waited for the elevator to take him to his partner's room on the seventh floor he noticed four men in teams of two standing on different sides of the room. They looked to be federal boys. Most likely, FBI. But until they interfered in his murder investigations or with him, he decided to ignore them. Sooner or later, Wells would find out just who they were and why they were following him. But at this moment in time, he was only concerned with questioning his suspect and visiting with his partner.

When the elevator doors opened, Wells entered the elevator and watched as the four men dressed in black came rushing towards him. At that moment he thought that maybe the four men weren't federal officers at all, but mobsters. And just as the men were within a few feet of the elevator, the doors suddenly closed, locking the four men out.

Wells thought nothing more about them as he was sure that other homicide detectives from his department would be hanging around and would scare away anyone that looked or acted suspicious.

Anyway, he was anxious to visit with his young partner. Lenda's room was one floor below his suspect's room so Wells decided to visit with his partner for ten minutes and then interrogate his suspect. And when he finished with his suspect, he would return to his partner's room and tell Lenda about the videotape – and play it for him if there was a video machine available, that is, if Lenda was up to it.

Wells got off the elevator at the seventh floor and walked to the end of the long hallway. A few of his brother detectives were standing near Lenda's room talking amongst themselves. Wells nodded to them and was just about to enter his partner's room when he saw two of the men dressed in black entering the floor from the stairway.

But as soon as the two men noticed that Wells had spotted them, they stopped dead in their tracks and acted like they were waiting for the elevator. Wells just shook his head in disgust and entered his partner's hospital room. Lenda was alone, sitting up and watching television. When he saw Wells, he turned the television off and greeted his partner.

"How are you, John?" asked Lenda.

"Detective Lenda, I think you're confused," said Wells as he walked over to his partner's bed and patted his wounded shoulder. "I'm the one that should be asking you that question. How are you doing?"

"I could be better," Lenda replied, as a smile broke across his face, "but I'm doing fine. I guess I'm not going to be of any help to you in your investigations."

"Don't worry about it," Wells replied.

"How is our suspect? Have you talked to him yet?" he asked Wells.

"Not yet," Wells replied. "I'll see him in a few minutes. I just wanted to stop by and see how you were doing. The suspect can wait, he's not going anywhere. He's under police guard one floor above yours."

Wells pulled the videotape out of his jacket pocket and Lenda noticed it. "What's that you're holding in your hand, John?" Lenda asked him.

But before Wells could answer him Captain Lawson walked into the room.

"Well look what the cat dropped in," joked Wells.

But Lawson ignored Wells' comment and spoke directly to Lenda. "Detective Lenda, it's good to see you sitting up. How are you feeling, son?" he asked.

"Good," Lenda answered. "I hope to be out of here in the next day or so...and be back at work in a few weeks."

"Don't over do it, son. You come back when you're well...and not before," said Captain Lawson.

"Yes sir. But this was my first real case and I get shot," said Lenda.

"You'll be back before you know it," Wells told him. "There'll be plenty of murder cases you'll be able to investigate. People will always be killing each other."

"Detective Wells, speaking of killing, what have you found out about the dead gunmen and the killer of Officer Diehl and the others that were found with the top of their skulls cut away? Have the forensic investigators come up with anything?" asked Captain Lawson.

Wells told him that they found a few sets of fingerprints and other pieces of evidence that could link their murders to the others. "The killers also left this videotape behind," he added, holding it up into the air so Captain Lawson could see it.

"What does the tape show?" Lawson asked him.

"Find me a video machine and I'll play it for you," Wells answered. "But I have to tell you, this videotape isn't rated P.G.-13. It might make you sick...if you have a weak stomach."

Lawson told him that he'd ask one of the nurses and said, "I'll see if I can't get a video machine in here. I'm curious now."

"I'll tell you what Captain, let me go talk with the suspect and I'll come right back. I'll leave the tape here, so if you get the machine before I return...play it. But let me warn you now, it's not for the weak at heart," said Wells, as he placed the tape on the table next to Lenda's bed.

Wells left the room and headed for the elevators. He breathed a sigh of relief when he noticed the men in black had disappeared. When the elevator doors took longer than usual to open, he decided to walk up the one flight of stairs instead, even though the stairway was at the opposite end of the hall.

When Wells reached the eighth floor tired and out of breath, he noticed many doctors and nurses running past him in a total panic and two men dressed in black getting on the elevator.

Detective Wells was troubled to see that the hospital staff was heading straight for his suspect's room. A policeman guarding the door directed them into the room, while keeping all others, including Wells, away until the trouble had cleared.

"Officer, what the hell's going on in there?" Wells asked him.

"You'll have to wait and speak with the doctor about that," he answered.

Wells showed him his identification and badge, saying, "I'm Detective Wells of Hollywood homicide. This guy was my suspect in a triple homicide. Now I'm talking to you and I want some answers."

He told Wells that he didn't know, and that he had stepped away for a few minutes to grab a newspaper at the other end of the hallway and as he was walking back, he saw two men leaving the patient's room. When he returned he opened the door to see how the suspect was doing and that's when he saw the patient sprawled out on the bed, choking and foaming at the mouth. "So I yelled for the doctor. I should have went after those two men...but I waited for the doctor instead."

"What did these men look like?" Wells asked him. "Were they dressed in black and wearing fedoras?"

"Yeah," he replied. "Why, do you know them?"

"No, but I will," Wells answered.

Just then the hospital staff came out of the room with sullen faces.

Wells reached out and grabbed one of the doctors by the arm and said, "Doc, I'm Detective Wells. What's wrong? How is my suspect? Is he all right?"

"I'm sorry," the doctor told him. "The patient died a few minutes ago. We couldn't save him."

"What happened to him!" Wells bellowed. "How did Mario Morrelli die!"

The doctor told Wells he didn't know. "But," he added, "whatever happened, he died within a few seconds. I don't believe I've seen anything like it before."

"Was it a heart attack or what?" Wells asked him.

"It could be," the doctor replied, "but I don't believe so. The autopsy should give us the answer." Just then a nurse passed by pushing a gurney into the room to transfer the dead suspect's body to the morgue.

"Why don't you think my suspect died from a heart attack?" Wells asked the doctor.

He told Wells that he never saw a heart attack cause bleeding from the ears, nose and mouth. "But like I said, the autopsy should give us the answer to the cause of death. Now if you'll excuse me, Detective, I have other patients to care for," said the doctor as he walked away pulling the gurney with the dead man's body.

Wells stopped the gurney and lifted the blanket off the suspect's face to see if there were tell tale signs of a homicide. But as the doctor told him, he would have to wait until the autopsy was completed. So Wells turned and walked to the elevator, returning to the seventh floor to his partner's room. Just as he entered the room, he saw Captain Lawson place the videotape into a video machine and press the on button.

"Captain Lawson, you better sit down. This videotape is off the ratings chart," said Wells, as he tried to get them ready for what they were about to witness.

After a minute or so the picture finally came onto the screen. Watching the facial expressions of Captain Lawson and Lenda, Wells knew they were very distraught at what they were viewing.

"John, I want you to catch these sick bastards and do it quick," said Captain Lawson as they watched the killer's gloved hands tape the mouths of the victims and then insert the large needle into each of the victim's vein. "This is beyond a rational mind. These killers are sadists. Do you have anything that might help you capture these animals?" he asked Wells.

Lenda at that moment took his eyes off the tv screen and asked Wells about their wounded suspect. "John, what did you get out of our suspect? You didn't interview him very long. Was the guy still weak from surgery?"

"Oh he was weak all right," Wells replied sarcastically. "So weak that he died."

"You've got to be kidding?" interjected Lawson not believing what Wells had just told them. "Did your suspect tell you anything about the killings?"

"How could he?" Wells answered angrily. "He was dead. By the time I reached his room the doctors and nurses were trying to revive him...but didn't have any luck. They won't know the cause of death until the autopsy is performed."

"Was it a natural death or foul play?" asked Lenda.

"Will you two guys be quiet," snapped Lawson, watching the film as it showed the victim's face as his skullcap was being cut off. "I want to watch this videotape. I can't believe what I'm seeing. How could one human being do that to another? I thought the mutilations were bad. This is got that beat, hands down. I wish these cowards would show their faces."

But Wells wanted to talk about his dead suspect and told Lawson that two men, possibly government agents, dressed in black and wearing black fedoras, were seen leaving the suspect's room and a minute later he turned up dead. "You wouldn't know who the two men dressed in black are or why they are following me, would you captain?" Wells asked him.

Lawson snapped back, telling Wells, "I don't know what the hell you're talking about, John."

"Captain Lawson," Wells retorted, "I'm talking about the people who took Susan Pelk's body away from our autopsy room before Dr. Terry could complete the autopsy. They were the same people who took away the male victim found at the murder scene with Officer Diehl and Benny "the baby" Benaldo of the Santini crime family? Are you covering up for the government?"

"John, you're too damn paranoid," Lawson told him. "Why would you think I would cover up for the government?"

"Because you didn't stop them from taking the bodies out of the morgue," Wells replied.

Lawson shot back. "Detective Wells, the two men that took away those bodies didn't even acknowledge that I even existed. I would like you to try and stop the federal government...from doing anything."

Wells then asked Lawson if the same men took both bodies away?

"As far as I know they did," Lawson replied. "You might want to speak with Dr. Terry about that. But what do they have to do with all these murders that are popping up all over the city?"

Wells told him that he didn't know just yet. "But I will," he added. "I believe these government agents are either trying to use me to help them catch these mobsters or they're mixed up with them somehow. It's funny how they were near my suspect one minute and the next minute they disappear and my suspect ends up dead. It's either a big coincidence...or it's a conspiracy."

Just then Lenda jumped back into the conversation and changed the subject. "John, what have you learned about the three dead victims from this video?" Lenda asked Wells.

"I'm still waiting for positive identification on them, especially the long-haired one, who I think is the male suspect in the tainted meat murders. I also want to interview Katie Brown again."

"Who's she?" asked Captain Lawson.

Wells answered, "She's Detective Smith's female suspect in the tainted meat murders. And I want to hear what she has to say about her boyfriend's death."

"Again? When did you interview Katie Brown?" Lenda asked Wells.

"About four days ago," Wells told him.

"Wait a minute," Lenda retorted. "You were suspended from duty. How could you interview Katie Brown when I did?"

Wells told him that he did it on his own time. Adding, "Smith allowed me to ask her a few questions. That was it. But now I want to ask her a few more questions about her boyfriend, Jarrett, the person who delivered and sold the tainted meat to all those mob owned butcher shops. I want to see Katie Brown's facial expression when I tell her that her boyfriend was tortured...and died while his brains were being scooped out of his head one big spoonful at a time...and while his blood was being drained from his body one drop at a time. Maybe then, she'll speak up and tell me the truth."

"I think I'm going to have to have a word with Smith about trust," said Lenda, shaking his head in disgust.

"I'll let him know you want to speak with him," Wells replied. "I'm having lunch tomorrow with him, along with Rodriguez and Wilmont. I want to go over the murders with them. Now I have even more pertinent information to tell them. They'll be surprised to learn about the death of our number one suspect in the tainted meat murder investigation."

Just then the visitor's bell rang throughout the hospital. It was time to leave. Wells grabbed the videotape out of the machine and said goodbye to his partner, as did Captain Lawson. They walked out of the room together promising to see him the following day.

Wells headed straight to the parking lot to his car. Before getting into his vehicle, he looked all around hoping to find the two guys that were following him in that black sedan. But there were too many cars in the lot and it was much too dark to see clearly. He was sure, however, that the black sedan would be following him again, sooner or later.

However, on this night, Detective Wells wanted nothing more to think about than having a drink and relaxing on his favorite couch. He had put in a long and hard day and now it was time for a little arm exercise. He should have driven to Hollywood police station to see if there were any reports sitting on his desk, but he felt it could wait until morning. He needed a drink more than he needed the reports.

Wells checked his rearview mirror periodically, but didn't see the black sedan following his car. He hoped that the people that had been following him since Susan Pelk's death had crawled back into the dark hole that they had come from? And the black sedan was still nowhere to be seen when Wells entered his home.

The minute he was inside he went directly for his bottle of liquid dreams. He grabbed a shot glass, a full bottle of scotch and headed for his favorite spot: the living room couch. However, before Wells began drinking, he pulled his briefcase to his lap and retrieved the stack of investigative, forensic and autopsy reports that he had neglected to read.

Wells mixed his reading with his drinking. He wasn't surprised to learn that the autopsy reports for the mutilation and first table murders stated that all the victims either had a sedative or heavy narcotic injected into their bodies' hours before they were butchered and killed.

Suddenly Detective Wells' reading and drinking was interrupted by the ringing of his telephone. Detective Rodriguez of the San Pedro homicide department was on the other end of the line. Rodriguez explained to Wells that they had arrested a female suspect in the tainted meat murders that had delivered the hamburger to the San Pedro butcher shop owned by Johnny Vega. He asked Wells to witness the female suspect's interrogation the following morning.

Wells explained to Rodriguez that he had to interview Katie Brown in the morning and then drive to the luncheon afterwards. Wells then asked Rodriguez to postpone the girl's interrogation until after the luncheon engagement so Wilmont and Smith could be included. That way Rodriguez could go over the girl's background with all of them.

Wells also mentioned to Rodriguez that he had some pertinent information to share with him and the other detectives, but didn't mention any of the particulars. And in turn, Rodriguez mentioned that he had tried contacting Wilmont and Smith at their stations concerning the female suspect's arrest. "But they had already left for the day so I left messages for them to contact me in the morning," he added.

Rodriguez then agreed to interrogate Kathy Fenton, his female suspect, after the luncheon engagement so the other detectives could participate and witness the interrogation of the homeless runaway. With that said, the two detectives ended their conversation and hung up their phones.

Wells went back to exercising his right arm and continued drinking and reading his reports until he passed out – fully clothed – on the couch and didn't awaken until his alarm clock went off the next morning. After slowly wiping the dew from his eyes and clearing the phlegm from his throat, he lit a cigarette.

As Wells stood erect, he straightened out the wrinkles in his disheveled suit of clothes, stumbled to the bathroom, where he quickly threw some cold water onto his face, shaved without cutting his throat and combed his little bit of greasy, dirty hair. And then, after plopping four aspirins into his mouth, he headed to the kitchen to drink his daily pot of hot, black Colombian nectar.

After pouring a cup of liquid speed, Wells then looked out his kitchen window thinking that the black sedan would be parked near his home waiting for him to leave for work. He figured as long as he was investigating these strange murders that the people in the black sedan would be following close behind. But it was nowhere to be seen – for once. Wells was actually relieved, hoping that they suddenly got a life and were now stalking somebody else.

After finishing a full pot of coffee, Wells grabbed his briefcase full of investigative reports and headed out the front door to his beat-up vehicle, where he jumped behind the wheel and placed the key in the ignition. Usually the car started right away, but this time it took three tries before it started. After taking a few deep breaths, he backed out of his driveway and headed to the station.

Looking into his rearview mirror, Wells didn't see the black sedan anywhere. However three miles later, it finally showed up. The black sedan crept up behind his vehicle but didn't follow him into the station's parking lot. But as Wells parked his vehicle, he noticed another black sedan already parked near the entrance doors. So he jumped out from behind the wheel of his car and headed straight for it, hoping to give its owner a few choice words. However, before confronting the person he jotted down the license plate number so he could run it for identification purposes. But when he looked into its tinted windows, there wasn't anyone inside.

So Wells entered the building to find the occupants of the vehicle. He figured that if they were government agents, they were probably visiting with Captain Lawson in his office. Most likely, ordering the Captain to follow their every whim without asking any questions.

Wells went directly to the front desk and signed in and then handed desk Sergeant Steiner a scrap of paper with the black sedan's license plate number written on it, saying, "Sergeant Steiner, would you please run this license plate number for its owner's identification. I'll be looking for Captain Lawson in the meantime. You wouldn't know where he is, would you Sergeant?"

"Detective Wells, it's not my turn to watch him," Steiner replied sarcastically. "But I did see him talking with two men all dressed in black and wearing black fedoras. I think they were G-men," he added.

"You could be right about that, Sergeant," Wells retorted. He then reminded Steiner to run the license plate number, adding, "Please get me the identification on that number I gave you. And if you happen to see Captain Lawson before I do, please tell him that I'm looking for him, would you?"

"Will do, Detective Wells," Steiner replied. And added, "I should have the information in a few minutes. I'll send it over to you when I get it back." With that said, Detective Wells nodded and walked away looking for Captain Lawson.

Wells first looked in Lawson's office but nobody was there. He then checked the snack bar thinking that Captain Lawson and friends would need coffee to sustain their energy flow. But that room was also empty of people.

Wells looked at his watch and saw that it was getting late. He needed to hurry to Santa Monica police station to meet with Smith to interrogate Katie Brown. So Wells gave up his search for Captain Lawson and went to his desk to retrieve any new reports that might be there. He wanted them for the luncheon engagement with Detectives Rodriguez, Wilmont and Smith.

Wells had a thin stack of reports sitting on his desk waiting for him. However, he had no time to waste. He grabbed the stack of reports, inserted them into his briefcase and headed for the front doors of the station. As he passed the front desk, Sergeant Steiner reached across the counter and handed Wells the information he had asked for.

By the time he reached the front doors, Wells had read it and had the answer he had expected. The words read: FBI, L. A. division. With that, Wells wadded up the piece of paper, threw it to the floor, and headed for the parking lot. But as he was walking out the doors, Captain Lawson was walking in and damn near bumped into him.

"Captain Lawson I was looking for you," Wells told him. "I wanted to speak with you about an important matter, but it can wait. I have to be in Santa Monica this morning to interrogate a witness. And by the way, another female suspect was arrested in San Pedro last night. So after lunch I'm going to meet with Detective Rodriguez and the other detectives that are involved in investigating these murders and witness her interrogation. I'll speak with you when I return." Wells then continued on his way, only to see the black sedan that had been parked near the station's front doors, racing out of the parking lot.

Wells just shook his head in disgust figuring that Captain Lawson had been speaking with its occupants just before their conversation. But Wells would have to wait to speak with Captain Lawson about that. He didn't want to miss his chance at interrogating Smith's female suspect.

Ten minutes into his drive to Santa Monica police station, Detective Wells noticed a bewildering sight: the black sedan was following him once again. But he refused to acknowledge it and continued towards Santa Monica.

Thirty minutes later, Wells was at the front desk of Santa Monica police station asking the officer behind the counter for Detective Smith. Within a few minutes, Smith was escorting him to the interrogation room, talking as they walked.

On the way Wells asked Smith if he had received Rodriguez's message.

Smith replied, "You mean about the recent arrest of the second female suspect in the tainted meat murders?"

Wells nodded, and added, "He's allowing us to participate in her interrogation. And I definitely have a few questions to ask her."

"Like what?" Smith asked him.

"Like what she has to say about this guy Jarrett," Wells replied. Adding, "And will she be surprised or even care that he's dead? And I want to see how your suspect reacts when she learns about Jarrett's death."

"Who...Katie Brown?"

"Who else? Of course, Katie Brown," Wells retorted. "What crime did you charge her with?"

"Involuntary manslaughter," Smith replied.

"Is that all?" Wells asked in disbelief.

"We were lucky to charge her with that," Smith answered. "In fact the district attorney was only going to charge her with a misdemeanor...for selling meat without a license."

"You've got to be kidding?" Wells said with an air of disgust.

Smith shook his head, saying, "Hell, I had to argue with the D.A. for thirty minutes before he finally gave in. I told him that the judge would set a low bond for a misdemeanor and if she got out of jail she would probably flee to another state and we'd never see her again. So even though he didn't want to, he finally agreed to charge her with involuntary manslaughter."

"So what was her bond set at?" Wells asked him.

"Twenty-five thousand – Cash."

"That was nice of the judge," Wells said, as a big smile filled his face.

But Smith wasn't as happy, and said, "Right now Katie Brown can't make bail. But if we don't come up with some decent evidence against her, she may walk." As the two detectives reached the outer office of the interrogation room, he added, "Oh, by the way, she has an attorney now."

Smith and Wells waited a few minutes before entering the room while Brown was brought in with her attorney. After taking their seats at the table, Smith and Wells took theirs, sitting directly across from them.

Smith then introduced Wells to them. "Detective Wells, I'd like you to meet Miss Brown's attorney, Mr. James Davis," Smith said, as Wells and Mr. Davis shook hands. Then he turned his attention to his suspect. "Miss Brown, you remember Detective Wells from Hollywood homicide division, don't you?"

She gave Smith a dirty look and said, "Yes, I remember him." Then she turned her evil gaze to Wells.

Smith told her that Detective Wells would like to ask her a few questions concerning his murder investigation. "If that's all right with you and your attorney, Mr. Davis?"

"I guess so," she replied, as her attorney nodded in agreement.

Wells wasn't at all happy about the attorney being present during the interrogation. However, he knew there was nothing that could be done about that now.

While the attorney lit his clients' cigarette for her, Wells reached for his briefcase that he carried with him and retrieved several photos of Katie Brown's boyfriend's dead body sitting strapped to a chair in the abandoned building, which he placed face down onto the table, then closed and set his briefcase on the floor beside his chair. Then he said, "Miss Brown, I would like to show you these photographs one at a time and get your opinion on them. They're a bit appalling to the naked eye…but I want you to get the full picture of the situation surrounding these photos." He then turned the first of four photos over and placed it in front of her.

The second she saw the photo her face lost color immediately. Her mouth dropped open and her eyes teared up as she recognized at least one person in the photo, her boyfriend Jarrett.

"Oh no. How did that happen?" she asked Wells as a tear flowed down her left cheek.

"Detective Wells, who are the people in this grisly photo?" asked Mr. Davis.

"I believe Miss Brown can tell you. Ask her," said Wells, as Smith stayed quiet and looked on.

"Katie, do you know any of these victims?" Davis asked her.

"Yes, I know at least one of them," she replied, pointing to Jarrett's dismembered skull. "This one looks like a boy I know named Jarrett." Then she turned to her attorney. "Mr. Davis, these two detectives have been looking for him to arrest him. But now they won't have to arrest him, they'll have to bury him."

"So you believe the person in the photo is your boyfriend, Jarrett?" Wells asked her.

She nodded, adding, "It sure looks like him, even though half his skull is missing."

Then Wells asked her if she knew any of the other victims in the photo?

She shrugged her shoulders, then said, "One of them looks familiar. I might have seen him with Jarrett from time to time. I'm not sure though."

"Katie, who do you know that would want your boyfriend dead? Do you have any idea who might have killed him?" Wells asked her, watching her smoke her cigarette right down to the filter.

She told him that she didn't know.

"Does that answer your question, Detective Wells?" asked Mr. Davis.

But Wells refused to give up and told her to look closely at the photo, saying, "Jarrett wasn't just killed. He was tortured…had his skull removed with a bone cutting saw, and had his brains scooped out a spoonful at a time, while his blood was being drained into a bucket a drop at a time. And all of this happened while he was still alive," Wells reminded her as he lit a cigarette.

"You're kidding?" interjected Davis.

Wells replied, "Does it look like I'm kidding? We don't know yet if he bled to death or if the disappearance of brain matter was the cause of death. Or maybe a combination of both killed him. The autopsy report should give us the answer. Who would do that to your boyfriend, Katie?" he asked her, looking deep into her teary eyes.

She again told Wells that she didn't know. But then added, "Unless it had something to do with the meat we delivered to those butcher shops."

"Why do you say that?" Wells asked her.

"That's the only reason I can think of," she retorted.

Wells then told her that they had one of her friends in custody.

"Who?" she asked.

"Kathy Fenton," Wells replied. "She's a good friend of yours, isn't she?"

She nodded, then said, "Yeah, she's a friend. Where was she arrested?"

Wells told her in San Pedro. Then asked her, "How do you think Kathy will feel when she learns that Jarrett is dead? Did she think of him as her boyfriend, too?"

She shrugged her shoulders, saying, "I don't know, Detective. Why don't you ask her?"

"Believe me, I will," Wells replied.

"Are you almost finished questioning my client, Detective Wells?" asked Mr. Davis.

"Just a few more and I won't bother her again. Not today, anyway."

"I'll let her answer a few more and that's it," said Mr. Davis.

Wells asked her what they did with the two meat grinding machines from Salvator Elmero's butcher shop?

She shrugged her shoulders and told him that she didn't know what he was talking about.

"You're lying," Wells snarled. "Why I don't know? But believe me, I will find out…and when I do the district attorney will change your charge from involuntary manslaughter to first degree murder."

"All right, that's enough," snapped Davis, as he advised his client to keep silent. "My client isn't answering anymore of your idiotic questions."

Wells then surprised them when he let it slip that he had found one of

116

the machines at a crime scene. Adding, "Maybe Kathy Fenton might have something to say about that? In fact, maybe she'll want to make a deal with the district attorney to spill her guts for a lenient sentence." Wells took a long drag on his cigarette and then flicked it to the floor.

"Detective Wells," interjected Davis, "I'm afraid you'll have to take that up with Kathy Fenton. My client and I are finished with this interview."

"We thank you for your time, counselor," said Smith.

The attorney then left the room as his client was taken back to her cell.

Detectives Smith and Wells stayed and argued about the interrogation of Katie Brown.

"Detective Wells, you certainly handled that interrogation well," Smith said sarcastically. "You're supposed to keep calm and not give away information about our evidence. When Davis learns that the meat grinder was found near a mutilated and dismembered victim, it'll be all over the news. You are aware of that, aren't you, Detective Wells?"

"Yes, I'm aware of that," Wells retorted. "I just couldn't help myself. That girl knows something about the connection between Jarrett and the mob that she's not telling."

"Let's hope we can get it out of Kathy Fenton," Smith told him. "In fact, we should be heading to Gabrielle's Hoagie House now. We have time for one cup of coffee before we leave. Would you like a cup, John?"

"Yeah, I could use one. I'm still hungover from last night," he said, as he followed Smith into a small snack room.

The two homicide detectives each poured a cup of black coffee, lit a cigarette, then headed for Smith's desk where the detective retrieved his important papers and reports so he would be prepared for their luncheon engagement.

With that, Wells and Smith, with briefcases in hand, left Santa Monica police station and headed for their cars, each driving their own to Gabrielle's Hoagie House just in case one of them had an emergency to contend with.

CHAPTER 9

As Smith's car pulled out of the parking lot, Wells' followed a few car lengths behind, all the while looking for the black sedan. But to Wells' relief, it wasn't anywhere in sight – which put him at ease.

By the time the two detectives had reached Gabrielle's Hoagie House it was a few minutes past one o'clock. Wilmont and Rodriguez had already arrived and were waiting near the restaurant's entrance smoking cigarettes with one hand while their other hands were holding onto their briefcases.

Smith and Wells jumped out of their cars with briefcases in hand, walked up to their comrades and shook hands, then entered the restaurant, walking to Wells' favorite table in the smoking section.

"Detective Wells, this luncheon is on me," said Smith, as the others thanked him and sat down around the table.

At nearly the same time all four detectives opened their briefcases to retrieve their important papers regarding their murder investigations. But before they got down to business, they ordered drinks. Detectives Wilmont, Smith and Rodriguez ordered Long Island ice teas, Wells – a double scotch on the rocks.

As the homicide detectives sipped their drinks and shot the bull, it wasn't until they had finished their meals and their second drinks before they began a serious discussion over their individual murder investigations.

"John," said Smith, "before we get started, I just want to know how your partner, Detective Lenda is doing? I hope to visit him at the hospital in a day or so. I hope he's feeling okay."

"Detective Lenda is doing well," replied Wells, "and should be out of the hospital in a couple of days. I'll let him know that you guys are thinking of him. But let's get down to some serious business. I know we're here today at Raul's request. He has some important information to tell us about his suspect in the tainted meat murders. And I have brought with me today some photos and videotape of six victims that I believe is linked to our other murder investigations. Raul can begin…and when all of you are finished speaking, I'll show you the video and photos I'm talking about. I don't want to show you any sooner because I'm afraid it would ruin your lunch."

"If it's that important," interjected Smith, "maybe you should show us now."

"No, it can wait," Wells retorted. "Why don't we let Raul begin."

"Very good, I'll start." Rodriguez set a photo in the middle of the table for all to see, saying, "Here is the photo of the woman who was seen delivering the tainted meat to the Hollywood and San Pedro butcher shops. Her name is Kathy Fenton. She was arrested by one of San Pedro's finest patrol officers. The patrolman spotted her and Janie Jenson near the beach and gave chase. He caught and arrested Fenton but lost Jenson. I have officers out canvassing the area for Jenson now. Hopefully, we'll have her in custody shortly."

"Has your female suspect been arraigned yet?" Smith asked Rodriguez.

"Not yet," he answered. "She's only been in custody for less than twelve hours and will probably be arraigned in a day or two. The district attorney is deciding what to charge her with."

"Good luck," interjected Smith. "We had a hell of a time with our D.A. over Katie Brown's arrest. He wanted to charge her with a misdemeanor and not a felony."

"Why? What crime did he want to charge her with?" Rodriguez asked him.

Smith replied, "Are you ready for this? Selling meat without a license. But we finally convinced him that our suspect would go free unless he charged her with at least manslaughter. He finally agreed and charged her with involuntary manslaughter. Now we have to come up with some new evidence to up the charge to murder."

Wilmont interjected his thoughts, saying, "We need a confession if we want to charge these people with murder."

"Has Fenton asked for an attorney yet?" Smith asked Rodriguez.

He shook his head no, adding, "And I hope she doesn't ask for one. Her interrogation would go much smoother without the interference of an attorney."

Smith looked to Wells and asked him about his wounded suspect in the hospital. "Have you interviewed him yet?"

"Oh, you mean Mario "the muscle" Morrelli," replied Wells. Smith nodded. Wells told him that he hadn't interviewed him yet.

Smith wanted to know when Wells was going to interrogate his suspect, asking, "Is he able to speak with you...or are his wounds so severe that he can't speak yet?"

"They're so severe that he can't speak yet," Wells retorted. Adding, "That's 'cause he's dead."

"Dead!" said the three detectives in unison, surprised by the news.

"Did he die in surgery...or from his wounds?" asked Wilmont.

"I won't know that until the autopsy is completed," Wells replied. "But I believe government agents killed him. Either that...or the mob silenced him."

Wilmont asked him why he thought that.

"Because," Wells retorted, "I have an eyewitness that saw two men dressed in black and wearing fedoras near Morelli's hospital room. And a minute later he was dead. I might have the autopsy report in my briefcase with all the other investigative reports. I'll look for it in a minute. But before I talk, I want Raul to tell us more about Kathy Fenton."

Rodriguez obliged, saying, "You guys heard what Katie Brown had to say about Kathy Fenton during her interrogation with Willard. Right?" The detectives nodded. "Well, since her arrest I've learned much more. I'm hoping she'll be able to tell us about this mob war between the Manzelli and Santini crime families."

"What do you know that Katie Brown didn't?" asked Wells.

"Well," Rodriguez replied, "evidently, Kathy Fenton didn't tell Katie Brown everything about her past. Not only did Kathy run away from her foster parents...but the police found them stabbed to death. They theorized that an intruder killed them and took Kathy as a hostage. They investigated the murders and Kathy's disappearance for more than a year before finally giving up."

"Raul, do you believe Kathy Fenton is behind the murders of her foster parents?" asked Smith.

Rodriguez shrugged his shoulders and said, "I don't know. But now we can confront her about those murders. Maybe she doesn't even know that they're dead. But we'll find out. That's one of the many questions I want to ask her."

"I have a few I might want to ask her, too," said Wells, as he glanced through the pile of reports that he had in his briefcase.

"Raul, is there anything else that you want to tell us about Kathy Fenton?" asked Smith.

"No, that's about it. But on my mutilation victim who was found in a San Pedro motel room, I'm still waiting for the DNA results for identification."

"I think all of us are waiting for the DNA results to identify the mutilated torsos," interjected Smith.

"I'm not," said Wells, looking at the report in his hand. "I just found the DNA test results amongst all of these reports on the five torsos found in Hollywood. In fact, now that I read it, I was right about the torsos being gangsters that were on our missing persons' list."

"Who are they?" asked Wilmont anxiously. "Do they belong to the Manzelli or Santini crime families?"

Wells took a drag on his cigarette, then a sip of his drink before telling them, "the torso found in the Hollywood motel room was Joseppi Vega, brother of the motel's owner, Johnny Vega, and brother-in-law to Salvator Elmero, whose torso was found with two others in an abandoned building in Hollywood only one day later. After finding Elmero's decapitated head at the crime scene, our coroner was able, through DNA, to match it to the torso. Then he had Elmero's wife brought to the morgue to identify his body parts. And she confirmed that the mangled body was Salvator Elmero, soldier of the Manzelli crime family."

"Raul, maybe that's why you couldn't find Joseppi Vega. It's hard to question a guy when he's no larger than second base," joked Smith.

"That's true," said Rodriguez as they all laughed over Smith's remark.

After the laughing died down, Smith asked Wells about the other three torsos. "Did you find out their identities?"

Wells nodded, then told them that the other two torsos found on the scene with Salvator Elmero's were identified as Johnny Vega and Tommy Elmero. Adding, "And the torso we found at an abandoned building a few blocks from the Elmero crime scene was another Manzelli soldier, which was identified as Jimmy "the grip" Graziano."

"But who's killing them?" asked Wilmont.

Wells replied, "That's what we have to find out. Somebody wiped out five members of the Manzelli crime family. Were the killers from the Manzelli crime family or the Santini crime family? And did the Manzelli family kill their own soldiers to keep them silent about the tainted human hamburger meat that was sold out of their establishments or did the Santini mob kill them to extract information about the Manzelli drug empire? That's the question we have to answer and we better answer it quick…or this mob war will get out of hand, if it hasn't already."

"I agree," interjected Wilmont, as the other three detectives nodded in agreement. "We need some answers and we need them fast."

Wells held up a sheet of paper and said, "Here's another report from my investigators concerning one of our prime suspects that was wanted in the tainted meat murders but was found just recently with the top of his head cut off. You know him as Jarrett." Then he told the guys something that surprised even him. "But it seems his fingerprint analysis shows that his name wasn't Jarrett at all…but rather Danny Jermaine."

"Then why did Katie Brown call him Jarrett?" asked Smith.

"I have no idea. We'll have to ask her," Wells replied.

"Katie Brown told us that she didn't know if the names that her friends used were their real names. So maybe this Jarrett used a phony name. That's not unusual," Smith told them.

"Do you have Jermaine's background report?" Wilmont asked Wells.

Wells nodded, then said, "There is a background report…but it only states that he is seventeen years old and had run away from a foster home when he was eleven. He ran away with two other boys, and that's all it says. We'll have to ask Kathy and Katie about Jarrett. Let's see if they're as surprised as we were to learn that his real name was Danny and not Jarrett."

"How did the kid get his skull smashed in?" Wilmont asked him.

"His head wasn't smashed in, per say, his skullcap was removed," replied Wells.

"How did that happen?" asked Wilmont.

"Why don't I explain that after you watch the videotape I have to show you," Wells told him.

"Why all the mystery, John?" asked Smith.

"Willard, you'll understand once you've viewed the tape," Wells retorted.

Calling the waitress to their table, the four detectives ordered more drinks before Wells asked the restaurant's manager for the use of the restaurant's special room, which is reserved for parties and other functions such as business meetings. The room was equipped with a television and VCR, which was needed for the viewing of Wells' videotape. The room was also equipped with a photocopying machine, which the detectives could use to copy each other's investigative reports that they thought were important and pertinent to their particular murder investigations.

The four detectives were given permission to use the room so they grabbed their drinks and headed for it, anxious to watch the video. Detectives Wilmont, Smith and Rodriguez sat around the table as Wells placed four photos of the second table murder crime scene in front of them, then placed his videotape into the machine. After pressing the play button he plopped down into a chair to watch his fellow homicide detectives' reactions.

Wells watched his friends' facial expressions as the film showed the three male victims strapped and tied in their chairs begging silently for their lives before their mouths were taped shut. Then they watched as the killer stuck a large needle into each victim's jugular vein before attaching a long plastic tube onto it, which ran down the length of the victim's body into an empty pale.

A few seconds later the detectives watched as the killer cut the skullcaps off of each victim with a small battery operated circular saw, which is used for cutting plaster casts. The detectives couldn't believe what they were seeing and couldn't take their eyes away from the screen as they saw the victims' eyes bulge out of their sockets as the killer cut away and then placed each skullcap on the table in front of them. Each skullcap took nearly ten minutes of brutal cutting. And each victim watched the others reaction from across the table as their brains were exposed and as their blood dripped slowly out of their bodies.

Disgusting grunts and groans from the detectives broke the silence in the room. They, like Wells, could barely hold back their anger and rage at the killers of the three male victims.

Wells knew that the homicide detectives were about to lose their lunch. For nearly sixty minutes they sat through this hideous "snuff" film concealing their frustration and anger, disgusted at themselves for not capturing the killers before these murders took place.

The detectives were upset that the cowardly killers never showed their faces in the video while torturing their victims. Rodriguez, Wilmont and Smith thought they had seen it all, until they viewed this film. They couldn't believe what they had just witnessed.

"We're going to have to catch these killers before they torture and kill anyone else," remarked Smith.

"I didn't tell you before," Wells interjected, "but this is the second murder scene of this sort that I have investigated. It's where we found the videotape. I don't know if the killers left it behind by mistake...or if they wanted us to find it. I just hope I don't run across anymore murder scenes like the one on the videotape."

After Wells ejected the tape from the machine the four detectives then left the room and returned to the table where they ordered more drinks and sat around talking over their investigations. Wilmont shared his knowledge of the murder investigation that they were conducting.

"After viewing the videotape, it's hard to believe that Jarrett and the other victims were involved in the tainted meat and mutilation murders," said Wilmont.

"Now he's really involved in the mutilation murders. He's not only involved, he is the mutilation," Smith said sarcastically.

Wells reminded Wilmont that Jarrett's real name was Danny Jermaine.

"Whatever," Smith answered. "Jarrett or Danny. It's only a name. But that kid was the only person that could have told us about his connection with the Manzelli crime family. Now that he's dead we don't have anyone that can finger the mob for all of these murders."

"Willard, don't be so pessimistic," Wells told him. "We still have Kathy Fenton to interrogate. And when we tell Miss Katie Brown about her boyfriend's real identity, maybe that news will dislodge some pertinent information from her."

"Let's hope so," interjected Rodriguez. "We need a break on our murder investigations. We had four suspects. Two are incarcerated and two are dead. One of them we've interrogated…and she's told us nothing. Let's hope Kathy Fenton knows more than Katie Brown."

Wells replied, "Speaking of Kathy Fenton…if none of you detectives have anything more to say about our murder investigations, I say we go to San Pedro police station and interrogate Raul's suspect. What do you say guys?"

But Wilmont wasn't ready to go just yet, saying, "Before we go I just have a few things to say about the mutilated torso and the fifty-five gallon container of ground human flesh that was found in my city."

"Like what?" asked Wells, anxious to leave.

Wilmont replied, "Well for one thing I have the identity on the torso…and there were at least four different bodies' ground up into hamburger in that plastic container. And that's not all. There was also an empty fifty-five gallon container found there that had dried blood stuck to its sides, which DNA tests showed belonged to the same four bodies that were ground up into hamburger. But I'm still waiting for confirmation to see if the DNA tests matched the hair samples that I sent along of the gangsters from our missing persons' list."

"You never told us who the torso belonged to. Who is it?" asked Smith.

"It's another gangster," replied Wilmont.

"From the Manzelli crime family?" asked Wells.

Shaking his head no, Wilmont answered, "It was Sammy Santini – soldier and brother of Don Louie Santini."

As Detective Wells looked through the rest of his reports, he found the ones that identified the other two victims in the second table murders. All were soldiers of the Santini crime family.

Holding the report in his hand and waving it for all to see, Wells told them happily, "I have found the identities of the other two victims in the videotape. They are both members of the Santini crime family. One was identified as Johnny "the wop" Walletti and the other was Benny "boy" DeBello. Fellows, I believe we have a crisis on our hands. We have to stop this run away train before it does anymore damage."

"But how? We need to speak with somebody that knows something," said Smith.

"Well...let's see if Kathy Fenton knows anything about Danny Jermaine's death and the men that he hung around with," said Wells.

After the four detectives finished their drinks, Smith paid the luncheon bill. As they stood up to leave Rodriguez's cell phone rang. The other three detectives watched and listened as Rodriguez answered it. After a two-minute conversation, Rodriguez hung up.

"I've got some good news, boys," said Rodriguez.

"What do you have for us, Raul?" asked Wells.

He answered happily, "Janie Jenson has just been arrested and is being booked at the station as we speak. Maybe we can get some information out of her...and Kathy."

"I just hope one of them cooperates with us," interjected Wilmont.

With that said the detectives left the restaurant, jumped into their cars and headed for San Pedro police station with Rodriguez leading the way.

But Detective Wells had made a big mistake when he left the restaurant. He had forgotten to retrieve the videotape from the machine and had left it behind. He wouldn't understand the ramifications from his terrible blunder until the following day.

But at that moment Wells' mind wasn't on the videotape. His eyes were looking into his rearview mirror and his mind was on the black sedan that had been following him since he left the restaurant's parking lot. This time though he had a trick up his sleeve for the occupants of that black sedan. He would just have to wait until the time was right to pull it out of his hat.

The detectives finally made it to the parking lot of San Pedro police station and quickly parked their cars. The black sedan didn't follow them into the parking lot and continued on its way. Only Detective Wells seemed to notice the government vehicle.

The detectives quickly stepped out of their vehicles and hurried into the police station as Rodriguez escorted his guests to the interrogation room.

Rodriguez quickly explained to them what he had in mind. "Listen up, Detectives," Rodriguez told them. "While the arresting officer is booking Janie Jenson and writing down her particulars, we'll interrogate Kathy Fenton. By the time we're finished interrogating her, Janie Jenson should be ready to answer our questions. How does that sound?"

"That sounds like a good plan to me," said Wells.

"Me too," said Wilmont and Smith in unison.

The detectives walked into the viewing room adjacent to the interrogation room hoping to get a quick glimpse of the suspect. But she hadn't been escorted in yet.

While anxiously awaiting Fenton's arrival, they decided who would conduct the interrogation and who would watch from behind the glass. Wells and Rodriguez were the two detectives selected to interrogate Kathy Fenton. Wells – for having the most experience amongst the four detectives and Rodriguez – because Kathy Fenton was his suspect.

Finally, after waiting more than ten minutes, Kathy Fenton was brought into the interrogation room. Bringing along a tape recorder, documents and photos, the two homicide detectives were ready to begin the interrogation of a suspect in the tainted meat murders. Rodriguez hoped to have Kathy Fenton charged with at least second degree murder and not involuntary manslaughter or selling meat without a license. He wanted to put this woman away forever, provided she was guilty.

The detectives waited and watched from behind the mirrored, one-way window as the suspect squirmed in her seat and struggled with her handcuffs and facial piercing.

The female suspect had at least six facial piercings, not including the five or so on each ear. She had one going through each nostril, one on her lip, two over each eyebrow and one in her tongue. The detectives wondered why the girl didn't get infections from her piercings? Her face looked as though it hadn't been washed in weeks.

After surveying the room from her chair, Fenton lit a cigarette then blew a big cloud of smoke into the air that made her disappear from the detectives view. With that cue, Rodriguez opened the door and he and Wells walked into the interrogation room to meet with their female suspect.

After turning on the tape recorder and placing it onto the table, Rodriguez quickly introduced himself and Wells to her while removing her handcuffs.

But she wasn't interested in the introduction. Only one thing was on her mind and she let it be known. "I'd like to know what the hell I've been arrested for!" she snarled.

But Rodriguez would have none of it. He shot back, "Miss Fenton, we ask the questions here. But if you must know, you're wanted for questioning."

"What do you mean?" she asked, taking a long drag from her cigarette before exhaling a big cloud of smoke.

"Miss Fenton," Rodriguez went on to say, "if a person is known to have committed a crime or is a suspect in a crime or conspiracy, then the police are allowed to hold that person for questioning before they charge them…or release them. Now do you understand?"

She shook her head in disgust, then asked, "What do you want to question me about? Shouldn't I have a lawyer present?"

Rodriguez replied, "For what? Why do you need an attorney? Do you think you have done something wrong? If you think you have, why don't you tell us about it?"

"That's what I mean," she whined. "I haven't done anything wrong. That's why I can't understand why I've been arrested."

As Rodriguez read from her booking report, he asked his suspect simple questions, like how old she was and where she was born, while Detective Wells was busy sorting through his photos of the dead victims in his murder investigations.

Wells picked out the photos that he wanted and set them on the table face down in front of him so Kathy Fenton couldn't see them until he was ready.

But the interrogation was going too slowly and Wells wanted to speed it up a little. He was disappointed in Rodriguez's questioning and interrupted the interrogation. "Excuse me, Detective Rodriguez," interjected Wells. "Ask her questions that mean something. Ask her about her boyfriend Jarrett…and her involvement in the delivery of tainted meat that killed innocent people because it was diseased ground human flesh. Ask her about that!"

Rodriguez replied, "Let's not get ahead of ourselves, Wells. Let me speak to Miss Fenton and let her know that if she cooperates with us and answers our questions to the best of her ability, she may well be released after this interview. Do you understand me, Miss Fenton?" he asked her, looking deep into her eyes.

"Yes, I understand. But I don't know anything about any diseased meat," she said as she threw the butt of her cigarette to the floor and quickly lit another from a fresh pack sitting on the table in front of her.

Rodriguez told her, "We have eyewitnesses, butcher shop employees, that say you and your boyfriend, Jarrett delivered the diseased ground human flesh to their butcher shops. What do you have to say about that? Are the eyewitnesses lying to us?"

"So what if I helped Jarrett deliver hamburger to butcher shops? That's not a crime," she replied, much wiser than her seventeen years.

Wells snapped, "It is when you deliver ground human flesh. Especially diseased ground human flesh."

"I know nothing about that!" she snapped.

"Come now, Detective Wells, let me handle this interview," Rodriguez told him, giving him a dirty look.

"I'm sorry for interrupting. Please continue," Wells answered sheepishly.

Rodriguez asked her who paid them to deliver the meat to the butcher shops? "Who asked you to do it? Do you know?" Rodriguez asked her.

She replied, "Jarrett asked me…and some fat man asked him. In fact, the fat man drove us in his car so we could deliver the meat."

"Does this man look like anyone in these photos?" Wells asked her, placing in front of her twelve different photos of mobsters of both the Manzelli and Santini crime families.

As Kathy Fenton looked at each photo, she suddenly recognized a familiar face. "This is him. This is the fat man that drove us to the butcher shops," she said, pointing to Salvator Elmero's picture.

"Miss Fenton, do you know that the person you just picked out was a member of the Manzelli crime family and owner of a butcher shop in Hollywood?" Wells asked her.

She shook her head no, saying, "I never got involved in Jarrett's business. He didn't like us to stick our noses where they didn't belong...so I always stayed away when he was talking with another person."

Rodriguez asked her if she knew where Jarrett was? "Do you know where we can find him?" he asked her, as Wells gave him a quizzical look.

She shrugged her shoulders, saying, "He's around. He's probably laying on a beach somewhere."

"Are you sure?" asked Rodriguez.

She answered, "Of course, I'm sure. He was with me just a few hours before your police officers chased and arrested me."

"Now we know you're lying," snapped Wells.

"Believe what you want," she said, taking another long drag from her cigarette, then exhaling a huge cloud of smoke that filled the entire room.

Wells reacted angrily to her answer and told her, "Miss Fenton, we know for a fact that Jarrett has been in police custody for nearly two days now. So how could you have been with him yesterday?"

"I'm telling you...Janie Jenson and I were with Jarrett not more than two hours before I was arrested."

"Miss Fenton, Jarrett has been lying to you from the beginning," Wells told her. "Did you know his name isn't Jarrett at all, but Danny? His real name is Danny Jermaine. Did you know that?" he asked her.

"No I didn't. I've always called him Jarrett and so did everyone else that he hung around with. But I know that he's not in police custody, unless he was arrested after me."

"Then look at this photo and tell me who it is?" Wells asked her, as he placed a recent police photo of Danny Jermaine, alias Jarrett, in front of the rebellious female suspect.

Holding the photo up to her face, she looked at it closely for nearly a minute, then answered, "Okay, it looks like Jarrett. So what? That doesn't mean that he's in police custody."

"Well, actually he's not in police custody anymore. We released him," remarked Wells.

"See, I told you he wasn't in police custody," she said with a big smile on her face.

"You're absolutely right. We released his body to the morgue," Wells retorted, looking deep into the suspect's eyes, trying to get a reaction from her.

"What do you mean, morgue? Is Jarrett all right!" she cried out, looking at Wells for the answer.

"When a person is taken to the morgue, it usually means that the person is dead," answered Wells sarcastically.

"I don't believe you," she told Wells.

"Look at this photo and you tell me, Miss Fenton," Wells told her, as he showed her the crime scene photo of her boyfriend strapped into a chair with his brains exposed and half gone.

Kathy Fenton stared at the photo for what seemed like forever. She just couldn't believe that the person in the photo was her boyfriend, Jarrett. She said, "This photo must be a phony. When was it taken?"

"Long before you were arrested," answered Wells.

"That can't be," she whined. "I'm telling you, Jarrett was with me just before I got arrested. So I know this photo can't be of him."

"Oh, but it is Jarrett," Wells retorted. "Or should I say Danny Jermaine. He used you and the other girls for his own selfishness and had ties to the mob. Now he's dead and you probably know who killed him." He stared into her eyes and asked her, "Who was angry enough to want him dead? Who would torture him this way?" He then explained to her that somebody actually cut off the top of his skull and scooped out his brains one spoonful at a time, while draining his blood out of his body one-drop at a time, while he was alive and conscious. He leaned across the table, putting his face near hers, then looking into her eyes, he said, "Miss Fenton, I believe he was being tortured for a reason and you know that reason. I'd bet my life on it. Now who do you think would torture and kill him?"

She told him that she didn't know. Adding, "But I do know that Jarrett is still alive. The person in the picture might look like Jarrett...but it can't possibly be him. Not if the person in the photo was killed more than two days ago. It just can't be Jarrett!"

But Wells didn't buy it and was angered by her statements. He replied, "Miss Fenton, I don't know why you keep on insisting your boyfriend is still alive...when we have the evidence and body that shows he's dead...and has been for nearly three days. I don't know who you think you're trying to protect...but your strategy won't work with us."

"Detective Wells, maybe Miss Fenton is telling us the truth? Let's give her the benefit of doubt for the time being. Remember. She is innocent until proven guilty," Rodriguez told him.

"Detective Rodriguez, you are absolutely right. I'll let you ask the questions and I'll just sit back and keep my mouth shut," said Wells, embarrassed at being reprimanded.

"Now Miss Fenton, let's talk about just before your arrest. You say that Jarrett and Janie Jenson was with you. Is that right?" Detective Rodriguez asked her.

"Only Janie was with me just before I was arrested. Jarrett had left us a few hours before that," she said, then threw her lit cigarette butt against the wall and quickly lit another.

"Did you know that we arrested Janie Jenson a few hours ago? She's being booked right now, as we speak. Is she going to back up your story about Jarrett? Will she help us find the people who are responsible for the deaths from the tainted meat?" asked Rodriguez.

"I don't know. Why don't you ask her?" she snapped.

"Miss Fenton, this is a serious matter!" snarled Rodriguez. "Not only did innocent victims die from eating the diseased meat...but many more died from being ground into hamburger. There's a serial killer on the loose and we want to stop the killings. And we need your help to do it. Now will you help us?"

"I'd like to help you," she whined, "but I don't know anything. Except that Jarrett is still alive!"

Wells broke in, saying, "Miss Fenton, your boyfriend's name was Danny Jermaine. The young man you knew as Jarrett...doesn't exist anymore. He's dead!"

"Ask Janie then if you don't believe me."

"Don't worry, we will," Rodriguez told her.

"I've told you everything," she whined, pounding her fist on the tabletop. "Now will you let me go home?" she asked Rodriguez as she puffed on her cigarette.

"If we did release you, Miss Fenton, where would you go?" Rodriguez asked her.

She answered, "I'd go back to the streets to find Jarrett."

Rodriguez shook his head in disgust and said, "I'll tell you what. Let me speak with the district attorney to see if he wants to charge you or release you."

Exhaling a big cloud of cigarette smoke from her lungs, she looked confused and asked, "Why would the district attorney want to charge me with a crime? I haven't done anything wrong!"

Wells snarled, "Miss Fenton, I guess it hasn't sunken into your pierced head yet. I think those facial piercings damaged your brain. Don't you understand...the meat you delivered to those butcher shops was not only diseased meat but diseased human meat! Many people died from it. If it were up to me...I'd charge you with first degree murder. But you lucked out...because I'm not the district attorney."

Fenton gave Wells a scowling look and clamored, "I'm not saying another word until I get a lawyer. So either charge me...or release me."

Fenton's words took Wells by surprise. He stopped the interrogation and asked Rodriguez to step into an adjacent room where they could talk.

Rodriguez agreed to Wells' commands and shut off the tape recorder, then both left the interrogation room to meet with the other two homicide detectives, Wilmont and Smith.

Rodriguez snapped, "What do you want, John! You screwed up this interview like you screwed up Katie Brown's interview. When will you learn to keep your mouth shut when you're angry?"

"Probably never," Wells replied. "But that's not important right now. If Fenton really believes that Jarrett is still alive, maybe she can lead us to the rest of her gang, which might lead us to the mobsters that have been on this killing spree."

"What are you saying?" Rodriguez asked him. "Do you want me to release her so we can follow her to her hideout?"

Wells answered, "That's exactly what I'm saying. If what she's saying is true...and we won't know until we interview Janie Jenson, then maybe we should let her out to find Jarrett. Maybe this guy has a twin. I really doubt it...but she could still lead us to the rest of her gang that helped deliver the tainted meat for those mobsters. One of them should be able to tell us who paid them to deliver the meat. When we know that answer...we'll have our killer."

"That sounds like an idea," Rodriguez told him. "But who would pay for her surveillance? I know Captain Helfman wouldn't sanction the overtime. He might put a few patrol officers to watch her...but I doubt if it would be around the clock."

Wells thought for a moment, then said, "Why don't we talk about that after we've interviewed Janie Jenson. If she doesn't back up Fenton's story about being with Jarrett a few hours before she was arrested, then we'll know Fenton is lying. But if she does back up Fenton's story...then it might do some good to release one of them and put to rest once and for all the question about Jarrett being dead or alive."

"Well, let's talk with Janie Jenson," Rodriguez replied.

Detective Rodriguez had Kathy Fenton escorted to her cell and had Janie Jenson brought to the interrogation room. Again the detectives agreed to have Detectives Rodriguez and Wells ask the questions. However, they did caution Wells not to lose his cool unless planned. To which he agreed.

After a cup of coffee and a cigarette, it was time to interview the female suspect. She was sitting in a chair and waiting. Janie Jenson was another throw back to the late sixties – a flower child and a Katie Brown look-alike with similar clothing – haltertop and cutoff jeans. Her hair – dirty and cropped short. Her feet – dirty and bare.

Detective Rodriguez entered the room and Detective Wells followed. Seconds later Rodriguez placed a new cassette tape into the machine and turned it on. Then he introduced himself and Wells to his suspect.

"Janie Jenson, I'd like to introduce us. I'm Detective Rodriguez and this is Detective Wells. We would like to ask you a few questions, if that's all right with you?"

"Before I answer anything...I want to know why I'm here. As far as I'm concerned I was kidnapped and brought to this place against my will," she snapped in a high-pitched voice, and then lit a cigarette from the pack that she carried with her.

"Get real, Miss Jenson," Rodriguez shot back. "When you're accused of committing a crime, the police have the right to hold you for seventy-two hours. How old are you Janie?"

She looked Rodriguez directly in the eyes and replied, "I'm twenty-two."

"You've been on the streets a long time, Miss Jenson. You know the ropes," Rodriguez told her.

"Yeah, I've been on the streets for a long time. So what? So have a lot of other people," she answered angrily.

Rodriguez shot back, saying, "These surroundings aren't new to you, Miss Jenson. You've been arrested more than a few times. Need I say more?"

Wells couldn't keep quiet and put his two cents in. "Miss Jenson," Wells interjected, "you know that Kathy was arrested and has already answered our questions. So I want you to know you can't lie to us or we'll know. Kathy Fenton has told us everything about Jarrett and your little gang of homeless street urchins…and your connection with the mob."

"I don't know what the hell you're talking about," she shot back.

Wells wouldn't give up and asked her who paid her to deliver the hamburger meat to the butcher shops? He then placed a dozen or so photos of different known mobsters on the table in front of her.

"Who are these people?" she asked, looking at the pictures.

"Take a close look," Wells told her. "Do you recognize any of these men as the one's that paid you and Jarrett to deliver that hamburger meat?"

"I've seen this one before," she answered, pointing to the photo of the late Salvator Elmero. "He drove us to one of the butcher shops. I think he also gave money to Jarrett for the meat."

"Miss Jenson, are you absolutely positive that this is the man that paid Jarrett to deliver the meat?" Wells asked her.

She nodded, adding, "I'm positive."

"Kathy told us that you and her were with Jarrett a few hours before the police arrested her. Is that true?" Rodriguez asked her.

"Kathy said we were with Jarrett when she was arrested?" she asked seemingly confused.

"That's what we're saying," replied Rodriguez.

"Then she's wrong!" exclaimed Jenson. "It's true that I was with her when the police chased us and arrested her, but I didn't see Jarrett at all that day. In fact, I haven't seen Jarrett in over three days. So I don't know what Kathy could be talking about. But she's definitely mistaken."

"What if we told you that Jarrett's real name is Danny Jermaine, would that surprise you?" Rodriguez asked her.

She quipped, "Honey, in this day and age, nothing surprises me. So his name is Danny and not Jarrett. So what?"

"A few days ago we found Danny Jermaine in an abandoned building. He was dead," Wells interjected.

"How did he die?" she asked.

"Before I tell you that," Wells replied, "I have two photos to show you. A recent photo of Danny Jermaine alive and a recent photo of him dead. I want you to take a close look at both photos and tell me if it's the guy you call Jarrett. Will you do that?" he asked her as he placed the two photos in front her.

Janie Jenson held each photo close to her face. When she saw the photo with her boyfriend's skullcap removed and his brains exposed, her face became white as a ghost. "I can't believe it! That is Jarrett! Who killed him?" she asked.

"Miss Jenson, are you sure the person in those two photos is your boyfriend, Jarrett?" asked Wells.

"Yes, I'm sure. That's him. When was he killed and where?"

Wells told her that her boyfriend was found dead a few days ago in an abandoned building in the city of Hollywood.

"I just can't believe that Jarrett's dead," she replied, stunned by the news.

"Who do you know that would cut the top of his head off and drain the blood out of his body? Do you have any ideas?" Wells asked her.

She thought for a minute, then blurted out, "Maybe it was the mob! The way Jarrett was tortured, it looked as though somebody was trying to extract information from him."

"Why would you say that Miss Jenson?" asked Rodriguez.

She replied, "Why else do people torture their victims? Usually to get information out of them."

But Wells told her, "In this day and age, Miss Jenson, I don't think people need a reason to do anything. Many kill just for kicks. They don't need a reason."

"You could be right, Detective," she told Wells. "But I still say someone tried to extract information out of him."

Wells told Jenson to relax for a few minutes. "Detective Rodriguez and I need to step outside and get a cup of coffee. Would you like a soft drink or a sandwich?" he asked her.

"I'd like something to drink," was her reply.

Wells and Rodriguez left the room for a few minutes to speak with Wilmont and Smith.

"I think we should let her out on the streets and follow her to her hangout. I think she'll lead us to the others and maybe the mobster that got them involved in all of this," said Wells.

"I agree," Smith interjected. "Now that Jarrett is out of the way, they'll have to contact somebody from his gang. If the mob uses these homeless kids to do their dirty work, I'm sure one of the gangsters will get in touch with them."

Rodriguez agreed and replied, "If I can get Captain Helfman's authorization to release her, I will. But it will take a little while to get all the paper work in order. I'll telephone each of you the minute Janie Jenson is released. But if my surveillance team follows her into one of your cities, your people will have to take over the surveillance. We're working with limited funds, which means we can't keep surveillance on her forever."

"We understand," said Smith, as Detectives Wells and Wilmont nodded their heads in agreement.

"Then it's agreed. Rodriguez will release Janie Jenson and his investigators will begin the surveillance. The rest of us will notify our superiors about the situation so we can have the officers waiting if our suspect comes into either of our cities," said Wells.

"Agreed," said Wilmont and Smith in unison.

"I don't know if this means anything…but each female suspect that we've interrogated has very short hair," Wells pointed out. "It's funny that their boyfriend has long hair and they have very short hair. Something just doesn't sit right with me for some reason."

"What does that mean?" Wilmont asked. "Maybe from being on the streets they caught lice and had to cut their hair for health reasons? It's nothing more than a coincidence."

Wells replied, "This whole murder investigation has been nothing but coincidence. But the more I investigate, the more I say there's a conspiracy in motion."

"Fellas, it's getting late," Smith opined. "I have to get back to my station and let my Captain know what's going on or he'll skin me alive. If we can, let's do lunch again in a couple of days from now. What do you say guys?"

"That sounds good to me," Rodriguez replied. "Maybe we'll have caught the killers by then. I sure hope so."

Wilmont told the detectives that he'd talk with them tomorrow, telling Rodriguez to, "Keep in touch and let me know the minute Janie Jenson is released. Okay?"

"Will do," Rodriguez replied.

Smith asked Wells if he wanted to follow him to Santa Monica to question Katie Brown about Jarrett's real name? "Maybe she'll tell us something useful this time," he added.

Wells nodded, telling him, "I have to travel that way anyway. But what about her attorney? He'll want to be present."

Smith told Wells that he'd contact her attorney when they get back to the station. "Maybe Katie Brown will agree to answer a few questions without having her attorney present. Especially when the conversation is about her boyfriend, Jarrett," he added.

"We can try," Wells replied. "It's getting late. We better get going."

The detectives agreed to meet for lunch within a few days and went their separate ways. Rodriguez returned to the interrogation room. He brought with him the soft drink that his female suspect had asked for, handed it to her then told her the good news about releasing her from jail within the next few hours if his superiors agreed to it. Miss Jenson was responsive and very happy to hear the news. She was then escorted back to her cell to wait her release.

Wilmont headed back to Redondo Beach while Detectives Smith and Wells drove to Santa Monica. Five minutes into the ride, Wells noticed the black sedan following a few car lengths behind his car. That's when Wells decided to find out more about the sedan's occupants. When the time was right he was going to get behind them and somehow cut them off, and then pull out his weapon to get their attention. He even thought about arresting them, but then thought against it. Especially if they worked for the federal government.

Detective Wells knew that the G-men always had the upper hand. He also felt that government law enforcement officials used tactics worse than that of the New York Mafia. There hasn't been a government agent that's ever been disciplined. When they do something wrong they get promoted. That's how Wells felt about the people following him in that black sedan and he was going to do everything in his power to do to them what they had done to him. He wanted them to feel powerless. However, he felt now wasn't the time.

Twenty minutes after leaving San Pedro police station Smith and Wells arrived at their destination. After parking their cars and entering the building, Smith excused himself to make a call to Katie Brown's attorney. He wanted Mr. Davis's authorization to question his client. But Davis wasn't in his office and was with another client.

The earliest Smith could speak to Katie Brown with her attorney present was the following morning. Smith reluctantly agreed to meet his suspect and her attorney at Santa Monica police station. But Smith was surprised to learn from Mr. Davis's secretary that Katie Brown had been transferred to the county jail. So the questioning would have to take place there.

Detective Smith ended the call and told Wells the bad news. He explained that the interview and questioning of Katie Brown would have to wait until the following morning. Wells was actually elated that Katie Brown had been transferred. He wanted to return home and have a few more drinks. After a long and tiring day Wells needed some time to himself.

Wells said his farewell to Smith and quickly left Santa Monica, driving directly to Hollywood station to pick up any reports that might have come in while he had been out. Once that chore was completed he would then drive to his home and bury his stress in a drink or two...or three. But after driving only a few miles, Wells noticed the black sedan once again following close behind. Now he believed the time was right to pull his ploy and find out once and for all the identification of the occupants of that mysterious government vehicle.

Wells waited for the right moment and stomped the accelerator to the floor, plowing through a red light and turning the corner as the black sedan waited in traffic. And by the time the government vehicle was able to move, Wells had circled the block and was a few car lengths behind it, doing this without its occupants noticing.

Wells quickly pulled his beat-up, old Ford alongside the black sedan and pushed the vehicle into a four foot deep ditch, then stopped his car, blocking the driver's door so the driver couldn't escape. The side of the ditch kept the passenger door closed which kept the passenger from escaping. Before the car's occupants could climb out of the windows, Detective Wells had pulled his gun out of its holster and had the two men dressed in black keep their hands in the air and their bodies inside the car.

While pointing his gun at the car's occupants, Detective Wells had them, one at a time, reach into their jacket pockets and retrieve their identification. The driver handed his identification to Wells first. Opening the wallet Wells saw that the man, Tim Wilkes was an agent for the FBI. He handed the identification back to the driver then had the passenger hand over his identification – which showed that his name was Dennis Boyd, also an agent with the FBI. Detective Wells then returned the identification to the agent but refused to let them go.

Agent Wilkes was the first to speak up, saying, "Detective Wells, now that you know our identities don't you think you should let us get out of our vehicle?"

Still pointing the gun at them, Wells replied, "Not before you explain to me how you know my name and why you two are always following my vehicle. And then I want to know why you killed my suspect, Mario Morrelli?"

"First of all, Detective Wells, it's our job to know your name. And as far as Mario Morrelli's concerned, we don't know what the hell you're talking about?" stuttered Agent Wilkes.

Wells didn't believe him and angrily told Wilkes, "I've got an eyewitness that put you at my suspect's hospital room just a few minutes before he died. I want to know why you were there and why the FBI killed him?" Wells snarled, threatening him with his gun if he didn't tell the truth.

"All right, we were there," Wilkes bellowed. "But we didn't kill him. When we went in to question him about his mob ties, he was laying in the hospital bed having some kind of fit. He was foaming at the mouth and blood was coming out of his ears so we just shut the door and left. We figured if we stayed…people would think we had something to do with his fit. So we hightailed it out of there."

"Then why are you following me?" Wells asked him, still pointing his weapon at him. "First it was Susan Pelk. But she ended up dead. She was on your team, wasn't she?"

Wilkes nodded, saying, "Yes, Susan Pelk was a government agent. That's one reason why we're following you. When you killed those two gunmen and one of them was found with your gun that was used in Pelk's murder, we figured you would lead us to the person that ordered her death. And eventually to Don Bruno Manzelli or Louie Santini." He went on to say, "We've been investigating organized crime for quite a while…and with all of these mutilated and tortured bodies that have been turning up, you were our trump card. But now it looks like our trump card's been played. And it looks like we've lost…unless you're willing to work for us just like Captain Lawson has been for the past few weeks. Will you work for us?"

Wells replied, "No thank you. I don't sell out my badge. If it were up to me, I'd arrest you for impersonating a law enforcement official. But then I'd just get in trouble for doing my job. That's why you G-men are called untouchable. You guys are never disciplined for overstepping your bounds. When one of you get in trouble…your superiors promote you. If I get in trouble, I'm either suspended, fired or arrested. So you two can go to hell! And the next time you interfere in my murder investigation, I will arrest you for obstruction of justice. Which I'm sure you guys know all about," snapped Detective Wells, as he kept his weapon pointed at the two agents the whole time. Seconds later, he holstered his weapon and jumped back into his beat-up vehicle then went on his way, leaving the two men dressed in black stuck in the ditch.

Detective Wells sped away, heading for Hollywood station. He felt elated that he had pulled one over on those over educated butt kissers. And patted himself on the back for a job well done. He figured it would be an hour or more before the two FBI agents would be able to catch up to him. And by that time he would be in his home kicking back on his couch drinking and reading the rest of his reports.

Twenty minutes after the incident with the agents, Wells was at his desk picking up more reports and visiting with Captain Lawson. He had a few choice words for his Captain.

Detective Wells knocked softly on Lawson's office door before entering the room.

"Yes, Detective Wells, what can I do for you so late in the day?" Captain Lawson asked.

Wells replied calmly, "I just had a talk with two FBI agents, Wilkes and Boyd. And I learned some interesting things from them."

"Such as?" Lawson asked.

Wells stared at his captain, giving him the evil eye, then replied, "Like...you were working for them when you told me you weren't. You knew who they were and why they were following me...but you never said a word to me. Captain, I trusted you. You told me the two bodies those agents took away from the autopsy room was without your knowledge. Now I learn that everything you told me was an out and out lie. What else are you holding back on, Captain? Who is your loyalty to? Your men that you work with...or somebody that doesn't give a damn about you or this department?"

Lawson's eyes buldged and his face turned beet red. "I don't have to answer that, Detective," Lawson snapped, angry with Wells' disdain. "I follow orders just like you. I do what I'm told...just like you. When I'm ordered to do something I follow those orders. Is that understood, Detective Wells?"

"Yes, sir, I understand. I understand that our thirty year friendship is finished," Wells retorted.

"Detective Wells, you just remember one thing. I was the one that got you your job back when you were suspended."

Wells replied, "You forget, Captain. You suspended me. You only got my suspension lifted because you needed me. You needed my experience and expertise. You figured that you could watch me while I investigated these murders. So you had Detective Lenda spy on me, telling you my every move, while the FBI followed me. I'll never trust you again as long as I live. Now if you'll excuse me, Captain Lawson, I need to get home and read my reports, then have a dozen drinks." With that said, he turned and stormed out of Lawson's office.

Walking away angry, Wells left Hollywood station and headed for his car. Getting behind the wheel, he looked around for the black sedan but it was nowhere in sight. He figured it was still in the ditch. He hoped so, anyway. He had to laugh at that.

After taking a few deep breaths, he started the car's engine, put it into gear and roared out of the parking lot, heading towards his abode.

All during the ride home, Wells repeatedly looked into his rearview mirror expecting to see the black sedan following him. But it wasn't to be. He hoped he had gotten rid of them once and for all.

When Wells arrived home, he parked his car in the driveway, then stepped out of the vehicle with briefcase in hand and ran up the front steps. He then inserted the door key into the lock and pushed the front door open.

Once inside his abode he went directly to the kitchen where he grabbed a new bottle of scotch and a shot glass and began pouring one drink after another down his throat. He didn't stop until he had guzzled eight large shots. That was the medicine he needed to shake the cobwebs out of his head before taking the goodies into his living room.

A few hours later, around ten that evening, Wells had finished the entire bottle of scotch while reading his reports. One of the reports he had picked up from his desk that afternoon was the autopsy of Mario Morrelli. It stated that he had died from poisoning. And that this particular poison had been banned more than twenty years ago and was only used by the military and CIA.

This particular poison was used basically for assassinations of world dignitaries and other enemies of the U.S. government. Wells couldn't believe what he was reading. He wondered how the poison got into his suspect's system. Then it dawned on him. It had to be those two men dressed in black – agents Wilkes and Boyd of the FBI.

As Wells thought more and more about the coincidence between the two agents and his suspect's death, he decided that he needed more answers on this subject. But his thoughts were suddenly interrupted by the ringing of his telephone. Answering it he was surprised and happy to hear Detective Rodriguez's voice on the other end.

Rodriguez had called Wells to tell him that the girl, Janie Jenson had been released just a few minutes before he made the phone call and was being followed by two of his best investigators. The surveillance had begun.

Wells was elated with the news. He also mentioned to Rodriguez about his run-in with the two men dressed in black. And told him to be wary of a black sedan and its occupants. Rodriguez didn't really understand the point Wells was trying to get across but he promised to heed his warning and advice.

When the phone call ended, Wells opened another new bottle of scotch and continued his drinking binge. He drank more than a liter before he passed out.

CHAPTER 10

Detective Wells was awakened from his drunken slumber by his noisy alarm clock. As he slowly sat up and wiped the cobwebs out of his eyes and cleared the phlegm from his throat, he felt a massive pounding in his head, as though someone was beating a bass drum inside it. But he was used to it by now. Lately it had become a daily occurrence. Trying to ignore the pain he lit a cigarette. And just at that moment he grimaced in agony when he saw his empty, wide-open briefcase and the reports that littered the living room floor. But not the videotape. It wasn't in his briefcase where it belonged. He was at a loss for words. He looked under the couch and all around the living room until it suddenly dawned on him. He had left the videotape in the machine at Gabrielle's Hoagie House. How stupid could he have been? He suddenly became sick to his stomach and completely forgot about his pounding head.

Wells was worried and somewhat anxious to find out if his stupidity and forgetfulness had caused him any harm. He turned on his thirteen-inch, ten-year-old, black and white television set to the local news station. What he saw made him want to throw up. There on the television screen his evidence, the videotape, was being shown to all that watched.

The station had no qualms about holding back. They showed one of the victim's being injected by two different needles: One in the arm and one in the jugular vein. Seconds later they showed the victim's skullcap being removed as the other victims stared in horror.

The station showed nearly two minutes of tape to their viewing audience. Wells couldn't stand it any longer and shut off the television in disgust and frustration. He regretted the fact that he would have to face Captain Lawson about this situation and wasn't happy about that at all.

Wells was able to shake off his terrible hangover after swallowing six aspirin, using scotch to wash them down. Straightening out the wrinkles in his suit clothes he then headed into the bathroom to wash his face, comb what little hair he had left and brush his teeth. He didn't have time to take a shower.

But before Wells could leave for work he had to have his daily fix of hot Colombian brew. That was his human gas – the energy – that he needed to face the day's unpredictable problems. Once he had finished the pot, he grabbed his briefcase full of reports and headed out the door to his car.

It took three tries to start the engine. But the old clunker did finally start. And just to be on the safe side, before backing out of the driveway he looked both ways so he wouldn't cause an accident – and to see if the black sedan was in the vicinity. He was relieved to see that it wasn't. But not for long.

It finally showed up a few car lengths behind Wells' vehicle within a mile of Hollywood station. Wells wanted to confront the occupants once again and put an end to this game of cat and mouse. But he figured he was already in enough trouble over the loss of the videotape and didn't want to start anymore.

Wells didn't need anything else for Captain Lawson to scold him about so he just ignored the vehicle and its occupants and proceeded to park his car. He watched in his rearview mirror as the black sedan parked a few rows behind his. But its occupants stayed inside the vehicle while Wells stepped out of his car and quickly walked into the station, hoping Captain Lawson wouldn't notice him.

As Wells was signing in at the front desk Sergeant Steiner warned him. "Detective Wells, watch out for Captain Lawson. He's in a rage this morning. He's been waiting for your arrival so be careful. I believe he wants to chew you out."

"So...that's nothing new," Wells replied, as he walked towards his desk.

But before Detective Wells could reach his desk, Captain Lawson stopped him in the hallway.

"Detective Wells, please come into my office. I have a little bone to pick with you," said Captain Lawson.

"I bet I know what you're going to say," Wells replied as he followed his captain into his office.

"I bet you don't," snarled Lawson as he shut his office door, returned to his chair and ordered Detective Wells to sit.

"Captain Lawson, before you say anything, I just want to say I'm sorry," Wells said as he took his seat.

"Sorry, Detective Wells, you don't know what that word means. You were plastered when you came into my office yesterday. But out of friendship I didn't say anything. I know how stress can take its toll. Then yesterday you told me our thirty-year friendship was over. I still overlooked it. But now this. Did you see the local news on the television this morning? Our department is the laughing stock of the state. Could you please tell me, Detective Wells, how the local television station got hold of your murder investigation evidence?"

Wells shrugged his shoulders and said, "I'm not sure, sir. But I will find out. It was my forgetfulness or stupidity. Whatever you want to call it. I left the videotape in the machine at the restaurant after playing it for the three out-of-town detectives. I don't know how I could have forgotten it...but I did. All I can say is that it will never happen again," he promised.

Lawson reminded him, saying, "Detective Wells, it seems I've been saving your ass a lot lately. I lifted your suspension when you let someone steal your weapon and use it to kill that woman. I look the other way at your constant drinking. Even this morning you look hungover and pale. But your my best homicide investigator and I need you sober and in control of all your faculties. Which you weren't in control of when you left the videotape for someone else to find and splatter all over the local television station."

"I said I was sorry," Wells said meekly, looking down at the floor.

"Sorry just doesn't get it, Detective Wells," Lawson told him. "If you're wondering why I'm chewing out your ass...it's because I had _my_ ass chewed out this morning."

Wells told him he was sorry to hear that.

Lawson went on to say that he had received a telephone call from the justice department earlier that morning concerning Wells' interference in the FBI's R.I.C.O. investigation on the southern California mob. "They said you assaulted two of their officers. Is that true, John?"

Wells nodded and sheepishly replied, "It's true. We had a slight run-in. But it was no big deal."

"No big deal! They said you forced them off the road and held them at gunpoint, then made them relinquish their wallets and identification. Is that true?" Lawson asked him.

Wells nodded, saying, "I just asked them for their identification and they obliged me. That was all there was to it, Captain."

"Detective Wells, I could lose my job over this," Lawson said angrily. "And believe me...if I lose my job, I won't go alone. I'll take you right along with me. Is that understood?" He gave Wells a dirty look.

Wells replied, "Yes, sir. Understood."

Lawson told him that, "The Justice department wants me to suspend you until further notice...and that's exactly what I should do. But with all these killings going on...I need my best investigator out there. You better try and stay off the sauce...and stay out of those agents' hair! I don't want anymore phone calls from the Justice department. And," he added, "Detective Lenda will be on disability for at least one month, so he won't be of any help to you. Let's see if we can't get these sadistic killers off the street before these killings get out of hand."

"I'll do my best, Captain," Wells replied. "If that's all...I have to go to County jail and interrogate one of the female suspects this morning with Detective Smith. So if it's all right with you I'll get my butt into gear."

"Fine. Just stay out of trouble," Captain Lawson told him, as Wells left his office.

Wells then walked directly to his desk and telephoned Detective Smith to coordinate the time of Katie Brown's interrogation. When that was settled, Smith mentioned to Wells that Janie Jenson was now visiting _his_ town and that he had _his_ surveillance team following her.

Smith also mentioned about seeing a minute or two of the videotape that they had watched the day before on the local television news program. But Wells refused to talk about that over the phone and promised Smith that he'd meet him within one hour at the L.A. County jail.

Wells grabbed his briefcase of reports and left Hollywood station for the County jail. As he departed he watched as the two government agents,

Wilkes and Boyd smoked cigarettes outside of their vehicle, then jumped into it as Detective Wells raced away from the parking lot. He kept an eye on his enemies by way of his rearview mirror as they followed close behind. Wells figured they hadn't gotten the message yet.

When Wells finally reached the L.A. County jail, Smith was near the entrance waiting for him. After parking his car, Wells then went to meet with the homicide detective. Just as the two detectives shook hands, Wells saw the black sedan slowly enter the parking lot.

"Detective Wells, I have some good news and some bad news," Smith told him.

"What news is that?" Wells asked, as they entered the County jail.

Smith replied, "Katie Brown's attorney's here. So we can have our interview with her."

"Is that the good news or the bad news?" Wells asked.

"That's the good news," Smith replied. "The bad news is that I had my rookie investigators following Janie Jenson."

"So?" Wells asked him.

"They lost her. She got away from them and they don't know where she went to."

"Have you told Rodriguez and Wilmont about this?" Wells asked him.

Smith nodded and said, "I telephoned them just before I left my station."

"Damn!" Wells replied under his breath.

Seconds later they had reached their destination. Once the two detectives had stored their weapons they were quickly escorted into the interview room where Katie Brown and her attorney, Mr. Davis were already sitting down and waiting.

"Good morning, Mr. Davis," said Smith as the attorney shook hands with the detectives. "We only have a few more questions to ask your client. It shouldn't take very long."

Wells began the questioning. "Miss Brown, I have a few questions concerning your boyfriend, Jarrett. We found out that his name wasn't Jarrett at all but rather Danny Jermaine. Did you know that?" he asked her as he placed photos of Katie's deceased boyfriend face down on the table in front of him.

"No. Everyone called him Jarrett," she said, then lit a cigarette, took a long drag and blew a big cloud of smoke into the two homicide detectives' faces.

"Well that's not his name," Wells replied, fanning the cloud of cigarette smoke away. "He's lied to you and your friends from the beginning. How do you feel about that?"

She shrugged her shoulders and replied, "It's no big deal. It's just a name. I still love him."

"Then you're in love with a dead man," said Wells, looking into her eyes for a reaction.

"What do you mean! Is Jarrett dead?" she asked as her face turned a pale white.

Wells nodded, telling her that, "Somebody tortured him to death."

"I don't believe you!" she snapped, putting out her cigarette and lighting another.

"Then believe this," said Wells, as he flipped over the photos and placed them on the table one at a time in front of her.

Katie Brown looked very closely at the photos. You could tell by her facial expressions that she knew the person in the photos.

"How did Jarrett die?" cried Katie Brown.

"Are you sure that the man in the photo with his brains exposed is your boyfriend?" Wells asked her.

She said she was. "When was he killed and where?" she asked him, taking a big drag of her cigarette and exhaling it into the detectives' faces again.

But before Wells would answer her questions he wanted to know if she knew who killed Jarret or wanted him killed?

"I wouldn't know," was her answer. "I just can't believe he's dead. Where was his body found?"

Wells told her that he was found in an abandoned building in the city of Hollywood.

"What day was he found?" she asked.

He told her that he died on a Tuesday night and was found the next day.

"I don't believe it," she said to no one in particular.

"What don't you believe, Miss Brown?" Wells asked.

She surprised Wells with her answer. She told him, "Jarrett wouldn't be in Hollywood on a Tuesday night. He only visited Hollywood on the weekends. During the week Jarrett would be near a beach...not in the city."

"Well...evidently he changed his plans," Wells interjected. "We found his mutilated body in Hollywood. Unless he's got a twin brother, you're boyfriend died on a Tuesday night in the city of Hollywood from being tortured to death...and I think you know who might have killed him. Do you know who killed your boyfriend, Miss Brown?"

She shook her head no and said, "He was friends with everybody. Why would someone want him dead?"

"That's what I want to know," Wells replied, looking deep into her eyes.

"I can't tell you if I don't know," she said, flicking the lit butt of her cigarette against the wall.

Wells thought for a few seconds then asked her, "Do you know if Jarrett had any brothers?"

She just shrugged her shoulders. "He never talked about any," she answered.

Wells asked her who she thought the person in the photo was if it wasn't Jarret?

She answered that she didn't know, adding,"I just know it's not Jarrett."

Wells shot back, "Two of your friends think it's Jarrett. Kathy and Janie think the person in the photos was Jarrett. Why don't you?"

"In my heart, I just feel Jarrett's not dead."

Brown's attorney suddenly interrupted the interrogation. "Detective Wells, this isn't getting us anywhere," Davis interjected. "Is there anything else you want to ask my client? If not, then I have another appointment to get to."

Wells and Smith looked at each other and just shrugged their shoulders. They had nothing more to ask the female suspect.

"Okay, Mr. Davis, that's it for now," Smith told him. "If we have anything else to ask your client, we'll get in touch with you."

Katie Brown was escorted back to her cell and the three men left the room and headed for the parking lot.

Standing next to Wells' car, Wells told Smith, "Well I have to get back to Hollywood and go over my reports. I have a lot of reading to catch up on." With that said he and Detective Smith shook hands then parted ways.

Detective Wells jumped behind the wheel of his car and headed for Hollywood station. Three miles from the station, he noticed the black sedan following a few car lengths behind his vehicle. But two miles before Detective Wells reached his destination the black sedan turned off onto another street.

After Wells parked his car and entered the station, he went to his desk and began reading reports. The reports that caught his eye were the ones that stated that many of the mutilated bodies and the table murder victims had been given the same type of poison that was used to kill Mario Morrelli in his hospital bed.

The U.S. government had banned this particular poison the same time that they banned assassinations. Only military personnel and the CIA had access to it. Detective Wells wondered what the hell was going on? Not only were these mutilated victims ground up into hamburger after their blood was drained from their bodies but they were also given a nasty poison that was banned and hadn't been used in over twenty years.

Just as Wells leaned back into his chair to think about his murder investigation he received a telephone call from Wilmont. He explained to Detective Wells that he had just arrived at another crime scene similar to the one shown on the videotape. He asked for Wells' assistance.

Wilmont also mentioned that he had asked Smith and Rodriguez for their assistance, to which they agreed and were on there way. Wells also agreed and promised Wilmont that he would be at the address within thirty minutes.

Detective Wells hung up the phone and left the building with his briefcase in hand. The minute he stepped outside he saw the black sedan parked nearby. Wells ignored their presence and jumped behind the wheel of his vehicle. A few minutes later he was heading for the city of Redondo Beach.

As soon as Wells left the parking lot, the black sedan followed his vehicle once again. This time Wells wasn't going to let them follow him.

He began to speed up and swerve in and out of traffic making other vehicles slam on their brakes and stop, until the traffic became so congested that the black sedan got snarled in it and couldn't move. While the black sedan was logjammed, Wells suddenly turned right on a red light. And by the time the traffic had cleared, Wells wasn't anywhere in sight.

Wells could relax and not worry about being followed for a while. He drove to the address that Wilmont had stated and parked his car without seeing the black sedan anywhere around. He noticed that Smith's Mercedes Benz was already there, but Rodriguez had not yet arrived.

The abandoned building was flooded with investigators and patrol officers. And the coroner's van was parked near the doorway. This building was only two blocks away from the last crime scene that Wells had visited in Redondo Beach.

As Wells neared the entranceway of the crime scene, Smith and Wilmont came through the door and greeted him with open arms. Or so he thought. But actually, the two homicide detectives were just waving away the distasteful stench from the crime scene.

"It's good to see you, Detective Wells," said Wilmont, lighting Detective Smith's cigarette and then his own. "We had to get out of that place for a minute to grab a breath of fresh air and a smoke. Now I know what you went through when you discovered your table murders. I have the same thing here."

"What have you got in there, Paul?" asked Wells.

"I'll show you in a minute," Wilmont replied. "Let me catch my breath and have a cigarette first. I've been in that smelly building for nearly an hour now and couldn't take another minute of it. I really needed some fresh air."

"Do you have your own table murders or is it more torsos?" Wells asked Wilmont.

"No, it's not torsos," Wilmont replied, puffing away on his cigarette. "It's another table murder. There's two bodies in there with the top of their heads cut off just like in the videotape that you showed us."

Wells asked him if the victims' blood was extracted from their bodies?

Wilmont nodded. "And their brains were half-gone as though someone ate them like cantaloupes. It's really a horrible sight." He added, "John, since I've been involved with you, I've seen more mutilated dead bodies in two weeks than in my twenty-five years on the job as a homicide detective."

"Boy, aren't you lucky," Wells said sarcastically.

The two detectives finished their cigarettes and then escorted Wells into the abandoned building to view the crime scene.

As the three Detectives entered the building, Wells put on a pair of rubber gloves. But there was so much garbage and human waste on the floor that it would be almost impossible to contaminate this crime scene.

Just like the two table murders he had investigated in Hollywood,

Wells saw two male victims strapped and tied to chairs with the tops of their heads removed and sitting on the table in front of them. Their brains were exposed and they each had a big welt on their jugular vein, where a large needle had been inserted, used to bleed the victims dry, which was the reason there were very few bloodstains on or near the bodies.

The victims had their hands, feet, chest and chins tied to the chairs with rope and duct tape and their mouths were taped shut. And the victims' brain matter had been scooped out just like the other victims found in this manner.

As Wells looked over the crime scene, the photographer was busy taking his photos.

"Detective Wilmont, was there any identification on the victims' bodies?" Wells asked.

"No, we haven't found any," was his reply.

"Was there a videotape found?" asked Wells.

"Not yet," Wilmont answered. "My investigators are still looking for evidence. I've also got my officers out canvassing the neighborhood to see if there are any eyewitnesses that might have seen somebody leaving the crime scene."

"This is getting to me," Wells quipped, wiping the sweat off his brow. "We have got to catch these sadistic killers. Someone is trying to extract information from these victims and I'd like to know why."

"Let's go outside and talk. I can't handle this putrid smell," Wilmont told the detectives.

"I second the motion," said Smith.

The three experienced homicide detectives walked outside to smoke a cigarette.

"Paul, when will you have the fingerprint analysis reports on the victims?" Wells asked him.

"Within a few hours," he answered. "When my forensic investigators are finished with the crime scene they'll run the victims' fingerprints through the data base when they return to the lab."

Just then the coroner came outside and spoke with Wilmont. He asked for permission to remove the bodies and Wilmont gave it. While the detectives smoked their cigarettes and conversed about the murder investigation, the coroner removed the bodies and began loading them into the coroner's van.

A black sedan suddenly came up alongside the van and a man dressed in black and wearing a fedora jumped out of the passenger's side and then showed the coroner his badge and identification. Then with the coroner's permission the man opened each body bag.

Then the man ordered his partner out of the car and the two men dressed in black began loading the two bodies into the back seat of their vehicle, laying one body on top of the other. By the time Wilmont, Wells and Smith had noticed what was happening, the black sedan was driving away with the victims' bodies.

The three detectives gave chase on foot, but it was too late. The black sedan had roared away from the crime scene with the dead bodies. When the coroner was asked about the identification of the two men and why they took away the bodies, the coroner was in utter shock. No reason was given to the coroner other than to telephone the Justice department if he wanted any information.

The three detectives were in an utter rage. They couldn't believe the arrogance of the government agents and the Justice department. They abused their powers at every level and nobody could stop them. The government could interfere in their murder investigation and not give them a reason for doing it. Government officials only had to show their badge and identification and city officials had to stand aside. They had no rights when the government was involved.

But just as Detective Wilmont was about to call the Justice department on his cell phone to find out why the bodies were taken away, three loud bangs rang out just a few doors down the block from them. They figured someone had discharged their weapon and ran to the sound of the gunfire, which led them to another abandoned and condemned building. It was a big garage that had been used at one time to repair large trucks.

When the detectives entered the building they saw an officer standing over a man and a young woman who were laying on the dirty cement floor. The man had been shot and wounded and the young woman's left side of her face had been crushed and beaten.

"What the hell happened here, officer?" asked Wilmont, as the detectives reached the two bodies and began checking for a pulse.

"This girl is dead," Wells interjected. "I can't really tell because her face is so beat up, but she looks like Janie Jenson. Let's get her fingerprints analyzed just to be sure."

"How did she die? Do you know, officer?" asked Wilmont.

He told the three detectives that while he was out canvassing the area for an eyewitness to Wilmont's murders, he saw the guy pistol whipping the young girl. "He had just hit her with the butt of his gun and she fell to the floor," he told them. "That's when I yelled for him to drop his weapon. When he didn't, I fired twice and he fired once. He missed...I didn't."

"What's your name son?" Wilmont asked the young officer.

"I'm Officer Mark Landers," he told Wilmont. "I was assigned to your murder investigation."

"Good work, Landers," Wilmont replied.

Checking the wounded man's pulse, Smith exclaimed, "This guy's unconscious but at least he's still breathing. If we get an ambulance here in time...maybe we'll be able to get some answers out of him. When he comes to, that is." He then began searching the man's body for his wallet and identification.

"If your coroner's still here, he could be of some help," said Detective Wells as he searched for the girl's identification. But she had none.

147

Just then the Redondo Beach coroner came on the scene.

"Speak of the devil. It's Dr. Wellman. We were just talking about you, Doc," said Detective Wilmont as Smith handed him the wounded man's wallet.

"When I heard the shots, I figured someone would need my help...so I retrieved my medical bag and came right over," said Dr. Wellman, as he bent over to check the bodies of the two victims.

"Work on the guy, Doc. The girl's dead," said Wells, as Dr. Wellman knelt down between the two victims.

"How bad is he, Doc?" asked Wilmont, as he placed the wounded man's wallet into his jacket pocket.

"He's been shot twice in the upper left shoulder. He's lost quite a bit of blood...but he should pull through. Unless he has a bad heart," replied Dr. Wellman.

As Dr. Wellman began treating the man's wounds to stop the bleeding, the ambulance arrived. The paramedics took control of the situation and bandaged the unconscious victim's shoulder and started an I.V. A few minutes later they placed the wounded man on a stretcher and the dead girl into a body bag then placed both into the ambulance before speeding away towards Redondo Beach Hospital.

The detectives ran and jumped into Detective Smith's Mercedes Benz and followed the ambulance to the hospital. They needed to question the wounded victim as soon as possible. They wanted to find out what information he was trying to get out of this young girl and why he needed it badly enough to kill her for it. These and many other questions needed to be answered.

While riding to the hospital, Wells turned and looked to see if the black sedan was following them. He was surprised to find that it wasn't. But as Smith's vehicle followed the ambulance to the emergency room entrance, Wells noticed a black sedan already parked in a far corner of the hospital parking lot. After parking their vehicle behind the ambulance, Wells, along with Smith and Wilmont jumped out of the car and ran into the hospital, following the stretcher that carried the wounded male suspect.

An emergency room doctor came out of another room and checked the suspect to see if the wounded man was in any immediate danger. Just at that moment the man came out of unconsciousness and began fighting with his handcuffs – each of his wrists were handcuffed to the rails of the stretcher. The emergency room doctor rushed the wounded suspect into another room, where it was off limits to anyone other than hospital staff, so the detectives had to remain in the hallway.

Wells had a gut feeling that something was amiss and decided to watch the doctor's actions through a little square glass in the door. He thought the doctor had taken the suspect away to operate on him but that wasn't the case. The doctor pushed the wounded man's stretcher to one side and hid the patient with wrap around curtains.

The doctor left the area, but Wells continued to sneak a peak every so often so he could keep an eye on the male suspect.

"Hey, Paul, do you have the suspect's wallet?" asked Wells.

"Yes, as a matter of fact...I do," he said, patting his jacket pocket. "I never got a chance to look at his identification. When Willard gave it to me I shoved it into my jacket pocket. Here it is." He pulled out the suspect's wallet and checked the driver's license.

"You know, I've seen this guy before but I just can't put my finger on it. What's his name? I'll bet you it's Italian," said Wells.

"You guessed right," Wilmont said, looking at the driver's license. "The name on his driver's license is Salvatore Peter Vanuchi. If that's not Italian, I don't know what is."

"Now all we have to do is find out if he's a Manzelli or Santini soldier. Do any of you experienced detectives want to take a guess?" asked Wells.

Just then Wells took a peak into the little door window to check on his suspect and suddenly saw two men dressed in black wearing fedoras. It looked like the two agents that he had a run in with not too long ago – Agents Wilkes and Boyd. He didn't think anything of it until he saw Wilkes pull back the curtain while Boyd walked over and stood near the suspect.

Detective Wells was angry. He didn't want the FBI agents to question the suspect before he did. And just as he reached to open the emergency room door, Wells saw Agent Boyd reach out with his left hand and cover the mouth of the suspect as Agent Wilkes pulled out a syringe from his jacket pocket. Wells wasted no time and ran into the room with his gun drawn. By the time Wilmont and Smith knew what was happening, Wells was already in the room.

"Stop or I'll shoot," Wells yelled as FBI Agent Wilkes tried desperately to inject the suspect with his syringe.

But when Agent Boyd pulled out his weapon and pointed it at Wells, Wells had no other recourse but to fire his weapon, hitting the agent directly in the sternum area. Detective Wells stood in shock for a second as Agent Boyd fell against the wall and then to the hospital floor. As Agent Boyd was falling to the floor, Agent Wilkes drew his weapon and shot at Wells. But as he did, Wilmont fired his weapon at the man in black at the same time Agent Wilkes fired his.

Agent Wilkes spun around after being hit in the chest by Wilmont's bullet and when Smith saw Wilmont go down, he fired his weapon which also hit Agent Wilkes in the chest. When the smoke had cleared, three law enforcement officers lay on the hospital floor bleeding from gunshot wounds: Two government agents and Wilmont. He had been hit by Agent Wilkes's bullet. The same bullet that had been aimed at Wells' body.

Once the gunfire subsided, the hospital staff rushed into the room to check the wounded and dead. Detective Wilmont and Agents Wilkes and Boyd lay on the floor, gasping for breath, dying. Detective Wells quickly picked up the syringe and checked out Agent Boyd. He was found to be alive and conscious. Wells wanted answers from him and wanted them fast.

"What the hell are you guys doing!" Wells screamed. "Why did you want to kill Vanuchi? Now I know you killed Morrelli." Holding up the syringe full of suspected poison, he exclaimed, "I bet you the stuff that's in this syringe is the same stuff that killed Morrelli and many others."

"Get me a doctor or I'm gonna bleed to death," whined Agent Boyd, as his blood began pooling around him.

"You answer my questions first," Wells snarled. "Then you'll get the doctor. Now why were you here?"

Coughing up blood as he spoke, he told Wells that they wanted to find out the whereabouts of their white van.

"What white van!" Wells snarled.

But before Agent Boyd could say another word, Agent Wilkes aimed his weapon and fired a bullet into his partner, killing him. Seconds later, Wilkes had succumbed to his wounds. Now both FBI agents lay dead.

Wells searched Agent Boyd's pockets hoping to find answers and found three different pieces of identification. One was for the Treasury department. One, for the FBI and the third was for the CIA.

Detective Wells also checked the pockets of Agent Wilkes for his identification and found the same three pieces of identification. Detective Wells figured, to be in possession of a syringe full of that particular poison – if it was that poison – they had to have been working for the CIA. But why? And why were they looking for a white van?

While Smith watched as the emergency room doctor tried to resuscitate Wilmont, Wells stood up and looked over the entire situation. He wondered how this shooting could have happened in a hospital emergency room.

While Wells pondered his thoughts, he saw two men dressed in black coming straight towards him. Wells pointed his gun at them, but was relieved when they passed by and went directly to the two dead agents' bodies.

When one of the men started checking the pockets of the dead agents, Wells interrupted them.

"Are you guys looking for these?" Wells asked, holding up six pieces of identification that belonged to the two dead agents.

"We'll take those," snapped one of the men dressed in black.

"Who are you guys?" asked Wells.

Showing Wells his badge and identification, he said, "I'm Agent Demler and this is my partner, Agent Bennett. We work for the CIA."

"And if I believe that you're CIA agents, what do you want with Wilkes and Boyd?" Wells asked him.

"They worked for the agency," said Demler.

"Why did they want to kill Vanuchi?" asked Wells, as he showed the dead agents' identification to Agent Demler and held up the syringe full of suspected poison.

"I'm sorry, what's your name?" Demler asked.

"I'm Detective John Wells from Hollywood Homicide division."

"Detective Wells, if you'll step over here, we'll tell you something that you can't repeat to anyone. If you give me your word that you will honor my request, I'll tell you why we are here and how Wilkes and Boyd were involved. Do we have a deal?"

Wells nodded. And the three men stepped to a far corner of the room while Smith stayed with Wilmont's body.

"Detective Wells, what I'm about to tell you goes no farther than this room. Is that understood?" asked Agent Demler.

Wells nodded.

Demler explained to Wells that two overseas cells in the agency have to find ways to run their covert operations when the U.S. government refuses to sanction them or cuts their budget. "But these two cells have gone too far by funding their operations using illegal means. We have people in Russia that are helping former KGB high-ranking officials sell and smuggle their illegal contraband into terrorist countries," said Agent Demler.

"What kind of illegal contraband are we talking about?" asked Wells.

Demler replied, "In this particular case, we're talking about plutonium, nuclear technology and nuclear weapons."

But Wells was confused and asked, "Why would they want to help Russia sell their nuclear weapons to terrorist countries. I thought the CIA was trying to stop that kind of stuff from happening."

"We do," Demler retorted. "But one cell doesn't want the cold war to end. If it ends…then they'll be out of a job…and they don't want that to happen."

But that was only the answer for one cell. Wells wanted to find out about the other. "Agent Demler, you said two cells. Now tell me about the other cell. How do they fund their covert operations? Do they smuggle illegal contraband, too?" he asked.

"That's right," Demler replied. "We found out that this particular cell has been smuggling narcotics into the United States for a long time now…and it's delivered to the southern California mob to distribute across the country. We believe the narcotics were hidden in the floor and walls of a white van that was to be delivered sometime last week."

"What mob family were the drugs going to?" asked Wells.

Demler paused for a few long seconds, then said, "We believe the drugs were to be delivered to the Manzelli crime family. But the agent in charge turned the tables on them and sold the van to the Santini family…and got twice as much money as planned. But then the agent did something stupid and parked the van one night in Hollywood and ended up not only losing the van…but his life as well. Now we're searching for the van…and thought that you might lead us to it through your murder investigations."

Wells shook his head in disgust. "Where do Wilkes and Boyd fit in to the scheme of things?" Wells asked.

Demler told him that the agency wasn't sure if they were part of the cell. "Evidently, they were. But once we were sure that Wilkes and Boyd were involved, we would have put a surveillance team on them until they led us to their boss," said Agent Delmer.

"They can't help you now," Wells interjected.

Just then the doctor came over to check the two agents' bodies. But they were both dead.

Demler told the doctor to get the bodies ready for transfer. Adding, "We'll be taking them with us when we leave here." Looking at Wells, he said, "Now if you don't mind, Detective Wells, I'll take the agents' identification. And that syringe." Demler held out his right hand and Wells handed him the six pieces of identification. But not the syringe.

Wells said, "Before I give you the syringe, I need to take a sample from it for evidence." He then stuffed a small piece of cotton into a small plastic evidence bag and sprayed the cotton with a few drops of the syringe's contents. "There. Now you can have it," he told Demler as he handed him the syringe.

"Thank you, Wells. You have been more than cooperative. Captain Lawson will hear about your good work," Demler told him.

Wells was still confused and needed some answers to a few questions and asked Demler, "If the solution in the syringe turns out to be the banned poison that has turned up in the mutilated torsos...why would Wilkes and Boyd use it to kill soldiers of the Manzelli crime family?"

Demler explained to Wells that they weren't trying to kill them but probably trying to extract information from them about the van. "They probably thought, like us, that the Manzelli crime family had found the van...and Santini wanted it back. It's as simple as that."

"Well I hope so," Wells retorted. "But I still have murders that haven't been solved yet. I have to convince Captain Lawson that your two agents were doing all of these killings. But why would they grind the bodies up into hamburger?"

Demler shrugged his shoulders and said, "Maybe someone from the Santini crime family was helping Wilkes and Boyd get rid of the evidence. But whoever it was, you seem to have some more work to do."

"You're absolutely right about that," said Wells.

"Well, sir...I think Agent Bennett and myself are finished here."

Wells asked him for a telephone number where he could be reached...if needed.

Demler told Wells to ask Captain Lawson. "He'll be able to help you."

"I'm sure you'll be hearing from me," said Wells.

Turning to the doctor, Demler said, "Now, Doc...if you'd be so kind as to have the two agents' bodies taken out to our vehicle I would be indebted to this hospital."

A minute later the doctor had the bodies removed from the hospital and placed into Agent Demler's vehicle.

Agents Demler and Bennett had disappeared with the agents' dead bodies, while Smith and Wells stayed behind to talk with their male suspect. Somehow the mobster had survived the ordeal but was still too weak to speak.

Wells remembered the suspect's wallet and identification was still in Wilmont's jacket pocket and quickly walked over to the dead detective's body before the doctor had placed it into a body bag, and retrieved the wallet. Searching through it he found the suspect's driver's license and other pieces of identification that didn't jive with his driver's license. The other pieces of identification showed the suspect's name not to be Salvatore Peter Vanuchi but one that Detective Wells had heard before, Tony Manzelli. Salvator Peter Vanuchi was just an alias. Tony Manzelli was the brother of reputed mob boss, Don Bruno Manzelli and had been reported missing for the last week or so.

Once Detective Wilmont had been bagged and taken away, the doctor began treating Tony Manzelli for pre-operative surgery to remove the bullets in his left shoulder.

"Doc, when will I be able to question my murder suspect?" asked Wells.

"After his surgery," was the doctor's reply.

"When will that be?" Wells asked anxiously.

Wells was told that he should be able to speak with his suspect, if everything went as expected, later that evening or the following day.

Wells didn't like the doctor's answer and said, "If I have to wait that long, Doc, I'm going to have an armed guard protect and watch this man until we can get him into our jail cell. Is that understood, Doctor?"

The doctor didn't like the tone in Wells' voice and snapped, "Just stay out of the hospital staff's way. We have work to do just as you do...and I'm sure you don't like to be interfered with, do you?"

"Don't worry, Doc. Nobody will get in your way. We just need to watch over our prominent murder suspect," said Wells, as he rechecked his suspect's handcuffs to make sure he couldn't escape.

Detective Wells had hospital security guard his suspect. No one would be allowed to question or speak with the wounded mobster other than the hospital staff that was treating him. The doctor was ordered to contact Wells by telephone if there was any change in the suspect's condition or any other problems that might arise.

Detective Smith was sitting out in the hallway still shocked over the gunfight and death of his brother homicide detective from Redondo Beach. Wells explained the situation to him about their suspect but didn't mention anything about the talk he had with the CIA agents. He would tell Smith about the conversation he had with them at a later time. Right now Wells wanted to take Detective Smith to Gabrielle's Hoagie House for a few drinks to settle their nerves.

Smith agreed to visit the restaurant with Wells for a few stiff drinks – which he needed badly. Anyway, the two detectives had a few hours to kill before they would check on their male suspect again.

Just as Detectives Wells and Smith walked out of the hospital, officers from the Redondo Beach police department began swarming the hospital grounds.

Wells told the senior officer what had transpired and that the suspect, Tony Manzelli, was under guard in the emergency room. He told the homicide detective, Tom Elder, that he and Detective Smith would return to the hospital once the suspect was out of surgery. He promised to answer any questions at that time because he and Smith were leaving the hospital to get a drink.

Detective Elder at first refused to let the two detectives depart without first answering some questions. But then, after giving it more thought, allowed them to do as they pleased as long as they promised to return later that evening. It was agreed upon between the three detectives that they would meet to question the suspect at seven that evening. That would give Wells and Smith more than four hours to calm their nerves.

With that said, Wells and Smith walked out of the hospital and drove away in Smith's Mercedes Benz. Detective Wells quickly looked around the parking lot and saw the black sedan still parked. He figured that was the vehicle Agents Wilkes and Boyd had used. He knew they wouldn't be following him any longer.

CHAPTER 11

As the two homicide detectives headed for Gabrielle's Hoagie House to relax and calm their frail nerves, Wells turned and looked to see if the black sedan was following the Mercedes Benz, but to his surprise it wasn't. Nonetheless, he checked his rearview mirror every few minutes waiting for it to appear.

During the entire drive, the two homicide detectives remained silent. But both were eager to get a drink under their belt. It had been a rather exciting and unfortunate day for the two experienced homicide detectives. Wells wanted to tell Smith about the conversation he had at the hospital with the two CIA agents and figured that after Smith had a few stiff drinks in his system, he would be in a better frame of mind to listen to his story of why all these people were being mutilated, tortured and killed.

Fifteen minutes after leaving the hospital they were sitting in the restaurant at Wells' favorite table in the smoking section. And one minute after they were seated, they were drinking their first drinks. Two minutes after that, they ordered and drank their second and third drinks. By the time their fourth drinks had arrived, Wells decided the time was right to let Smith know what was going on and why these bodies were showing up in their cities.

"Willard, what I say to you now can't leave this room," Wells told him after lighting a cigarette. "This conversation is for your ears only. Is that understood?"

"If you say so. Why all the mystery?" he asked.

Wells asked him if he had noticed the two men dressed in black that he was talking with at the hospital?

Smith replied, "John, once the shooting started I wasn't really aware of anything." He told Wells that was the very first time in his twenty-five year career in law enforcement that he had ever pulled his gun out of its holster to fire at a human target. Adding, "That was also the first time that I ever had someone shooting bullets at me...and I really didn't like it. Now that I think about it, considering how close I came to dying, I don't like my profession. I didn't join the force to get into gunfights and get shot at. I think I need another drink." He then ordered his sixth drink within a ten-minute period.

"Don't feel so bad, Willard. I never fired my weapon at another person in more than thirty years. Now, within the last couple of days I have fired it and killed or wounded five people. I don't have any bad feelings about it, though. At least the people I killed or wounded were either gangsters or dirty CIA agents. So I don't feel so bad at all," said Wells, toasting his drink high into the air before guzzling it down.

The drinks continued to come for the next four hours, until it was time

155

to return to Redondo Beach hospital to talk with Elder and the wounded mobster. If he was still alive that is. However, Wells would have heard something if the suspect had turned for the worse or died. He was sure of that.

"Who were those two men that we killed in the hospital? Were they mobsters?" Smith asked Wells.

Wells shook his head no, telling him, "That's what I wanted to talk with you about. The two men shot were government agents that worked for the CIA. But they were dirty."

"Dirty? What do you mean?" Smith asked.

Wells replied, "Did you see the two men dressed in black that were speaking with me after the shooting?"

"Like I told you before, John, I don't remember too much about that entire episode...and I don't think I want to remember it," said a drunken Smith.

Wells told him that the two men he spoke with were also CIA agents. "They told me a story that's hard to believe...but it makes sense. They explained to me that the two men we killed at the hospital were also agents with the CIA and had been stationed overseas. In order for the agents to run their covert and sometimes illegal operations, they had to resort to smuggling illegal contraband to the United States and other destinations in order to fund the operations that our government wouldn't. If the Congress even knew about the CIA's covert operations, many of the agents would be sitting in prison for life. But with no one to prosecute them, they can sometimes get away with murder. Just like Agents Wilkes and Boyd did. It seems they were the people who mutilated and killed all of the Manzelli soldiers," Wells told him, as he finished his sixth drink and ordered another double scotch on the rocks.

"Why would those two agents kill these people?" asked Smith.

Wells told him that they were looking for a white van that was supposed to be filled with lots of narcotics. "It was explained to me" Wells went on to say, "that there are two cells within the CIA that are smuggling illegal contraband to fund their illegal operations. One cell smuggles nuclear technology and nuclear weapons to terrorist countries, while the other cell smuggles narcotics. I never asked how much drugs were in the van...but we should be able to get that information from Tony Manzelli. That's the name of our suspect. He's the brother of crime boss Don Bruno Manzelli."

"But why would those two agents kill and mutilate all of these mobsters?"

Wells explained that the agents that brought the van into the United States had sold it to the Manzelli crime family first for distribution across the United States through their drug network. "But then," he added, "the agents decided to sell it to the Santini crime family instead...and for twice the money. Unfortunately one of them made a stupid mistake."

"Why? What did he do?" asked Smith.

Wells told him that the agent and a Santini soldier drove the van to Hollywood to find some women to party. "But the van was stolen. So they went looking for it...and ended up dead. And when two other agents from the same cell found out about the van being stolen they went looking for it...but so did the Manzelli and Santini soldiers. And when they all crossed paths...some of them ended up dead, too."

"Yeah, I know...they died from being ground up into hamburger," Smith replied jokingly.

"From my autopsy reports," Wells interjected, "most of the victims died from a poison that was banned more than twenty years ago and had only been used by the military and CIA for the purpose of assassinations. But when the victims died their blood was drained and they were ground up into hamburger to get rid of the evidence."

"So these victims were actually assassinated?"

"Not really," Wells replied. "The agent I spoke with today said that the poison was probably used to extract information from the victims about the whereabouts of the white van."

"Then this wasn't a mob war like we thought it was, was it?" Smith asked.

"I beg to differ," Wells retorted. "It is a mob war. And the CIA is right in the middle of it. The only question I have is...are the two agents that I spoke with at the hospital also involved in the smuggling...or are they trying to put an end to it? Let's see what our suspect has to say. In fact, we should be getting to the hospital now. We promised to be there by seven o'clock to talk with Elder. And it's nearly seven now. Which means that we have five minutes to make a thirty-minute drive. Are you able to drive without causing any accidents?" he asked Smith.

"I think I can handle it," Smith replied.

Wells paid the bill and the two detectives headed out the door to Smith's Mercedes Benz. As Wells stepped outside onto the steps of the restaurant he viewed the parking lot, expecting to see a black sedan parked nearby. But to his amazement, he didn't see one. He was relieved to know that he had lost his black shadow.

The detectives jumped into Smith's car and headed for the hospital to question the suspect and to answer Elder's questions.

"Willard, let me answer any questions that Detective Elder might ask of us. Is that okay with you?" Wells asked him.

"That's fine with me. I don't know that much about what happened, anyway," said a tipsy Smith.

Smith had no trouble with his driving. However, Wells couldn't shake the feeling that someone was still following him. A few miles from the hospital he thought he had seen a black sedan following behind the Mercedes but he couldn't be certain. The car was much too far away and Wells was a little too tipsy himself to be sure. So he put the thought to the back of his mind and watched as Smith turned his vehicle into the Redondo Beach hospital parking lot.

But just as the two detectives stumbled out of the vehicle and staggered towards the hospital, Wells thought he saw a black sedan slowly drive past, but it didn't enter the hospital parking lot. At that particular moment though, he wasn't seeing very clearly due to extreme intoxication.

Wells and Smith slowly passed through the electronic door and entered the hospital emergency room. Detective Elder was patiently awaiting their arrival and escorted them to the suspect's well-guarded room. While walking to the room, Elder talked to the detectives about the girl that Tony Manzelli was suspected of killing. He told them that the fingerprint analysis report stated the girl's name was Belinda Bannister, who was nearly nineteen years of age, a runaway and part of Jarrett's gang of street urchins. She was also a pickpocket and thief, which was the main reason the mob was after her.

When the three detectives finally reached the suspect's room, Tony Manzelli had been out of surgery for more than two hours and was awake and eating a light dinner.

Elder introduced himself and the two detectives to the mobster. "Tony Manzelli, I'm Detective Elder from Redondo Beach homicide. This is Detective Wells from Hollywood division and this gentleman is Detective Smith from Santa Monica homicide. Have you been read your rights?" he asked the mobster.

"How the hell do I know!" he snapped. "I've been in and out of consciousness since I was shot. I can't remember. But I know my rights. You guys have read them to me often enough."

"I'll bet your family will be happy to know that you're alive," said Wells.

"That's enough of that, Wells," cautioned Elder. "Let's do this by the book. Mr. Manzelli, you're being held for the murder of that young girl that we found you with in that abandoned garage. You could face the death penalty...so you don't have to talk with us if you don't want to. But if you do...we could probably save you from dying. And maybe you'll be able to get back out on the street one day."

"Hell, I'd be a dead man," he admitted. "If I talk to you...you'll have to give me protection. Maybe even put me into the witness protection program."

"Witness protection!" quipped Wells. "Are you kidding! You'll have all the protection you'll need. You'll be sitting all alone in a cell twenty-three hours a day. You can't get more protected than that."

"What can you tell us that would be worth your going into the witness protection program?" Elder asked him. "What information do you have that we would want? We already have you for murder."

"Why did you kill that young girl! Did you know her?" Wells asked as he interrupted Elder's questioning.

"It was an accident!" Manzelli exclaimed. "I didn't mean to kill her. She had something that I wanted."

"What could that young girl have that you had to kill her for it?" asked Wells.

"Easy, Detective Wells, he'll answer the question," Elder reminded him.

"Who was this girl? What did she have of yours?" asked Wells.

After a long pause, Manzelli replied, "She stole a van from a friend of mine and I was trying to get it back."

"Was it a white van that was stolen from Hollywood Boulevard?" asked Wells.

"It could be? But the girl's death was an accident. Honest," whined Tony Manzelli.

Elder jumped back into the interrogation and said, "You were going to tell us why we should place you into the witness protection program. Why should you deserve that?"

"Because I can tell you about the drugs that the CIA brings into this country," Manzelli replied.

"Be real!" Elder snapped. "Are you trying to tell us that the CIA is involved in smuggling narcotics into this country? I thought you guys did that."

He told them that the CIA wouldn't allow them to smuggle narcotics into the country.

"And why is that?" asked Elder.

Wells knew, but he promised the CIA that he wouldn't say anything. So he had to sit back and listen to what the mobster had to say. Smith remained silent throughout the entire interrogation.

"That would cut into their profits," Manzelli retorted.

Elder asked him if the CIA was the only government agency involved in the smuggling of illegal narcotics?

He told Elder that the CIA was supported and helped by the U.S. military.

"Wait a minute! Are you saying the U.S. military and the CIA smuggle large quantities of illegal narcotics into this country?" asked Elder.

"That's right. They've been doing it since 1942 when the U.S. Navy became involved with Lucky Luciano."

"And why did the U.S. Navy become involved with him?" Elder asked him.

Manzelli remained silent for about thirty seconds and then replied, "The Navy promised to get Luciano released from prison if he helped the U.S. military in their fight against the Germans when they invaded Sicily. So using his Mafia connections and with the help of the Italian resistance, Luciano kept his part of the agreement. But after he was released from prison he was deported to Italy. Then after the war, the CIA hired Lucky Luciano and his crime family for their covert operations. That's how the mob and the CIA became partners in crime. And since then...their relationship has evolved into a worldwide operation."

"What do you mean by worldwide?" asked Elder.

He told him that the CIA and the U.S. military are now involved with the Pakistani and Thai militaries. "That's how the third world country leaders stay in power," he added.

"How's that?" asked Elder.

He explained how the leaders of the countries allowed their military elite to be involved in the illegal narcotic trade with other military establishments. Adding, "When their military is paid well, they won't bring about a coup and make sure their leader stays in power."

"Do you expect us to believe this garbage?" Elder asked him.

"How do you think the cocaine cartels got their information for flying planeloads of drugs into this country?" he retorted.

"I give up. How?" asked Elder.

Manzelli explained that it started back in the early eighties when Ronald Reagan was president. "One of his military officers, an advisor that worked for the National Security Agency and the Contras, gave the cocaine cartels the U.S. military and Coast Guard flight plans of their drug intervention program. That way, the cartel's planes could bypass the US's security blanket. How else do you think they could bring in twenty tons of coke at a time into our country? Think about it!"

"I don't believe what I'm hearing," snapped Elder.

Manzelli went on to say, "Hell, the U.S. government stops bad fruit, Cuban cigars, bad meat, counterfeit clothes and any drugs that aren't under military protection. Why? Because many of the generals in our military are either selling military weapons illegally or smuggling drugs with the CIA. How else do you think these generals come out of the service as millionaires? It's not from their monthly salary. Why do you think the Pentagon's accounting is always screwed up? So they can steal their budget blind. That's why!"

"If this is true, what kind of evidence can you give us that proves what you are saying is true?" asked Elder.

He replied, "I can give you names of more than a dozen elite military and CIA officers. I can also give you the dates when these leaders of our government brought the drugs into this country."

Elder asked him how they get the narcotics into the U.S.?

He said that they bring it in using vans and trucks. "They usually hide the narcotics in the sides and floor of an Econoline type van and then bring it in a military cargo plane with a general or CIA agent driving it off the military base two minutes after the plane lands. Then it's given to my family to distribute and sell across the country. But this time after we paid for the load, the CIA reneged and sold it to the Santini family. By the time we caught up with them, the drugs had been stolen." He added, "I'm lucky to still be alive. The information I know can send a lot of big boys away for a long time. That's why I need to be in the witness protection program. Or my life isn't worth two cents."

"Don't worry, Tony, you'll be safe here," Elder promised. "The best law enforcement officers that we have are guarding this room. And as soon as I leave here I'll speak with our district attorney and the Justice department about getting you in the witness protection program. I'm sure, if what you told us is true, we'll be able to accommodate you."

"The drugs were hidden in that white van, weren't they, Tony?" Wells asked.

He nodded. Adding, "That's why I was questioning Belinda. I wanted to know what she did with the van. But she never told me."

"That's because you killed her before she could tell you!" snapped Wells.

"That's enough of that, Wells," cautioned Elder. "Tony, let's talk about all of the mobsters from your crime family that have been found mutilated and dead. What do you know about them?"

But before Tony Manzelli could answer the question and continue the conversation, a nurse came into the room to check on her injured patient.

"Excuse me gentlemen. Visiting hours is over. It's time for my patient's pain shot. If he expects to get better, he should rest now," said the nurse.

"Tony, we'll talk to you in the morning. I'll bring the district attorney and a court reporter to take down your information," Elder told him, as the nurse was about to inject him intravenously with the pain medication.

The three detectives quickly left the room and walked to the hospital's restaurant to talk about Manzelli's story. They each bought a cup of coffee and sat down at a table. But before starting their conversation they each had to light a cigarette.

"How are your fellow detectives taking the death of Detective Wilmont? Were you able to catch up on all of the murders he was investigating?" Wells asked Elder.

Elder told him that Wilmont was their first homicide detective killed in action. "Everyone at Redondo Beach station is pretty shook up right now. I'm doing everything I can to keep it together. I was Paul's number one assistant." He explained how he read many of the investigative, forensic and autopsy reports and then updated Wilmont on them and any that stood out. "I know everything about his recent murder investigations," he added.

"Then you shouldn't have any trouble taking over Paul's murder investigations," said Wells.

Elder asked Wells what he thought about Tony Manzelli's story and if he was telling the truth?

"I think there's something to it," Wells replied. "Especially if he can give us names and dates." Wells was about to break a promise that he had made earlier that day. He said, "You'll have to give me your word that what I'm about to tell you can't be repeated to anyone. It's for our ears only. I've already told Smith...now I'll tell you."

"I'm all ears," said Elder, as he sipped his coffee then took a long drag from his cigarette.

"I'm sure you have the names of the two CIA agents that came and took the two dead agents away from the hospital today, don't you?" Wells asked him.

He nodded, saying, "They gave their names to the emergency room doctor before they left the hospital with the bodies. I believe their names are Demler and Bennett. You're not gonna tell me that they are involved in smuggling narcotics into this country, are you?"

Wells shook his head and replied, "No. At least I don't think they're involved. What Demler told me…was that two cells within the CIA are smuggling illegal contraband into many different countries, including the United States. But he never said anything about the military being involved."

"Boy! This news is making my head ache," Elder griped. "I think I need a drink instead of this coffee. Would you gentlemen like to visit my favorite bar with me and talk about this over a few stiff drinks?" he asked his brother detectives.

"Sure. Why not!" Wells replied. "But I came here with Willard. If he wants to go, I'll go along."

Smith agreed. "Let's go," he said. And the detectives left the hospital grounds.

In the parking lot Elder said, "Smith, follow me in your car."

Instead of using one car, Elder told Smith to follow him just in case he had an emergency of some kind. And it turned out – he did.

While Elder was driving to his favorite bar, he received a radio call telling him that Jarrett, the long-haired male suspect (who was supposed to be dead) in the tainted murder investigation had been seen in the Redondo Beach area, but the officers that had been following him lost him at the Redondo Beach Pier and he had gotten away.

Elder figured that it had to be a case of mistaken identity because he knew that Danny Jermaine (alias Jarrett) had been found dead with the top of his head cut off. So he ignored the call and continued on his way to the bar.

Five minutes after leaving the hospital, they had arrived at their destination safely and upon entering the empty cop bar, began drinking immediately. Wells and Smith were still pretty tipsy and had quite a head start on Elder, who needed at least five drinks to catch up. Before a word was said about their suspect, they each had downed three stiff drinks. But Elder still had a long ways to go to catch up to his brother detectives.

Elder was the first to speak up, telling them about the radio call he had received. "I just thought I'd mention that I received a radio message a few minutes ago concerning Danny Jermaine."

"What!" said Smith and Wells in unison.

"Let me explain," Elder pleaded.

"Go ahead," Wells replied.

"As I was saying. Jermaine was supposedly seen near Redondo Beach pier. But his identity couldn't be verified due to the inadequacy of the rookie officer's experience at following suspects. The Jarrett look-alike got away from him."

"Unless Danny Jermaine had a twin, the officer must have been mistaken," Wells interjected. "As far as I know, Danny Jermaine...or Jarrett, whatever you want to call him, had no brothers."

"That's what I figured," Elder replied. "That's the reason why I ignored the call. I wasn't going to say anything about it...but I thought you might want to know."

"Well at least it's nice to know that we're keeping each other updated on things like that," opined Wells.

Elder then asked Wells to finish his story about the conspiracy between the CIA and the mob. "I'm having a hard time believing it," he said.

"Well one thing Demler and I do believe," Wells admitted, "is that those two dead agents from the hospital killed many of the people that we found in our respective cities."

"Why do you say that?" asked Elder.

"Because most of those bodies had been poisoned before their bodies were ground up. And this poison, which was used only by the military and CIA, has been banned since the mid-seventies. Demler thinks that they used the poison...like Tony Manzelli used his gun...to extract information," said Wells.

"What do you mean?" asked Elder.

"Just what I said!" Wells replied. "Tony Manzelli pistol whipped the young girl to extract information about the stolen van. The agents used poison. But sometimes they used more than needed and their victims ended up dead. Just like Manzelli did to the girl. He got a little carried away and the girl ended up dead. But I'm not sure if the agents used too much poison during the questioning and killed their victims accidentally or if they poisoned them to kill them before grinding up their bodies. Either way...the victims ended up dead. Then the ground round ended up being sold out of the mob's own butcher shops. Whether the butcher shop owners knew that they were selling their own brother mobsters as exotic "Ostrich meat", I'm not sure. Most of the people that had the answers were either ground into hamburger or tortured to death."

"But why the brain drain," quipped Elder.

"Same reason – to extract information. And to make a point. The CIA can be sadistic S.O.B.'s when they don't get what they want," Wells replied.

"So what about those street urchins? What part do they play in this sick game?" asked Elder.

Smith interjected, "I believe the Santini family had the young kids deliver the tainted meat to the Manzelli family owned butcher shops. I think they were duped by a Santini soldier into delivering the meat to take away suspicion from their own crime family."

"You could be right," Wells replied. "Those young kids might have been duped. But until we have positive proof of the true killers, the two young women that we have in custody and Janie Jenson who's still on the street, are still considered suspects in the murders and possibly the mutilations."

"We don't have one shred of evidence that these young kids had anything to do with the mutilations," opined Smith.

"If the CIA really is involved with the two crime families," Elder interjected, "maybe they played one against the other and tortured both Manzelli and Santiti soldiers believing that one of them knew the whereabouts of the white van. And" he added, "when the mobsters failed to produce the correct answers, they were poisoned. Afterwards the agents had other mobsters grind them up to get rid of the evidence."

"That's also a possibility," interjected Wells. "But we won't know for sure until we have a confession from someone."

"I can believe that the CIA agents poisoned the victims. But who ground them into hamburger?" asked Smith.

Wells replied, "Take your pick...either the Santini or Manzelli people...depending on who the agents were questioning at the time."

"Maybe," interjected Elder, "a few of the Manzelli soldiers went looking for the agents and the van...and when they ran into them, the agents poisoned them then had the Santini soldiers mutilate and grind up the bodies to get rid of the evidence."

Smith jumped into the conversation and said, "Maybe the kids found the meat in the abandoned buildings and sold it to the butcher shops for drug money. That's basically what Katie Brown told us. Then," he added, "Jarrett called these butcher shops to give them a special deal on some exotic "Ostrich meat" and had the owners drive over and pick it up, while Jarrett and his friends went along for the ride to carry it into the shop and get their money."

"That's also a good theory," Wells replied. "But until we have the evidence to back it up, we won't know for sure."

"I've got another one for you," Elder suggested. "What if the Manzelli family thought one or more of their own soldiers stole the van? Maybe Don Bruno, along with the two agents, questioned them, killed them and then ground them up. And used the kids to take suspicion away from their own crime family."

Wells nodded. "I thought about that possibility when I first began the tainted meat murder investigation," Wells admitted. "But that was before I knew the CIA was involved. Hell...if people hadn't gotten sick and died...we wouldn't be sitting here now talking about it."

"Like you said before, John, we won't really know for sure unless we get a confession," Smith remarked.

The three detectives had finished more than ten alcoholic drinks each. It was very late and they needed to get home for some well needed rest. And Smith still had to drive Wells back to his vehicle at Santa Monica police station parking lot. Wells wouldn't arrive home until after midnight.

Driving drunk in Hollywood on a Friday night near midnight was an accident waiting to happen. But Wells was an old horse at driving while intoxicated. He had done it for more than thirty years and had never been ticketed.

"I guess it's time we leave this place before they have to carry us out," quipped Elder.

"I agree," said Wells.

The detectives left the bar and stumbled to their cars. Elder was the first to leave and Smith followed, driving Wells to his car before going their separate ways. Wells intended to continue his drinking ways when he returned home figuring he would have the whole weekend to recuperate.

As Wells drove through downtown Hollywood, different thoughts swirled through his head. One that he honed in on concerned the nurse that had injected Tony Manzelli with the pain medication. Instead of giving him the injection in his buttocks or his upper arm, she had injected him intravenously. Even as drunk as he was, Wells sensed something wasn't right with that picture.

Just at that moment Wells received a radio call from his dispatcher telling him to return to the hospital as soon as possible because his suspect, Tony Manzelli was just found dead in his hospital bed. But there was more. He also was told that a patrol officer in the Hollywood area a few hours earlier had spotted a person who resembled Danny Jermaine, but the officer had lost him in a crowd of tourists. But Wells thought – like Elder – that it was just another case of mistaken identity.

Wells quickly made a U-turn and headed for Redondo Beach hospital. But only a quarter mile after he had made the U-turn, he saw Janie Jenson walking along the sidewalk on Hollywood boulevard, heading towards a row of abandoned buildings. He thought for a split second about the hospital and figured that his suspect was already dead, so he decided that the important thing to do at that moment was to go after Janie Jenson and bring her in for questioning.

Wells pulled his car over to the side of the road and then ran after the female suspect. But she was more than fifty yards ahead of him, and after two minutes of running he was out of breath. He didn't want to be seen, but he knew that if he didn't get closer, fast, he could lose her again. As drunk and out of shape as Wells was, he still ran after the young woman.

Janie Jenson dashed into one of the buildings just three blocks from the second table murder crime scene that Wells had investigated a few days before. And even though he was drunk and out of shape, Wells continued his chase, trying not to stumble so he wouldn't attract attention, and entered through the back door of the abandoned building.

It was well past midnight and very dark outside. And even darker inside the smelly building. Wells looked around as he walked from room to room. He didn't see Janie Jenson anywhere in the building and thought he had lost her once again. That is until he heard some strange, disturbing sounds coming from a second floor room.

Detective Wells heard people chanting some type of weird language and began walking carefully and very quietly up a small staircase to the sound of the chanting. When he reached the room where the strange noise was coming from, he slowly peeked around a corner and through an open door where he could see hundreds of lit candles on top of and surrounding a wooden altar. And on top of the altar, a large crystal bowl that was filled to the brim with a dark substance, which stood in front of a wall that was adorned with satanic symbols and pagan idols.

Detective Wells had seen enough. He figured there were at least three people and possibly more, chanting – and one of them was Janie Jenson. He left the building as quietly as could be, ran back to his vehicle and radioed for silent back up. His radio crackled and his voice was barely audible to his dispatcher but he had gotten his message through. After signing off, he ran back to the abandoned building to make sure none of the trespassers got away – especially Janie Jenson.

Entering the condemned dwelling, Wells again heard loud chanting coming from the second floor room. Climbing the steps once again he reached the second floor without being heard. But his heart pounded so loud that he thought he would either have a heart attack or the noise would give him away to the devil worshipers.

Once Wells had pulled his gun from its holster, he again peeked around the corner and into the room without anyone seeing or hearing him, then stepped closer to the doorway to get a better view and a complete picture of what was going on and who was in the room. But his eyes were drawn to that six-foot long wooden alter which was surrounded by pagan statues and hundreds of small lit candles. And in the middle of the altar – the crystal bowl.

Then suddenly something else caught Wells' attention – something he had seen a few times before, which made him very sick to his stomach. Sitting around a small square table were two male victims, strapped into their chairs with their mouths taped shut. And sitting on the table in front of each victim – their hairy scalp. A large needle had been inserted into each of the victim's jugular veins which was connected to a small, clear plastic tube that ran the length of the victim to a small gallon pail sitting on the floor next to their tortured bodies.

Stretching his neck a little more, Wells was able to see four females (or so he thought) chanting – three with short hair, one with long. Suddenly the long haired sicko began scooping out large portions of the exposed brains of the two male victims. But Wells couldn't see the sicko's face. But he could see one of the victim's facial expression change as his brain slowly disappeared.

As the chanting continued and became louder, the sicko held the spoonful of brain matter high into the air as though he was toasting the gods and then turned towards his chanting shorthaired female companions. That's when Wells got the surprise of his life and couldn't believe who he was seeing. The sicko wasn't a female at all, but a male. And not just any male. He looked exactly like Danny Jermaine, (alias Jarrett).

As Jermaine held the spoonful of brain matter into the air, Wells noticed that one of his chanting companions was recording the episode with a video camera.

Seconds later the four chanting sickos surrounded the table – one on each side – and began swaying back and forth. And after a few seconds of this behavior, with all eyes focused on Jermaine, he suddenly inhaled the brain matter from his spoon – eating it in one gulp. After swallowing it, he then spewed out some unintelligible words before scooping out more brain from his victims. But this time he shared it with his companions. Each of them eating one or two spoonfuls. After swallowing it, they too spewed out some unintelligible words, which Wells believed to be Latin.

After losing quite a bit of their brains, the two victims became unresponsive and in a zombi-like state.

Wells couldn't tell if the victims were still alive or dead. He wanted to arrest the four devil worshipers right then but voted against it. He didn't want to take a chance of losing them and decided to wait until his back up arrived.

Detective Wells continued to watch their evil ritual. After eating their spoonfuls of brain matter, the four devil worshippers then scooped out small glasses of blood from the victims' pail beneath the table and drank it, evidently to wash down the brain matter.

Another item that Wells had seen before (at previous crime scenes) that was in the room was a large bowl of ground meat. And lying next to it was a rather large piece of human leg.

Once the devil worshipers had their fill of brain matter, the long-haired Jarrett look-alike wandered over to the wooden altar, picked up the crystal bowl, hoisted it into the air, then brought it to his mouth and began drinking it as the others continued to chant while the cameraman videotaped the entire episode.

Wells tried to remain in control throughout the entire ordeal and not bring attention to himself, at least until help arrived. But he wasn't that fortunate.

When the others began wandering over to the wooden altar to share the bowl of dark liquid – which Wells believed to be blood – Janie Jenson was the first to notice him standing in the doorway watching their every move.

"Get out of here! The guy's got a gun!" Janie Jenson yelled to her comrades.

The girl who was videotaping the episode suddenly threw the video camera at Wells. But Wells, too drunk to move, couldn't get out of the way fast enough and the camera hit him on the left knee causing his legs to buckle. As Wells hit the floor, the assailants tried to escape – and nearly got away. The only thing Wells could think of doing without shooting and killing them was to fire his weapon into the air.

"Stop! Police!" Wells yelled, as his assailants barreled over him, knocking him to the ground.

Wells tried to run after them but his legs gave out running down the stairs and tumbled down the last ten steps, landing at the base of the staircase.

Luckily, the four young assailants didn't get very far. Because Wells' back up finally arrived on the scene and apprehended the fleeing subjects on the main floor.

As the patrol officers confronted Wells, he slowly staggered to his feet and showed them his badge and identification.

"Detective Wells, are you all right?" asked the patrol officer.

When Wells' drunken eyes finally focused on the face of the officer, he suddenly recognized the face as one he had seen before. "Oh, it's you Officer Tobin. I'm glad you could make it. Good job, son," beamed Wells.

"Detective Wells, we have apprehended four suspects and they are now in custody: One male and three females. Was that all of them?" asked Tobin.

"As far as I know. Radio for the coroner and forensic team. We have one horrendous murder scene in the room upstairs. We have two male victims up there. I'm not sure if they are alive or dead," said an overworked Wells, as he slowly limped over to the four devil worshipers to get a better look at them.

Wells was dumbfounded when he saw the clone of Danny Jermaine.

"Officer Tobin, did you find this boy's identification?" asked Wells pointing at Jermaine.

"No, sir. He doesn't have any on his person."

"What's your name boy?" asked Wells, staring into the dark, evil eyes of his male suspect.

"That's for me to know and for you to find out," snapped the young, long-haired male devil worshipper.

"Is your name Jarrett?" asked Wells.

"I don't have to talk with you and neither do they," he said, nodding his head in the direction of his female comrades.

"Son, you might be looking at the death penalty if those two victims upstairs don't make it. Do you have a brain eating fetish?" Wells asked him.

"Don't knock it till you've tried it. It tastes just like caviar," he said, as he licked his lips, angering Detective Wells.

"Officer Tobin, would you please get these sick animals out of my sight and take them to a holding cell. Make sure that you separate them...so they can't speak to each other," Wells told him, as he turned away from the suspects who were escorted to the patrol cars.

Wells slowly limped up the stairs, picked up the video camera that had been thrown at him, removed the video and placed it into his jacket pocket. Then, after placing the empty video camera back onto the floor, Wells entered the room to search for anything that would connect the four sadistic devil worshipers with any other crimes that they may have committed. Just as he entered the room, the coroner and forensic team entered the premises and the patrol officers secured the crime scene.

Detective Wells was drawn to the wooden altar and the bowl of dark liquid. Dipping his fingertip into the liquid, he rubbed it between his fingers and smelled it. He was sure that it was blood. But whether it was human blood or not would later be determined at the forensic lab.

To the left side of the altar sitting on the floor were two medium-sized cardboard boxes that held clear plastic bags of ground up meat. The forensic lab would determine if that meat was human or not. But most of it had turned rancid.

To the left of the two boxes was another bag of hamburger that was being mixed into a small meat grinder with fresh hamburger. Behind the grinder full of meat, lying on the floor, was a small cardboard box that contained four more videotapes.

While Wells was searching the room, the coroner was checking the two victims that were still tied to their chairs and the forensic team was gathering up pieces of evidence that would tie the four devil worshippers to this crime scene and possibly many others.

Then Wells made a startling discovery. A phony wall that could slide back and forth and hide the altar and the small area behind it from prying eyes, making it look as though it was the real wall. He then realized that the other crime scenes where the table murders had occurred must be checked again to see if they had similar phony walls that might be hiding evidence of a murder or murders.

By the time Dr. Terry checked the victims to see if they were still alive, it was too late. They had already succumbed to their torture and had bled to death.

Dr. Terry had also made a startling discovery. When he checked the two dead victims' pockets for identification, he came across three different pieces of I.D. from one victim showing him to be either a Treasury agent, an FBI agent or a CIA agent whose name was Agent John Belford. The other victim's name was Dennis Sellers, one of the police officers who had spotted Jarrett but was thought to have lost him. Evidently, the two men had bumped into each other – and apparently Jarrett had gotten the upper hand.

While Dr. Terry had been searching the victims for identification, Detective Wells had made yet another discovery. He found in a small metal container, two police badges, two pair of handcuffs with keys, one nearly empty bottle of liquid morphine, and five different full bottles of prescription narcotics, which held one hundred pills each of Percodan, Dilaudid, Morphine, Oxi-Contin and Demerol.

Also in the container was unused syringes and a bottle of the banned poison that was used on many of the victims who had been discovered in his city over the last few weeks. As Wells placed the evidence back into the container, he noticed, just three feet from where the container was found, evidence that would put a noose around the suspects' necks. Wells came across a bag full of wallets, identification and three more videotapes, most likely recordings of other episodes of torture. He took the videotape that he had in his jacket pocket and placed it with the box of others he had just found and left them for the investigators to tag and bag.

A couple minutes after Wells' discovery, the forensic team came upon another startling find. In the corner of the candle lit room, lay on the floor, covered over with garbage and newspapers, a freshly discarded torso. The detectives figured its missing parts were being ground up and mixed with the rancid hamburger meat that was found next to the altar.

The torso was found just like the others. No arms, legs or head and large patches of skin had been peeled away along with a large needle mark on the victim's jugular vein. This sight overwhelmed Wells. He had experienced more on-the-job training in this one day than all of his thirty years as a homicide detective.

After having such a long and exhausting day, he needed to get home for some rest and relaxation. He thought he had the weekend to do that, but now he wasn't so certain.

Anxious to get home, Wells left the investigation up to his crew and gave Dr. Terry permission to move the bodies to the morgue. Then he left the abandoned building for home. It was nearly two o'clock in the morning.

But just as Wells entered his car, he received an urgent radio message from a Redondo Beach dispatcher telling him to meet Detective Elder near the same address of Wilmont's table murders that Wells and Smith had viewed nearly fifteen hours earlier. That was all that was relayed to Detective Wells.

He didn't want to go but reluctantly did as asked. Wells wondered why Elder needed his help. However, thirty minutes later, he would know why.

When Wells reached his destination, he saw that it was only two doors down from the abandoned building he had visited earlier that day. A large number of detective and patrol vehicles were already there, along with the coroner's wagon.

As uniformed officers secured the area, Wells wondered why he was there? But his question was soon answered.

As Wells walked towards the building's front entrance, Elder was there to meet him.

"I'm glad you could make it, Detective Wells," said Elder as the two homicide detectives shook hands.

"Detective Elder," Wells retorted. "I've got a few developments to tell you about our murder investigations. But first tell me why I'm here?"

Elder replied, "I want you to see something that I think might be of interest to you. I came upon this crime scene just thirty minutes ago while driving home. On my way home I decided to go by Wilmont's crime scene to see if it had been secured…and I saw a shorthaired female running away from the building and into the one we're searching now."

"But couldn't you have told me this tomorrow morning?" Wells asked him as they walked towards one of the patrol cars.

Elder shook his head no, adding, "This was too important to wait. I also called Detective Smith but they couldn't contact him. He is gone for the weekend. So I left a message."

"So...what do you want to show me?" Wells asked, as they stood next to the patrol car.

"John, do you recognize the guy laying down in the back seat?" asked Elder pointing to the back seat of the police car.

When Wells bent down to look through the cruiser's side window, he got the surprise of his life. It was another young man with long hair that resembled Danny Jermaine. And in the police car next to him was two shorthaired females sitting handcuffed in the back seat.

"What the hell's going on?" Wells asked, scratching his head in confusion before lighting a cigarette. "I just arrested a guy not more than an hour ago in Hollywood that looks exactly like him."

"If you have a person that could be this guy's clone, then they must be twins," said Elder.

"Not twins, but triplets," Wells replied, as they walked towards the building. "The first guy that we thought was Jarrett...was found dead. Now we have two more. Did he have any identification on him?"

"Yep," Elder answered. "His name is Samuel Jermaine. But the two females only knew him as Jarrett. What was the name of your clone?"

"I don't know. The kid wasn't carrying any identification. When I asked him his name, he just gave me a stupid answer. So I had the officers take him to jail where he could be interrogated," said Wells, as the two detectives entered the abandoned building.

Elder escorted Wells through the building to an upstairs, windowless room just like the one he had left in Hollywood. And he saw the same exact scene – a long wooden altar adorned by candles, satanic symbols and pagan statues. And in one corner of the dimly lit room was a small kitchen table.

And sitting at the table were two dead male victims facing each other with their hands, feet, chests and chins bound by rope and duct tape. This was an instant replay of the crime scene Wells had just left, right down to the skullcaps sitting on the table and their partially exposed brains.

But when Detective Wells got a closer look at the victims, he knew he had seen and talked to them before. It was Agents Demler and Boyd. Evidently the two men had met their match when they ran into their killers.

"Tom, do you know who these two victims are?" Wells asked.

"Yeah," he replied. "We found about ten different pieces of identification on them. I believe these two gentlemen are the agents we talked about, Demler and Boyd. These guys were professionals. How in the hell did they get trapped by these young kids?"

"I don't know, but I'm sure we'll know after we interrogate our suspects. By the way, did your investigators find any other evidence – like wallets or identification?" asked Wells.

Elder nodded, adding, "We found lots of stuff behind the altar. Most of it has been carried out and taken away. We even found a few videotapes. I'm sure we'll learn a lot from those." Then pointing to a false wall, he said, "And look at this phony wall. When it's closed, it hides the altar and all of their satanic possessions." Then he showed Wells how the wall worked.

"I know," Wells told him. "I found a phony wall just like it in the room where I discovered the devil worshippers as they were chanting some kind of demonic ritual." Adding, "It made my skin quiver when I saw them eating their victims' brains. I'll tell you what, though. I sobered up right away watching them. I've never seen anything like it in my life. They even drank blood out of the same type of bowl that's sitting on this altar...and they were videotaping it."

"My suspects were videotaping their ritual, too," Elder told him. "This is really weird. We discovered two male clones that were caught nearly at the same moment with their victims and their female partners. I too saw and heard them chanting and going through a demonic ritual of blood drinking and brain eating. I've never witnessed anything like it in my life either. I wonder if Katie and Kathy knew that there were three Jarretts?"

"I don't know, but I'm sure anxious to ask them. I thought I would have the weekend to myself, but now I guess I'll be interrogating suspects. I'd like to be at your interrogation. And I think it's important that you, Smith and Rodriguez be there, too. But we should each interrogate our own suspects first."

"That sounds like a good idea," Elder said.

"Hey. I just realized that this was Friday the thirteenth," Wells quipped. "Their rituals must have begun at midnight. That's about when I discovered my four suspects, including Janie Jenson."

"She was involved in more than just delivering tainted meat then," Elder quipped.

"I guess so. She ate the victims' brains just as much as her boyfriend did."

Elder then told Wells that Tony Manzelli was found dead three and a half hours after they left his hospital room.

"I know. I received the radio call from my dispatcher. I had just made a U-turn to return to the hospital when I saw Janie Jenson and decided to follow her instead. And I'm glad I did," said Wells.

"Hell, I thought I was gonna surprise you with my news about capturing Jarrett and his gang. But you surprised me instead," Elder quipped.

But Wells wasn't sure about one thing and told Elder. "There's only one thing, Tom that I don't see here that I had at my crime scene...and that's a torso and ground meat. Or was that taken away already?"

Elder shook his head no and said, "We didn't find anything like that – just the two male bodies and a ton of satanic symbols and statues. We even found a stash of pills and poison. It might even be the type that was used to poison and kill many of the victims. The serial number and label on the bottle is being checked now and we should know if it's the banned poison or not. We also found a small bottle of the same poison and two syringes on Agent Demler. All of our answers to these murder investigations may be right in this room."

"I found the same poison at my murder scene," Wells replied. "I'm sure it's the same stuff that was banned more than twenty years ago by the military. The only way these young kids could have gotten a hold of the stuff was to take it from one of their victims, like one of the CIA agents."

"I'm sure you're right, John. But we have lots of work to do yet. I have at least three videotapes to watch that was found behind the altar and the one found in the video camera before I question my suspects. Since Paul's death, I've experienced more on this crime scene than I had in the five years I've been a homicide detective. This kind of crap is just too overwhelming for me."

"I know what you mean," Wells exclaimed. "I've been on this job for over thirty years and never experienced anything that even comes close to this case. But I want to find out just how these young kids were involved in this conspiracy between the mob and the CIA. Right now though...I want to get home and get some sleep. I'm drunk, tired and overworked."

"It has been a rather long day, hasn't it?" Elder retorted.

"Well...Tom, I'm going to let you finish your investigation. If I don't go home and get some much needed rest, I'll never be able to get up in the morning. I also have many things to take care of before I can interrogate my suspects. I too have a few videotapes to watch...and many reports to read before I can even think of questioning them. I'll talk with you sometime tomorrow to see how your interrogation is going." Wells then left Detective Elder's murder scene and headed for home.

Forty minutes after Wells left Redondo Beach he was sitting on his couch relaxing. And before long was fast asleep. He didn't awaken until early the next morning, and with a pounding headache. Having only five hours of sleep, he reluctantly dragged himself off the couch and went into the kitchen where he splashed cold water on his face, swallowed four aspirins and drank a pot of hot, black coffee. Two minutes later he was out the door heading for work.

Wells was anxious to question his suspects. He was just hoping that they would speak with him and not ask for attorneys. And with over thirty years of experience as a homicide detective, he was certain that he knew the questions to ask so they would want to answer him.

He believed his murder investigations would be wrapped up within the next few hours, if he was lucky. Then he would turn it over to the district attorney for prosecution.

Just as Wells turned into the Hollywood police station parking lot, he saw a black sedan cruise by. But it didn't follow him into the lot. He figured the agents had other things on their minds and wouldn't bother him. They were still looking for the white van – he wasn't.

When Wells entered the police station the whole place was full of people: Media, politicians, uniformed police officers, detectives and even a few men dressed in black and wearing fedoras. The two men dressed in black were busy speaking with Captain Lawson.

After Wells signed in at the front desk, the media overwhelmed him with questions concerning his murder investigations. But he ignored them and headed towards his desk, but only got a few feet before Lawson stopped him, as the men in black stood nearby.

"Detective Wells, would you please come with us?" asked Captain Lawson.

"Yes, sir," he said, and followed his Captain and the two men dressed in black that he had never seen before.

The four men walked into a small, windowless room and shut the door behind them. The room contained a color television and a video machine. On top of the machine lay four videotapes. As Wells and the two men dressed in black sat down in chairs, Captain Lawson inserted the first of four videotapes into the machine, then pressed the play button and sat down to view the film.

The four men remained silent as the tape began – which had been found by Detective Wells just six hours earlier. They watched the snuff film for nearly an hour before placing the second videotape into the machine.

The first videotape showed three mobsters entering an abandoned building in Hollywood with the girl named Belinda. As soon as they entered, two girls, both with short-cropped hair came out from behind a staircase and began undressing for the men. While the girls stripped, each man was given a glass filled with a liquid substance – most likely alcohol. And within fifteen minutes all three men had passed out onto the dirty floor.

Then the young women stripped the mens' clothing from their bodies, searching them for money and valuables. They also stripped them of any jewelry and watches before a young man came into the picture – one of the Jarrett triplets.

When the long-haired young man entered the room, he was handed the wallets, money and valuables, which he placed into a small paper sack and then set it to the side. He then dragged each unconscious mobster to the center of the room and placed them next to each other before starting his evil deeds.

First, the young man injected each male victim with some type of drug and then placed a large needle into each one's jugular vein, which was then hooked up to a long, round plastic tube, which was connected to a super large syringe. This was used to suck out the victim's blood.

When the syringe was full, they unhooked the plastic tube and squirted its contents into a large pale. When the pale became full they dumped the liquid into a larger plastic container – a garbage can. Once the blood was depleted from one victim, it was the next victim's turn.

Once the victims' blood had been sucked from their bodies, Jarrett began cutting their hands, feet and head, using a saw like the one used to cut the victims' skullcaps. But before sawing the appendages, Jarrett placed a black garbage bag under them to catch any pieces of tissue or bone.

And while Jarrett was cutting off the victims' appendages, the three women were busy scraping away any tattoos or birthmarks by freezing the skin with dry ice and then scraping away the identifying marks with a knife or by simply cutting it away. Once they had completed their chores, the appendages and skin were then ground into hamburger using a small meat grinder. It looked similar to the one found at Wilmont's mutilation murder scene.

While grinding the human flesh into hamburger, the sadistic devil worshippers also drank their victims' blood. At that point the videotape ended and Captain Lawson placed another into the machine. And repeated the process until they had watched them all.

All four videos showed young women seducing their male victims to their deaths.

Why the males fell prey to these psychopathic women was a complete mystery to Wells. But Wells hoped that question would be answered either at the suspects' interrogation or at their murder trials? The tapes showed that Katie Brown, Kathy Fenton, Janie Jenson and other females assisted one of the Jarrett triplets in the sadistic murders.

Many questions had to be answered. Were these three young male psychopaths, brothers? Or were they clones? But whatever the answer, Wells was sure he had the evidence to connect his suspects to his tainted meat, mutilation and table murder investigations to get a conviction of first degree murder. The district attorney would have to decide if the death penalty was warranted. Wells was sure it was.

When the four men finished watching the videotapes, they were utterly disgusted. Only Captain Lawson expressed his view out loud.

"Detective Wells, I want you to hang those people on these videotapes. They're the pond scum of society and should be exterminated. It's just too bad we can't exterminate them like they exterminated their victims. Even if most of them were mobsters," snapped Lawson.

Wells replied, "I'll do my best, Captain. I'm gonna interrogate the suspects within the hour."

"Can we watch?" asked one of the men dressed in black.

"Detective Wells," interjected Lawson, "let me introduce you to Agents Thomas and Reeves. These two gentlemen are here from the Justice department. They want to see what federal charges can be brought against your suspects. Killing a government agent brings the death penalty…and the federal government has more money in their budget to bring about a trial of this magnitude."

"But it's my case," Wells reminded him. "I don't need their help. The state of California will execute these satanic devil worshipers…not the federal government!"

"Don't worry about us. We're just here for support and to view your suspects' interrogation," said Agent Thomas.

"I thought you guys would be out searching for your white van," Wells quipped.

"What white van? What are you talking about, Detective Wells?" asked Agent Thomas.

"Never mind, it's not important," Wells retorted. "Captain Lawson, if you're finished with me, I need to get ready for the interrogation. If your two friends want to watch, they can do it from the viewing room. I don't want any interference from the federal government."

With that said, Wells returned to his desk and was happy to see reports already there waiting for him. The first report he picked up was the complete life story of Danny Jermaine. It stated that Jermaine and his two brothers, Samuel and Luther, were identical triplets that had been born to a homeless fourteen-year-old girl. The triplets' life with their alcoholic mother was pure hell. And just before their tenth birthday, the brothers were taken away from her and placed into three different foster homes. However, within a day or two they had all disappeared and run away, never being heard from until now.

So now, Wells knew that his male suspect's name was Luther Jermaine – and was seen in at least one of the video films that were found at the crime scene. But Wells had a problem – which triplet was in the other videos. He had to prove, beyond a reasonable doubt, that his suspect was the person in the video and not one of his brothers, Samuel or Danny. Identical triplets looked exactly alike. Only if the brothers confessed to their crimes and to the murders they had committed, could this question be resolved. But Luther and Samuel were caught at the crime scenes. That was irrefutable evidence enough, not including the video taken at the time of the crime.

So Wells had his investigations all but wrapped up. He was wrong when he thought the CIA agents had been poisoning the victims. It had been these homeless street urchins all the time. They were the real killers. The shorthaired females seduced their victims to the crime scene and then fed them drinks laced with poison or drugs. Once the victims were knocked out, their blood was taken from their bodies and then were decapitated, mutilated or had their brains eaten for devilish reasons. But one thing was certain – these satanic devil worshipers would kill no more. Detective Wells was sure of that.

After reading a few other reports concerning his newly caught suspects, Wells decided it was time to interrogate Luther Jermaine.

As Wells entered the viewing room, he was surprised to see it packed with wall to wall law enforcement officers. Looking through the mirrored window, he saw that his male suspect was already sitting in the interrogation room.

So Wells entered the room and introduced himself to his suspect.

"Hello, Jarrett, I'm Detective Wells. I spoke with you for a few seconds just after you were arrested. Do you remember me?" he asked, as he turned on the tape recorder that was sitting on the table.

"What was I arrested for? Why am I here?" asked the hyper young man.

"We'll talk about that in a minute. Do you go by the name Jarrett or Luther?"

"My name is Jarrett!"

Wells played along. "Okay. For now, I'll call you Jarrett. You've been given your rights, haven't you?"

"Yes, I know my rights," Jarrett replied. "Anything I say can and will be used against me in a court of law."

"Do you want a lawyer?" Wells asked him.

"Will it do me any good?" he asked as he stared into Wells' eyes, sending chills down the detective's spine.

"You are likely to get the death penalty once the jury hears the evidence and sees your videos," Wells replied.

"You can't kill me. Nobody can," sneered Jarrett.

"Why not?"

Jarrett gave Wells an evil look and boasted, "I drank the blood of my victims and stole their souls. I'm gonna live forever."

"We'll see," Wells snickered.

"Yes we will," Jarrett responded.

"Jarrett, I have a few questions I'd like to ask you. Do you feel like answering them or would you like an attorney present during questioning?" Wells asked.

"Be my guest. Ask away."

"Good. Why do you use the name of Jarrett when your birth name is Luther?" Wells asked him.

"Jarrett is my name. Luther is dead," he answered.

"No, your brother Danny is dead. Do you know who killed him?"

"Yeah! My brother Samuel."

"Why?"

"You'll have to ask him," Jarrett replied.

"I'm asking you, Luther...and I think you know the answer," Wells said, looking deep into his dark, evil eyes.

"I told you...my name is Jarrett. I'm king of the street people and a road scholar," he quipped.

Wells asked him why he killed and mutilated all of those people? "Was it for your devil worshipping?"

Jarrett replied matter-of-factly that they were sacrificed for his god, Lucifer.

Wells then asked him whose idea it was to grind up his victims into hamburger and sell it as exotic Ostrich meat?

"We did."

"Who's we?" Wells asked.

"Me and my brothers, Samuel and Danny. We figured we had to do something with our victims' bodies after we used them in our satanic rituals."

Wells shook his head in disgust and asked, "What did you do in those rituals?"

Jarrett replied, "Haven't you watched the videos yet? They'll give you the answers."

Wells nodded. "Yes, I've watched them. But why did you do it? Was it to torture your victims before you killed them…or was it to get information out of them?"

Jarrett gave Wells a devilish look and said, "You mean to get information about the white van, don't you?"

"Were you trying to find the white van? Is that why you tortured your victims?" Wells asked.

Jarrett smiled an evil smile. "Sometimes we drained the victim's blood very slowly to watch his last gasp of breath leave his body. But the best was cutting off the top of their heads and then eating their brains one spoonful at a time, while they watched their friends sitting across the table having their brains eaten," sneered Jarrett.

"You really got a kick out of that, didn't you?" Wells said, trying to hold back his anger.

Jarrett nodded. "I sure did, but it took a little bit of experimentation."

"What do you mean?"

"The first victim died as I cut away the top of his head," Jarrett told him with a smile on his face. "I think he died from shock. So I had to shoot the others up with liquid morphine so they wouldn't feel the pain. Then me and my disciples would eat either the right or left side of the brain, then watch and listen as their speech and other motor functions evaporated…and then disappeared altogether. We had a ball watching their facial expressions as we dipped our spoons into their brains and scooped up a big spoonful…and let them watch as we ate it. And it tastes similar to Russian caviar. It was great entertainment…and good food for my gang of homeless derelicts." He laughed.

Wells shook his head in disgust and said, "Luther, you are one sick individual. You need to have your brains eaten while you're alive…and have others watch as you lose your mind. That is, if you have any brains at all."

"I'm not sick at all," Jarrett quipped, "I'm ingenious. In fact, I got a brilliant idea from one guy I did in. I made small, b.b. sized holes in a small piece of dry ice. Then I filled the holes with some poison I had gotten from another victim and made about twenty small pellets of poison. Then I replaced the lead b.b.'s from a shotgun shell with the frozen pellets of poison…and shot the guy in the chest. Detective Wells, guess what he died of?"

"I give up. What?"

"Spread poisoning," Jarrett snickered. "Get it? But most of the time I didn't have the time to play around. I had a purpose to my insanity."

"Insanity is right, Luther," Wells replied. "But an insanity plea won't help you in your defense. You and your gang of homeless derelicts are responsible for lots of deaths in my city and many others."

"I told you...I go by the name of Jarrett...and so do my brothers."

"All three of you used the name, Jarrett. Why?" Wells asked.

Jarrett smiled. "That way we stayed a mystery. While I was doing crimes in one city, my identical brothers were doing crimes in other cities. If the police placed me in a particular city at a particular time, I would have an alibi. None of our disciples knew that we were triplets...because we were never seen together. We made sure of that. In fact, you don't know if it's me or my brothers on the videotapes."

Wells sneered, "We know you're the killer in at least one videotape...and that's all we need to convict you and send you to death row."

"You might be right. But you'll never kill me,"snapped a defiant Jarrett.

"Did you kill these people for your devil worshiping...or was there another reason you killed and tortured them?" asked Wells.

"That's for me to know and for you to find out," Jarrett replied. "But I will tell you this. We needed to survive...and when we drink our victims blood...we add years and years to our lives. And I plan to live forever!"

"I'd bet money you don't," Wells quipped.

"Say what you will, but I know better," Jarrett shot back, with a big smile on his face.

Wells asked him how he picked the places that he delivered and sold the hamburger meat to? "Why did you sell it as exotic Ostrich meat?"

"Did you want me to tell our customers that we were selling ground up human flesh? I don't think so. But we knew the people that we sold the meat to. The owners of the butcher shops always gave us handouts when we were hungry...so I thought I would help them out. We needed money...and we needed to get rid of our victims' bodies so we ground them up into hamburger and sold it to people we knew."

Wells scratched his head. "So when these gangsters helped you deliver the meat to their shops they didn't know about the meat being human. Is that right, Luther...I mean Jarrett?"

"That's true. They were just helping a friend in need."

"When did you learn about the white van?" Wells asked.

Jarrett smiled. "I wondered when you were gonna get around to asking me questions about that."

"So give me an answer," Wells retorted.

Jarrett looked Wells in the eyes and told him, "I learned about the van when one of the Manzelli soldiers came to see me in a run-down motel room and gave me twenty dollars to keep an eye out for a white Econoline van that had been stolen from them by the Santini crime family. I was to tell him anything that might help them find the white van."

"So did you tell him?" asked Wells.

"Not him. He never left the room. He was one of our first victims," said a smiling Jarrett.

"Do you remember your victim's name?"

Jarrett shook his head no, adding, "Names aren't important. It's what they have inside that counts."

Wells asked him where he got the poison?

"We got it from a government agent that was also looking for the van," he replied.

"How did you run into the agent?"

Jarrett told him that the agent ran into them. "I guess he had been following me for a few days. He thought I had stolen the van with Belinda."

"Did you?" Wells asked him.

He shook his head no and replied, "Danny stole the van. I didn't know anything about it until I was confronted by the agent."

"What kind of government agent was he?"

"He showed me I.D. that said he was from the FBI. But I learned later that he had lots of different pieces of identification. One being for the CIA."

"What was his name? Do you remember?" Wells asked.

He shook his head no and replied, "I told you, names aren't important."

Wells asked him why the agent would give him the poison?

Jarrett replied, "I was to use it on my brother Danny…to threaten him into telling me where he had hidden the white van."

Wells couldn't believe his answer. Shaking his head in disgust he snarled, "You killed your brother for someone that you didn't even know!"

But Jarrett wouldn't admit to his brother's killing. After a few long seconds of silence he replied, "I didn't say I killed my brother. You didn't see my face on the videotape, did you?"

"So tell me what happened when you saw your brother Danny?" Wells asked him.

"I was to telephone the agent so he could question him about the van."

"Did your brother tell you where the van was hidden?"

He shook his head no, adding, "I guess someone scooped out one spoonful of brains too many and he lost his speech and motor faculties. But before he lost his speech, he told me that him and Belinda parked the van on a side street when they went to a dope house to buy drugs and get high. And when they came out, the van was gone. Danny said that someone stole it while they were at the dope house."

Wells asked him what Belinda had to say about the van?

Jarrett shrugged his shoulders and said, "When she found out that people were after her…she split."

Suddenly Wells remembered a question he had asked Jarrett about the poisoning of his brother Danny and wasn't sure about the answer. So he wanted clarification and asked him about it. "Jarrett, you told me that you were to use the poison on your brother. But your brother's autopsy report stated...that there was no poison in his system."

"You're right...he was just threatened with it. When that didn't work...other methods were tried," snickered Jarrett, as an evil smile crossed his face.

"Like cutting off the top of his head and eating his brains...while bleeding him dry," Wells sneered.

"Yep! Him and that agent. The agent had me torture my brother...so I tortured him, too. But it didn't do any good. I still don't know what happened to that white van."

Wells looked at him in disgust and bewilderment and mused, "So all of these people that you and your brothers tortured, mutilated and ground into hamburger were all involved in searching for the white van. Is that right, Jarrett?"

"Yep. They were the reason that I began killing in the first place. If they hadn't ordered me to find that van...I would be sitting on the beach right now."

"So you killed these people because they annoyed you?"

"To a point," Jarrett replied. "But Lucifer gave me the power and instructed me and my disciples to steal their souls by eating their energy source."

"You are really a sick person," Wells told him.

Wells questioned the sick, evil killer for a few more hours before finally calling it a day, and left the interrogation room disgusted, dumbfounded, nervous, shaking and wanting a few drinks. He had questioned his suspect until he literally became sick to his stomach.

While the male killer was being escorted to his cell, Wells telephoned Elder wanting to know what had transpired in the interrogation of his suspect. After speaking with him for a few minutes Wells learned that the two homicide detectives basically had received the same information from their male suspects. Neither killer admitted to knowing the whereabouts of the white van or which victims they had killed.

The two detectives would have to rely on the videotapes to tell the story.

All ten defendants, including Katie Brown, Kathy Fenton and Janie Jenson were all charged with first degree murder with special circumstances, which, if convicted, they would receive the death penalty. However, three months after their arraignment the devil worshipers began dying one by one because they had drunk their victims' blood, and two of their victims were HIV positive and in the last stages of the aids' virus.

Before their trial began, all ten defendants had died from a torturous disease that no pill could fix. So, to a point, justice was served.

Detective Wells soon forgot about the devil worshipers. But not his peers, He stayed in close contact and remained good friends with Detectives Rodriguez, Elder, and Smith, the three homicide detectives who had also been involved in the devil worshiper case that began as the tainted meat murders but turned into something more grotesque than anyone could ever have imagined.

But Wells seemed to forget about me. I'm still out searching for the white van full of narcotics. I was also the person behind the wheel of the black sedan who had been following Wells. Who am I? I'm Bobby Legend: Investigative Reporter.

Read the sequel to "Raw Meat" as Bobby Legend, Investigative Reporter continues to search for the white van. What was really hidden in the white van? Was it really narcotics or was there something even more sinister and devastating that the CIA doesn't want known to the public? Are the Manzelli and Santini crime families warring over the loss of the van? Read "Raw Meat Revisited" and find out.